To Tim,

The Staff of Moses
An Oliver Lucas Adventure

In the footsteps of
Dr. Jones.

Andrew Linke

Thanks for reading!

~ Linke

The Staff of Moses
Copyright © 2012 by Andrew Linke

Cover art based on Egypt Saved by Joseph, painted by Abel de Pujol in 1827. The author was inspired to write the book you now hold by seeing this mural, which is painted on the ceiling of the Louvre, during a vacation in Paris in the summer of 2010.

Visit and connect with Andrew Linke online for more novels, short stories, and blog updates.
Website   www.alinke.com
Twitter   @darkillumine
Google+   Andrew Linke

To my parents...
for giving me the time to read.

And my wife...
for giving me the time to write.

Chapter One

Oliver fumbled with the tap, doing his best to keep the blood on his knuckles from smearing onto the spring loaded knob as he attempted to wash the battered fingers of his left hand. It was quite the challenge and he was starting to get angry. If only airlines had regular taps, he thought, or even those timed pressure taps. But no, the mandates of efficiency and conservation stood head and shoulders above the needs of passengers whose day-old scars started to crack and bleed in the dry cabin air of an eight hour flight.

He finished washing his left hand and started in on the right, rushing to finish before the newly washed knuckles began to bleed again. He succeeded for the most part, then reached into his toiletry bag for a washcloth. He gingerly padded at his fingers until they were mostly dry, hardly noticing as fresh red splotches joined the faded brown blood stains already speckled across the washcloth. He fished the last remaining packet of liquid bandage from the bag, ripped it open with his teeth, and began slathering its contents across his abused knuckles. The antiseptic in the bandage burned, but he hardly noticed. He tossed the packet into the trash slot and began waving his hands gently up and down in front of him to dry the bandage.

"Not a bad price to pay," he muttered to his reflection in the dingy plastic mirror. The man in the mirror nodded back at him and quirked a smile with one corner of his mouth.

Oliver leaned forward, inspecting his appearance. His khaki shirt was threadbare at the shoulders and bore the wrinkles of a transatlantic flight. His face was tanned from the unrelenting sun and snow glare of the last two weeks and the scraggly stubble of an underdeveloped beard was starting to show. His red hair was a disheveled mess from sleeping on the airplane. He ran a hand across the stubble on his chin and considered shaving before returning to his seat.

A soft knock sounded on the door of the tiny bathroom. Oliver started and reached for his bag, then remembered that he was aboard an international flight. The handgun he had carried for the last two weeks was locked away in a safe in Reykjavik. Besides, he chided himself, this was most likely just another passenger in need of the toilet.

The knock came again. This time it was followed by the softly accented voice of a flight attendant, "Sir, are you alright in there?"

"Yes. Fine," he replied, zipping his bag and reaching to unlock the door. "Coming out now."

Oliver had hardly left the restroom when he was nearly knocked over by a small boy pushing past him. The boy slammed the restroom door shut and Oliver looked to the flight attendant. She was about his height, with a thin frame and blond hair. Not exactly his type, but certainly pleasing to look at.

She smiled apologetically at Oliver. "I'm sorry sir, he was quite desperate and your compartment had been occupied the longest."

He stole a glance at her name tag. "No worries, Eowyn. Just a bit of first aid for my hands. Had a bit of a rough time of it on a glacier in Iceland." He flashed her a grin and waved one hand, knuckles towards her. As Oliver had expected, the flight attendant's eyes lit up at the sight of his newly bandaged fingers.

"Are you a scientist?" she asked.

"You could say that, but not studying the ice or volcanoes. More of a historian looking for clues to the early settlers," he explained.

"Fascinating. My sister is studying history at university."

"Oh? What's her favorite time period?"

Eoywn frowned and appeared to concentrate for a few seconds, then replied, "I don't really know. She talks about the Celts a good deal though."

Oliver smiled at that. "Neat people, the Celts. Can't say I'm an expert on them myself, but I have a friend who worked at dig in Brittany."

She nodded and seemed about say more, but at that moment a soft tone sounded from the service compartment.

"It's been lovely chatting with you, sir, but I have a call to attend to. I hope the remainder of your flight is enjoyable." She dipped her head to him and slipped past, catching hold of the beverage cart and pushing it down the aisle in front of her.

Oliver watched her go, feeling a vague guilt at noticing the pleasing curves of her uniform as she moved down the rows and paused to dispense a cup of hot tea to an elderly woman. Social mores could be so confusing these days, he thought. Thirty years ago, a man would have felt no compunction about noticing a stewardess, but now it was hard to tell if the lovely woman chatting you up outside the toilet was genuinely interested, or merely providing top-notch customer service with a smile. They weren't even called stewardesses anymore on most airlines, instead the generic term "flight attendant" had been applied to the entire profession. He considered waiting for her to return and trying to rekindle the conversation anyway, just to see where things went.

Then he noticed the man out of the corner of his eye.

He sat three rows away from the restroom compartment, between Oliver and the place where the lovely Eowyn stood dispensing a cola to an elderly woman. There was nothing remarkable about the man, except that he was staring at Oliver with undisguised interest. His dark eyes, small holes of black under a heavy brow, bored into Oliver across the rows. Oliver had never seen the man before, but he certainly didn't like the way he was looking at him.

Oliver turned away and returned to his seat. He didn't need any trouble on the plane, but he would have to be careful when they debarked. Hopefully he was simply being paranoid.

The remainder of the flight was uneventful. Oliver tried to get back to sleep, but the competing images of Eowyn's enticing curves and the dark-eyed man's threatening gaze kept him from resting peacefully. He passed some time reading, but after a short while, a baby began to cry several rows over, distracting him. He plugged his headset into the plane's entertainment system and selected a recent film from the media menu. Midway through the movie, he paused it and went to the toilet, half hoping to see Eowyn sitting on the crew bench, but she was nowhere to be seen. Oliver caught the man staring at him again as he emerged from the compartment.

Oliver traveled under his own name, of course. Airline security being what it was these days it wasn't safe for an average person to cross borders under a false name. But as soon as he was through Icelandic immigration control, Oliver had switched to one of the false identities he had purchased anonymously online several years back. He had scrupulously maintained that persona throughout his time in Iceland until the moment he stepped up the ticket counter in Reykjavik to pick up his returning ticket. If he was being followed, and that had yet to be proven, the people responsible had probably just booked a last minute seat when they heard the ticket agent announce which gate his flight would leave from.

Oliver settled back into his seat for the remainder of the flight. There was nothing he could do until the plane landed.

There was no point in worrying unless the dark-eyed man continued to watch him in the airport.

Debarking at Dulles International Airport, Oliver found himself crammed into a gangly large wheeled passenger transport with a hundred other weary travelers, including the dark-eyed stranger. Oliver made an effort to appear unconcerned. He neither watched nor obviously avoided the man from the plane. He still suspected that he might be suffering from a touch of paranoia. For all he knew, the man would clear immigration and walk right past the baggage claim to board a plane to California or New York.

As the travelers spilled from the hallways of the unloading terminal and began sorting themselves into the lines for immigration, Oliver slipped through the crowd and made for the restrooms located across from the roped-off queues. He spun on his heel and backed through the door to the men's room, using the moment before the door swung shut to scan the crowd for his pursuer. He didn't spot the man, but decided to wait a few minutes and see what happened. If he really was being followed, there was no telling whether the dark-eyed man was a citizen or not. Oliver couldn't count on losing him in the tangle of the immigration lines. Better to find out now whether the man was a threat or not.

He walked past the first row of stalls and turned a corner. He tossed his backpack onto the counter between two sinks and and leaned against the wall. From here he could just catch the reflection of the door in the mirror, but didn't think it likely that anyone coming through the door would notice him in the narrow sliver of dressing mirror that was visible from the first row.

Oliver pulled his phone out of his pocket and flicked it out of airplane mode, then waited for it to acquire a signal while he watched the door. The phone buzzed in his hand as the data connection activated and pulled down his e-mails. He glanced away from the door and skimmed the titles of the e-mails in his priority inbox. One of them caught his eye and he pulled it up. Delivery confirmed. One side of his mouth turned up in a crooked smile.

Just then, the restroom door opened.

Oliver glanced at the sliver of a reflection visible from where he stood. The man entering the restroom weighed at least three hundred pounds and had blond hair. Obviously not the dark-eyed stalker. Oliver slipped his phone back in a pocket and pulled a comb out of his bag. He waved a hand under the sink to wet his fingers, then started slowly combing his hair, but stopped when the man didn't turn the corner to the second row of stalls. A moment later he heard the clatter of a stall door locking.

The door opened again.

It was the dark-eyed man.

Oliver watched him in the sliver of mirror. The man paused and surveyed the first row of stalls, sinks, and urinals. Then he moved forward and out of the field of the reflection. Oliver tensed, listening carefully, ready to spring if the man came around the corner. He heard a stall door bang open. Then another. Then Oliver heard a loud thudding, followed by an angry shout as the man's hand pounded on the stall occupied by the blond traveler.

"What the hell, man! Occupied here." An angry New York accent, most likely the large blond man who had entered the bathroom after Oliver.

The banging of stall doors continued as the stranger worked his way down the rest of the row. Oliver waited, tense, his battered fingers flexing.

The stranger rounded the corner and spotted Oliver.

He swung a fist at Oliver's gut.

Oliver spun to the side and ducked, letting the swing slip past him as he rammed his elbow into the stranger's ribs. The stranger's dark eyes bulged and he let out a huff of air, then he seemed to recover and brought his fist down on Oliver's neck. The blow dazed Oliver and he dropped to his knees. He grabbed at the man's jacket as he fell. That caught the stranger off balance and Oliver heard a dull crack as the man's chin slammed into the countertop. The stranger went limp and Oliver pulled his feet back under himself and sprung up, slamming into the stranger's right side and spinning him round so he leaned stunned against the counter.

Oliver stood straight and grasped the man's collar with one hand, holding the other up in a tightly balled fist. He pushed his face in close and hissed, "Who. Are. You? Why the hell are you following me?"

The man's eyes came into focus and he glared at Oliver. He worked his jaw slowly and with obvious pain, but his gaze never left Oliver's face as he spoke. "You took something that doesn't belong to you." He growled in a thick accent that Oliver took to be Eastern European. "Give it back and we won't kill you."

Oliver chuckled and pressed his thumb up against the stranger's bruised jaw. The man clenched his teeth and groaned in agony. "I don't recall stealing anything from your part of the world recently," he whispered. "So unless I miss my guess, you're just pissed that I stole something before you had the chance to steal it yourself."

He slid his thumb back down the man's throat and waited, his gaze questioning.

The man spat, the spray spattering across Oliver's chest and right shoulder. He growled at Oliver, "Such details don't matter. You're playing a dangerous game, Mr. Croft. The people I work for have connections. What have you got? Nothing but a dangerous hobby and a target on your..."

A toilet flushed in the first row of stalls and both Oliver and the dark eyed stranger froze. Their eyes locked. Oliver tightened his grip on the man's collar, but dropped his fist to reach in the man's jacket and grab his belt. "If he comes round the corner, you slipped and I'm helping you up," he hissed. The man nodded. Whatever enmity existed between them, both knew it would be bad news to have airport security alerted to their tussle.

They waited. There was a click, followed by the hiss and splash of water running from an automatic sink tap in the next row. The blond New Yorker could be heard muttering something to himself, then the faucet stopped running and the restroom door squeaked open and banged shut.

Without breaking eye contact with the dark eyed stranger, Oliver rammed his knee into the stranger's groin, at the same moment releasing his grip on the man's collar and slamming his fist into his already bruised chin. The stranger's eyes rolled up in his head and he gasped. His knees went weak and Oliver let the man collapse onto the floor, then delivered one swift kick to the man's stomach before grabbing his backpack from the counter and running for the exit.

Oliver slowed just before he reached the door and left the restroom at a stroll, not letting himself look back as the door swung shut behind him. He strode directly to the citizen's check-in line and fished his battered passport from the side pocket of his khaki cargo pants. The line moved forward at a shuffle and Oliver pulled out his phone, both to kill time and to look as normal as possible as he kept one eye on the bathroom door. About three minutes later, he saw the restroom door swing open and the dark-eyed stranger walked slowly out, wincing with every step. The man scanned the crowded check-in line and locked eyes with Oliver, who smiled, waved, then gestured towards the check-in line with his free hand. The man glowered, then limped towards the line marked for visitors holding European citizenship.

Thirty minutes later, Oliver was through security and heading towards the immigration exit when he heard raised voices from behind him. He turned and saw his pursuer gesticulating wildly as three security officers moved in on him, stun guns out and pointed at him. Oliver smiled and reached into his pocket where he felt the worn pages of the burgundy passport he had slipped out of his attacker's jacket pocket during their encounter in the restroom. He figured it would take a few hours for the man to convince the TSA that he wasn't a terrorist, then a while longer for him to establish his citizenship and contact his embassy to work things out. Chances were that even then the man would be sent right back to his homeland.

All told, Oliver was pretty sure that he was rid of his pursuer. Still, whoever was behind this had arranged for him to be followed all the way from Iceland to Virginia, so it would be wise to take precautions. He pulled out his phone and tapped the name of his cousin, Amber, who was supposed to pick him up at the airport. She picked up immediately.

"Welcome home Ollie. Where you at?"

"Just got through immigration. Listen, I had some company on the plane. Looks like another collector isn't pleased with me winning this round. Would you mind picking me up at the Tysons Corner food court instead? I don't want to risk anyone spotting your car."

Amber didn't miss a beat. "Sure, but you'll have to tell me the story when I get you."

"I promise."

Oliver ended the call and shrugged his backpack on, then headed past the crowds surrounding the baggage claim, rode the long escalator to the ground floor, and pushed his way through the revolving glass doors into the sweltering heat of northern Virginia. He joined the line at the cab station and was soon settled into a barebones hybrid with vinyl seats and rubber floor mats.

"Where you going man?" The driver asked, his head bobbing slightly side to side to the rhythms of the jazz music coming from his radio.

"Tysons Corner Mall."

"At this time of day? Man, sit back and chill. You're in for a long ride."

Oliver did just that. He kept an eye out the window until the taxi had pulled away from the curb, just in case the dark eyed man had somehow managed to get past security and come after him, but the man never appeared and nobody in the throng appeared concerned with Oliver's ride. As the taxi pulled out of Dulles, merging into the crawl of Beltway traffic, Oliver finally allowed himself to breathe easy.

He pulled the passport out of his jacket pocket. The cover was even more battered than his own. He flipped it open and examined the photo on the first page. It was his man.

Nikola Simo. Latvian citizen. 36 years old and well traveled, by the stamps nearly filling the little book. No way to know if this was the man's real name, but Oliver was willing to bet that it was. False passports were growing more difficult to come by these days and in this business, the rewards really weren't worth the risk of being caught with false identity papers. In the grand scheme of things, a few relics acquired for a wealthy collector weren't worth a stint in federal prison or, worse, the holding tank of some third world nation that somehow caught you in a lie during immigration.

This Nikola character was probably a fellow treasure hunter who had been just few steps behind him in tracking down that particular piece of the puzzle. Dangerous, sure, but certainly not as deadly or well-organized as the Creed or its agents might be if they turned out to exist after all. The man hadn't even penetrated the false identity of Howard Croft that Oliver had used while in Iceland.

He pocketed the passport and closed his eyes, smiling a little as he recalled capturing his most recent prize. It had been quite an adventure, with more than one near brush with death, several broken bones on the part of people who got in his way and, if he was being completely honest with himself, a good dose of betrayal all around. But he had got what he came for and managed to slip out of Iceland with his false identity intact and his prize safely bundled off to home.

Oliver pulled out his phone and once again checked the delivery confirmation message. The package had arrived yesterday, right before he boarded the airplane. A smile crept its way onto his face as he settled back into the seat to wait out the ride.

Chapter Two

Oliver tipped the taxi driver and watched him drive off into the bright, sticky air of the Virginia afternoon. For once, Oliver didn't mind the heat. After two weeks in Iceland, he was glad to finally be warm. He lingered near the door for a moment, still wary of being followed, but none of the arriving shoppers appeared to pay him any mind as they dashed past him into the cold air of the mall interior. Eventually he turned and took the twisting staircase up to the third floor of the parking garage, crossed the pedestrian bridge, and entered the mall by the heavy glass doors of the food court entrance.

Amber was waiting for him at a table near the entrance. She was dressed in her typical style: a purple, retro-style flower dress with a tight bodice and a loose-hanging skirt. Her hair was topped with a flapper cap that he was fairly certain had been purchased from a handicrafts website. Some girls Oliver knew had gone through dozens of fashions over the years, but with Amber there had been a neat line of demarcation between her pre-teen years of coveralls and tennis shoes, and the switch to a 1920s retro style the same week that Oliver's mother had informed her, in no uncertain terms, that she had to, "stop dressing like an lowborn little waif and start wearing skirts, or you're never going out of the house again." She had disappeared into her bedroom for hours the next two nights, then pulled Oliver out to his car on Saturday morning and insisted that he drive her to a series of consignment shops. Amber spent that weekend draining her allowance on clothes that were certainly less revealing and tattered than her beloved coveralls, but nowhere near the modern fashions that Oliver's mother had in mind when she issued her ultimatum.

Although Oliver was three years older than Amber, the two had been best friends since she had come to live with his family at the age of twelve. She might have come from the unstylish side of the Lucas clan, born to his uncle Norman and his wife and raised on their dig sites throughout South America, but she could hold her own against Oliver's prep-school education and his parents' efforts to civilize her. They had bonded over a mutual love of history, his gathered from books and documentaries, hers from being raised by archaeologist parents, and it hadn't hurt that neither of them got on with Oliver's parents or the children of their high society friends.

"Ollie!" she shouted, jumping up and throwing her arms around his neck as soon as she spotted him.

Oliver hugged her back, then bowed formally and kissed her hand.

"Amber, my dear. And how are you this fine afternoon?"

She swatted him on the shoulder with a set of white gloves pulled from the belt of her dress. "Don't be an ass, Ollie. I'm an intentional anachronism from the Jazz Age, not a relic of the Gilded."

He smiled crookedly and offered her his elbow. "Right. That's why we'll be listening to piano punk in your car. Or is it back to steampunk death metal this month? Honestly, Amber, I can't think of the last time I heard you listen to jazz."

Amber took his arm and they strode together across the food court, heading towards the long escalators in the middle of the expanse. "Neither. This month I'm sampling artists from the neo-new wave movement. Really quite exciting, though most of them are indies with real jobs and families, so I'm having a devil of a time scheduling interviews."

"I'm sure it will all come together for you, it always does."

Amber squeezed his arm. "Thanks, but what about you, my intrepid cousin? Here I am wiling away the hours blogging about music while you're off galavanting across the globe. I saw your tweets, but I need more details."

"You could be having adventures with me, you know. After all, I'm not the one who fell in love with a homebody." Oliver teased, looking sideways at Amber.

She giggled the way he had known she would, then hit him with her gloves again. "Don't try to change the subject. You know perfectly well that I'm happy with Tom. Besides, I've grown accustomed to the comforts of home in the States."

Oliver nodded. When he had first started adventuring, as he liked to call it, he had invited Amber along. She had gone with him on one expedition to the Amazon, where they had revisited the scene of her parents' deaths and secured a relic that they, and later Oliver, had been searching for. Despite some near misses, everything had turned out well and Amber had no difficulty keeping up with him. But when he had invited her along on a journey to India to explore a long lost temple two years later, she had refused to come along. When he returned, he found that she had met a web developer named Tom and was already planning their life together.

"Well, I shot a few thousand photos of the glaciers and about as many of nude hot spring spas." Oliver began. "About a week of touch up work and I should have no trouble selling the best to my usual 'zine and website clients. I'll toss the middling ones on stock photo sites and should have my expenses covered no problem."

Amber rolled her eyes and leaned heavily against him. "Right, Ollie. You only go traipsing across the world to take photos of retired Scandinavians in their mud baths. Oh, and did you hear, I've decided to throw out my wardrobe and start dressing in black turtlenecks and plaid shorts?"

"So, you didn't want to hear about the legitimate reasons for my expedition? Well, then, as it happens I actually found... but oh, here we are."

Oliver slipped quickly away from Amber before she could hit him again and darted into a nearby camera shop.

The man behind the counter looked up at the sound of his entry and smiled broadly. He was large and bald, his light brown scalp polished to a glint. He wore round wire rim glasses over a thick black goatee and seemed to dress exclusively in tailored blue suits.

"Hey Oliver, welcome back. Iceland, huh?"

Oliver nodded and shook his friend's hand enthusiastically. He leaned against the counter and shrugged. "You know me Hank. Always looking for exciting photo ops."

"So you always say. And always sending your equipment back to my store after you have made a mess of it," Hank said with feigned annoyance.

"Hey man, I just don't want to risk my equipment getting dumped on the steps of the apartment. Besides, it's always nice to give the camera a good cleaning when I get back. Speaking of which..."

Hank nodded enthusiastically and held up a finger before disappearing into the back of the store. Oliver watched him go then he turned to smile at Amber, who had been examining a set of macro lenses through the glass countertop.

"You ever think of switching to this sort of work, Ollie?" She asked. "Maybe building miniatures and photographing them to look like real ships and towns."

Oliver grimaced. "You're not serious, are you?"

"I don't know. It might keep you out of trouble. If not miniatures, maybe get in on the wedding racket. Those guys make a steal for a day's work." She looked up at him and, while he was pretty sure she had been joking about the miniatures, Oliver thought he caught a note of concern in her eyes.

"Amber, are you worried about me?"

She gave a little shrug and broke eye contact.

"I'll be fine. Look, I made it back again without a scratch."

Amber slipped a little closer and gestured down at his hands. "Without a scratch, Ollie? What about your hands? Those cuts don't look like frostbite. Matter of fact, they look a lot like what I had to patch up down in Brazil."

Oliver sighed. He had almost forgotten his hands and, now that he looked at them, they were worse off than when he had patched them up on the airplane. Probably some extra damage picked up during his encounter with Nickola in the airport bathroom.

He looked up at his cousin and put on his best reassuring smile. "One of us has to be adventurous. You found Tom, and he makes you happy. And you got some closure on your parents down in Brazil. I'm still looking for my prize... looking for the answer."

Amber held his gaze for a moment, seeming to look for something in his eyes. Then she smiled and let out a little laugh. "I get it. Just be careful. I'm happy with Tom, but I still like to hear about your adventures, and I don't want one to have a bad ending."

Oliver chuckled. "Don't worry. I'll keep bringing you stories in person. This one is pretty good."

"As touching as this little moment is," Hank interrupted, "I've got your equipment right here." He set a large black bag down on the counter and unzipped it to reveal an SLR camera, half a dozen lenses, and several zipper cases for memory cards, all nestled into padded compartments and secured with elastic straps. "Your special lens is still in there too, looks intact."

Oliver zipped the bag shut and slung it over his shoulder. "Thanks, Hank. You put the cleaning on my card?"

"Certainly. As much as it pains me to charge a friend, one must keep up appearances." Hank winked at Oliver and pushed his spectacles higher on his nose. "Do I get to hear the story this time?"

Oliver nodded and took Amber's arm, speaking as he turned away. "Sure thing Hank. Dinner next weekend?"

"I'll be therem" Hank called after them.

They strode out of the camera shop and made their way through the crowded mall to the parking garage, Amber filling Oliver in on all the happenings in her life since he had been away. He listened attentively, but couldn't resist glancing at his bag every few seconds as they walked. Once in the garage, Amber broke away from him and led the way to a battered old Civic, fishing her keys out of her clutch bag as they walked. She unlocked the car and slid behind the wheel. Oliver dropped heavily into the passenger seat, laying his bag of equipment on the floor between his feet. They left the garage and pulled onto the busy streets.

"So when do I get to hear about your adventure?" Amber queried. "I only waited this long because I figured you wouldn't want to tell me about it in public."

"Just a minute. I need to check something first."

Oliver reached down and rummaged through the bag. He came up with a large black camera lens. He grasped the front and back of the lens gently and rotated, twisting the halves as if he were adjusting the zoom, but the barrel of the lens did not retract or extend. He continued twisting, first counter clockwise, then clockwise, then counterclockwise again. The lens grated as he turned it, as if there were grains of sand jammed in the gears. Then there was an audible clicking sound and the two halves of the lens split apart, revealing a chamber within.

Amber glanced away from the road to gawk at the device in Oliver's hands. "What is that? Did Hank mess up one of your lenses?"

Oliver grinned. "Nope. This is just something he cooked up for me a year or two ago. It looks like a normal medium range telephoto lens, but it's actually a little combination lockbox." He held up the two halves so she could peek into them. "It'd take a real thorough examination to tell that the barrel isn't just jammed with grit. Even has a small pass-though fiber optic so you can see light through the scratched up glass, just in case someone held it up to try and look through."

"I suppose that's where you keep all your treasures then," Amber said.

Oliver nodded. "Yep. At least the ones small enough to send by mail, which this one happens to be."

He upended the lockbox and dumped two clear plastic zipper bags out onto his lap.

The first bag contained what appeared to be a scrap of cloth covered in faded marks. Amber couldn't tell if there were drawings or words, but there did appear to be some bold lines drawn across the face of the cloth. The second bag contained a small piece of metal, about the size of Oliver's thumb.

Oliver picked up the metal piece and turned it slowly over and around between his fingers without removing it from the plastic bag. It was extraordinarily heavy for its size, crafted from some dark metal that he had yet to identify, and so cold that it felt like a cube of ice between his fingers. The sides were decorated in an intricate scrollwork of engraved lines. Two sides were irregularly marked with protrusions and divots of different shapes and sizes. He squinted closely at it, trying to imagine how it might slot into the other pieces he had already collected and wondering, not for the first time, how many fragments might remain to be found. He had already collected five from various hiding places scattered across the globe. Of course, if Nikola was any indication, he was not the only modern adventurer to discover this trail. For all he knew, one or more of the remaining fragments might have already been captured by a rival.

"Is that a part of the mechanism?" Amber asked. Her voice was suddenly serious, almost reverent. They had both learned of the device from her father's research journals and it was on their shared adventure in Brazil that Oliver had collected his first fragment.

Oliver nodded. "Yes. It's why I went to Iceland. I pieced together enough rumors and hints to find the cave where it was hidden. Had a hell of a time getting to it, but it was there."

Amber let out a long breath. "Wow. Do you think you have enough to prove your theory yet?"

Oliver shook his head and slipped the metal piece back into the lockbox. He picked up the bag containing the scrap of cloth and briefly examined it, then returned it also. He put the two halves of the lockbox lens back together and gave the front a single counterclockwise twist before pushing lockbox, which once again appeared to be nothing more than a camera lens, back into his equipment bag.

"No. Maybe half of it," he said. "But I've found enough that I've convinced myself that I'm not crazy."

Amber nodded and fixed her gaze on the road ahead. They drove together in silence for a few minutes, both contemplating what Oliver had just shown her. Ten years ago Oliver had been a promising young doctoral candidate making waves through the history department at Old Dominion University in Norfolk, Virginia. He'd taken semesters abroad at Cambridge throughout his accelerated undergraduate career, had a strong reputation as a meticulous researcher during his graduate work, and even succeeded in gaining a reputation among the undergraduates as a passionate and entertaining lecturer during the first year of his doctoral research. Then, over the course of two semesters, it had all come crashing down.

Oliver stirred from his reverie and looked out the car window.

"Where are we going?" he asked. "I thought we were going back to your place for dinner with Tom and the details of my adventure."

Amber grimaced. "We'll go soon, but first I need to take you somewhere. To see someone."

Oliver glared at his cousin. "Is this what I think it is?"

"Yes. And no. We are going to see him, but only because he has some business for you."

Oliver groaned and slumped against the back of his seat, letting his head loll beside the headrest dramatically. "You know I don't want to talk to him. It always ends in a fight."

"That's what you always say, but he really misses you. You haven't even seen him for three years. Don't you think it's time to bury the hatchet and mend some bridges?"

"I'm pretty sure you're mixing metaphors there, not to mention that a hatchet would probably be pretty useful when building a bridge."

Amber flushed and reached over to whack Oliver's knee with one hand while she kept the other steady on the steering wheel. "Don't be petulant. It's not my fault."

"And you think it's my fault? Come on, Amber. I tried to stay in academia but nobody would hire me. Not even the community colleges wanted anything to do with me once they called for references."

"And why is that?" she interrupted.

"Because..." Oliver paused, trying to think of an excuse that didn't sound hollow. "Because I was just following the truth where it led."

Amber barked a single laugh and nearly choked, trying to keep from laughing more. Oliver crossed his arms and sank lower in his seat, turning to look out the window at the landscape of rolling fields and oversized houses. He knew he was acting childish, but his fall from academic grace had been bad enough without his family refusing to support his decision.

A few minutes later Amber had herself under control. She glanced over at Oliver and said, "I'm not laughing at your theories, you big baby. That was one of the most ridiculous excuses I've heard from you yet. You weren't a journalist tracking down government corruption who got too close to the source. You were a hotshot young academic who made a lot of enemies just by outshining them. Enemies who were more than happy to snuff you out when you started spouting crazy philosophies instead of focusing on your historical research."

Oliver turned his head and glowered. "You just saw it Amber. How can you call what I'm looking for 'crazy philosophies' when you've seen part of it with your own eyes."

"You're being over sensitive, darling. I only said that because it's how everyone outside your small, and ever diminishing, club of supporters saw you."

He sighed and nodded, but stayed slumped in the seat. "I know you're right, Amber. Hell, I wondered if I was crazy for a while when all the kooky Internet people started glomming on to my work as evidence of their theories. But I've see it! I know the mechanism is real and there must be some way of proving it to the world. And then..."

He trailed off. Partly because he had already said all of this to Amber before, and partly because he didn't know what would come of his research. If Oliver was right about the relics he had been tracking down and assembling over the last decade, then he was also probably right about the global conspiracy that had disassembled the device and scattered it across the globe over three thousand years before. He hadn't found any evidence that the Creed, as he called the cult that had scattered the device, still existed, but that didn't mean he was safe. They might just be leaving him alone until it was more clear that he was a threat, and then... but he didn't like to think of that. Down that path lay true paranoia.

"This might help." Amber interrupted his thoughts.

"What?"

"When your dad called last week, he said that he had been contacted by someone who needed help finding something special. Someone powerful enough that they might be able to help you find what you're looking for."

Oliver sneered. "Really? After all he's said, he is willing to help me now?"

"He never said he wouldn't. Just that you should back off making any public comments and refocus your research."

"'Refocus.' Great word for throwing away the truth and caving to political pressure."

Amber shook her head and didn't reply.

Oliver returned to musing over the mechanism and his failed career as an academic. If only he had never found his uncle Norman's private research notes, or simply chosen to not believe them. He lapsed into contemplation of the events that had destroyed his career.

A few minutes of silence passed between them until Oliver shook his head, sat upright in his seat, and sighed. "Alright. I'll give him a chance."

"That's a good boy. Now stop pouting and tell me how you got that chunk of metal."

Chapter Three

Amber drove west from Fairfax, pushing the car through thick summer afternoon traffic for nearly an hour. As they drove, Oliver filled her in on his adventure in Iceland. Everything had gone well, he explained, until he had reached the cave where the object of his hunt had lain hidden for so many years. There, he had nearly been killed by a concealed deadfall and the animated corpses of three Viking warriors. Despite being low on ammunition, and here Oliver treated Amber to a lengthy rant on the difficulty of purchasing ammunition in Iceland, he had dispatched the ghouls and successfully captured his prize.

It was a token of their long friendship and shared experiences in the South American jungle that Amber saved her mockery for Oliver's inability to secure sufficient firepower, rather than his claims of fending off undead foes. Normally, when relating the tale to an editor or acquaintance at a party, Oliver would have excised the supernatural aspects of his adventure from the story, but he knew that Amber would believe him. After all, as she had reminded him in the camera shop, it was she who had cleaned his wounds after an encounter with a particularly pissed off snake god in the jungles of Brazil.

Amber eventually navigated the car off the main highway and began steering it along winding roads that wound through rolling hills and deep valleys. Oliver was familiar with this area, if not this particular road, from having grown up on the family estate in Loudoun County, west of Washington D.C. The valleys between the hills were crisscrossed with streams and narrow roads that connected the patchwork of small towns. The hillsides were covered in vast tracts of pastureland for beef cattle and racing horses, as well as the large and widely spaced homes of the wealthy landowners whose political machinations were perhaps even more famous than the products of their pastures.

Oliver had grown up on one of those farms. His parents had made a comfortable fortune breeding some of the best race horses on the East Coast and had started to carve out a name for the Lucas clan amongst the Washington area elite long before he had come along. As a child, he had spent many an evening helping the horse wranglers in the stables and most weekends exploring the limits of the family estate. When Amber joined the family, she became his companion in many of those rambles, injecting their escapades with a shot of exoticism from her intimate knowledge of Mayan mythology. It had been a good childhood and in many ways Oliver regretted not visiting his family more often. The chasm between him and his parents wasn't very wide, but it was deep and bridges had grown few and rickety over the last decade.

It had all started when Oliver had chosen to follow in the footsteps of his dead uncle and study history and archaeology at the college of William and Mary in Williamsburg, rather than launch a career in politics or finance through studies at Georgetown. His father had taken the news in stride, encouraging Oliver to "dig deep" and learn all he could about the past. His mother, on the other hand, had long hoped that her son would carry the family name to greater heights of fortune and influence, so she took the news rather poorly. He had been a diligent student, however, and had nearly managed to win back her approval when he had fallen from grace with such publicity and force that even his father had refused to speak with him for six months.

"We're here!" Amber exclaimed, breaking Oliver out of his reverie.

She braked sharply and turned the car into the gravel drive of a large house that stood at the head of a cluster of buildings near the top of a hill. The house was painted a faded goldenrod yellow with pale blue shutters over the windows. The wide front porch was screened in and adorned with simple white support columns and a double screen door. Wide granite steps led down to a series of stepping stones leading from the steps to the gravel driveway. A dozen or more cats were lounging about the place, sitting on the stone retaining wall, curled up in the grass, or batting at stalks of catnip growing in clumps throughout a flower garden that stretched along the front of the porch and around the corner of the house.

"What is this place?" Oliver asked. "Did my parents move while I was away at camp in Iceland?"

Amber giggled at that, then replied, "Of course not. This is the Rabbit Warren, a cozy little bed and breakfast nestled in the hills of Virginia wine country, only minutes from the highway and just outside a lovely little community of stuffy antique dealers."

Amber pulled the car around the back of the house and parked it between two large black SUVs. "The perfect place for a romantic getaway with your spouse, or a private tryst with the intern of the month."

"Something tells me not all of that is in the advertising materiel."

Amber shrugged and flashed Oliver a wicked grin. "I just call it how I see it."

Oliver grinned back at her, then his face grew more somber as he inquired, "Why are we here? My parents' place is just as close to D.C."

"My best guess would be that this is neutral ground."

"For what?"

"Your father wasn't specific, but I got the impression that he won't be the only person at this little heart to heart. Honestly, I'm not sure if he's offering you a patron as a conciliatory gift, or using your unique skill set to gain leverage with someone in power."

Oliver nodded, chewing silently on the inside of his lip.

"Ready?"

In answer, Oliver pushed the car door open and climbed out into the sticky heat of the afternoon air. Amber followed and the two of them walked together back along the path to the front steps of the house.

Passing through the screened porch they entered a large sitting room decorated in shades of yellow and blue, with dozens of small framed sketches of rabbits hung all over the walls. The room smelled heavily of cedar from a set of lightly smoking incense sticks arranged artfully on the coffee table in the center, between the overstuffed yellow paisley love seats.

"Nice place," Amber commented.

Oliver shrugged.

A short and plump woman with gray hair and a broad smile came bustling into the room and welcomed them with enthusiastic handshakes.

"Welcome to the Rabbit Warren. I'm Gwen, the owner of this fine little inn. How may I help you on this lovely day?"

Oliver shook her hand and smiled. "Hi, Gwen. My cousin and I are here to meet someone. Elderly man, dark hair, thin as a stick and about twice your height."

"Oh! You must be Oliver. Can't believe I didn't recognize you from the photo. Mr. Lucas told me to expect you." She turned to Amber and pulled her into a hug. "And you must be Amber. I've heard so much about you both."

Amber appeared startled by the sudden familiarity, but managed to return Gwen's hug with what passed for enthusiasm.

"You know my father?" Oliver asked.

"Know him? We're old business associates!" Gwen enthused, gesturing for the two of them to follow her through a doorway and down a hall. "We met at some fund raiser in town and it turned out that we both had something the other needed. He had connections and I had a quiet place where people could arrange to meet in private."

She led them through a gleaming steal and granite kitchen to what appeared to be a large broom closet. She opened a circuit breaker panel set into the wall and flipped several switches. There was a soft hum and the rear wall of the closet slid back and up, revealing a set of brightly lit steps leading down to a heavy steel door.

Gwen stepped aside and gestured for Oliver to go down the steps. He thanked her and did, descending the steps without hesitation. Amber made to follow him, but Gwen held up a hand. "I'm sorry dear, but Mr. Lucas said that only Oliver could come to this meeting."

Oliver paused his descent and turned around. "Then why did you even let her see the steps?"

Gwen smiled. "Oh, she'll be allowed down soon enough, I wouldn't deny her a peek at the room, but my clients pay for discretion and this particular gentleman needs to leave before Amber is allowed down there."

Amber grimaced and waved Oliver on. "Don't worry Ollie, I'll just have a cup of coffee and wait. Make sure you let him know I'm annoyed though. I don't like playing messenger without knowing whose messages I'm carrying."

She turned away and disappeared from the closet door. Gwen flipped a switch and the false wall lowered back into place at the top of the steps.

Oliver sighed and continued down the steps. It wasn't like this was out of character for his father. Michael Lucas was a good man, despite their differences Oliver would be the first to admit that, but his concepts of honor were perhaps a little more flexible than average. He had convinced Amber to lure Oliver to this meeting, and offered Oliver's services to someone without consulting him, so it wasn't inconceivable that he would bar her from the meeting if it suited his plans. The man would never harm Oliver or Amber, but he wasn't above using them as tools.

Oliver reached the bottom of the steps and tried the knob on the door. Locked. A glance told Oliver that the door was set in an equally heavy frame, which was probably anchored deep into the concrete surrounding the door. He knocked, knuckles sounding loud on the heavy steel of the door, then looked directly into the domed glass eye of the peephole.

The door swung silently open and Oliver found himself face to neck with a muscular man in a dark suit. A wire coiled from his left ear into the collar of his jacket and Oliver immediately noted the gentle bulge of an under arm holster. He looked up into the man's square face, noting the cold intelligence of his eyes. The man's expression remained blank as he looked Oliver up and down.

"Are you armed?" His voice was much softer than Oliver had expected.

"I just got off an international flight and was shanghaied into this meeting by my darling little cousin. So, yeh, I've got an arsenal in my back pocket."

"Don't fool yourself Oliver. That little girl probably has more firepower in her car than our Secret Service gentleman here." Oliver's father appeared behind the guard, a drink in one hand. "It's him, Ted. Frisk him if you must, but let's get this meeting started."

The guard nodded slightly and stepped aside, gesturing for Oliver to enter the room.

It was surprisingly bright and pleasant for an underground room, especially after the caves Oliver had been crawling through just a few days before. Comfortable white light filtered through panels set in the ceiling to illuminate a sitting area with four high backed leather chairs arranged around a polished wood table. The walls were painted a soft eggshell white, which extended into the thick carpet on the floor. One of the chairs was occupied, judging from the dark gray pinstriped pent legs that Oliver could see past the body of the guard.

The legs uncrossed and a man leaned forward to set a thick glass of dark liquor on the table. Oliver's eyes widened and one eyebrow moved up in surprise, but he stepped casually around the guard and extended a hand to the gray haired man.

"Senator Wheeler, now this is a surprise."

The Senator rose to his feet, flashed a charismatic smile, and shook Oliver's hand enthusiastically.

"It's good to meet you boy. Your father has just been filling me in on some of your little adventures."

Oliver glanced at his father, who winked at him over the rim of his glass.

"Seems to me you've been having quite the adventure of your own. I've been out of the news loop for a couple weeks, but the last I heard, you were your party's last remaining hope for a respectable nominee."

The Senator laughed and settled back into his seat, snaking his glass off the table and bringing it to his lips in a single smooth action. He sipped at it, licked his lips, and said, "Things certainly have advanced since then. In fact, I am the nominee now, hence Ted over there." He stabbed a finger of his drinking hand in the general direction of the large Secret Service guard standing in front of the door and continued. "However, I'd be lying if I didn't admit that I have some concerns about the general election. It's never easy going up against an incumbent, no matter her popularity."

Oliver felt something brush his elbow and turned to see his father holding out a glass of the same dark liquor the older men were enjoying. He took the glass and sniffed at it suspiciously.

"Jack. Good solid bourbon." Senator Wheeler said.

Oliver sipped at dark liquid. It burned this lips and tongue before slipping down his throat and spreading a fire through his chest. He made a face and set the glass on the table before dropping heavily into the armchair across from the Senator. His father walked around and settled quietly into the chair directly facing the door. Oliver slid the glass towards his father and looked inquiringly at the Senator.

"What can I do for you, sir?" he asked.

The Senator rested his glass on the arm of his chair and gazed steadily at Oliver. "Not a bourbon man, eh?"

"No. I try it every now and again to be polite, but I prefer craft beer myself."

The Senator cleared his throat. "I suppose I can respect that. Small brewers and their customers are a growing constituency in my home state. Tell me Oliver, are you a praying man?"

Oliver was taken aback by the non sequitur. "Excuse me?"

The Senator glanced from Oliver to his father, who shrugged. "Give him a break Wheeler. He didn't know you would be here. Boy's still surprised."

"That right, Oliver?"

Oliver nodded slowly, but didn't say anything. He was still trying to figure out what was going on here. Obviously his father had arranged for him to meet with Senator Wheeler, and it was equally clear that the Senator was trying to get some sort of measure of him, but he couldn't fathom where this might be going.

The Senator grinned again, a politician smile that reached every bit of his face and eyes, yet still struck Oliver as superficial. Perhaps because it was just a little too enthusiastic.

"I'm just wondering if you're a man of faith, Oliver. I like to know who I'm dealing with, and the question is absolutely relevant to our topic this afternoon."

Oliver stood and looked from the Senator to his father and back again. "Why don't we start from the top. Hi, I'm Oliver Lucas. I'm a travel photographer just returned from a trip to Iceland and I'm exhausted. Depending on what my father has told you, I'm also either a dithering crackpot conspiracy theorist, or a dedicated historian who believes that most of our myths and urban legends have roots in historical events." Oliver paused and glanced at Ted, who was standing impassively by the door, eyes fixed on him but not giving any sign that he considered Oliver a threat. He continued, "You're Senator Gary Wheeler, a career politician with a decent shot at the White House, sitting here in a secret bunker with my father, a self-made businessman who likes to play political power games in his spare time. Obviously I've been brought here for a reason, so why don't you stop dithering about whiskey and religion and just tell me what the hell you want."

Senator Wheeler leaned back in his chair, apparently surprised at Oliver's outburst. Oliver's father chuckled and took a sip of his drink.

"Alright." The Senator said, after studying Oliver's face for a moment. "Sit back down and I'll tell you why you're here."

Oliver returned to his seat and leaned back, crossing one leg across his knee and resting his hands on his lap. He looked at the Senator expectantly.

"Tim. If you could step outside."

The Secret Service guard nodded, pulled the heavy door open, and stepped into the landing at the base of the staircase, pulling the door shut behind him.

"Are you familiar with the Old Testament?"

Oliver nodded.

"Specifically, the tale of the Exodus from Egypt, when the children of Israel threw off their chains of servitude and began the long journey to the promised land."

Oliver nodded again and gestured for the Senator to continue.

"The Bible speaks of many wondrous events during that time. Plagues. Burning bushes. Pillars of fire. All signs from God that the Pharaoh must, 'let my people go' as Moses put it."

"I'm familiar with the story, Senator. All Sunday school stories and historical studies aside, I've seen The Ten Commandments over a dozen times."

Senator Wheeler smiled at that, and continued. "Then I don't have to go into detail about the origins of the legends concerning the Staff of Moses."

Oliver nodded his head in agreement. "I'm familiar with that bit of history. Moses carried it throughout the Exodus story, from the moment he spoke to God at the burning bush until he died just outside the promised land. It's supposed to have had many powers."

"Are you familiar with the fate of this particular relic?"

Oliver pondered that for a minute. It had been a long time since he had investigated that particular line of history. Finally he replied, "As I recall, the staff was supposed to have been passed from generation to generation among the kings of Judah, then lost during one of the invasions of biblical Israel.

Some scholars believe that it might be the same as the rod of Aaron, which was placed in the Ark of the Covenant and remained there until the Ark was lost."

"But what if the staff wasn't lost? Both scenarios you describe say it is gone, but I've heard other versions of the story. What do you make of the story that Moses's staff is actually in a museum in Turkey?"

"I've heard of that. Personally, I doubt it. In my experience most true relics were destroyed in arguments over what king, religion, or church should be allowed to control them. Only a few were kept safe by leaders of the religion that holds them sacred or hidden away in remote monasteries or caves."

The Senator nodded and reached for his liquor glass. He held the glass up the the light and contemplated the dark liquid within. "You say, 'in your experience.' What do you mean by that?"

Oliver contemplated how much to reveal to the Senator. He was cautious to cover his adventuring with a legitimate career, but there was no denying that his actions occasionally crossed the borders of legality. Then there was the matter of just how much the Senator knew of his academic past.

His father interrupted Oliver's train of through. "Just tell him, Oliver. You're here because Senator Wheeler mentioned something to me and I told him you might be able to help out."

"What did you tell him?" Oliver kept his voice level, but inside he was beginning to feel the pressure rise. After the collapse of his academic career, Oliver had kept the truth of his adventures to a small group of friends and a few pseudonymous internet forums. The thought of someone as powerful as Senator Wheeler knowing the truth about his international travel and research efforts gave him chills.

Michael Lucas shrugged. "He knows about some of your theories, and I mentioned your trip to Brazil a few years ago."

"As it happens," the Senator interjected, "I share some of your theories. Maybe not all of them, but I do sympathize with your plight. It's a hard thing to stand for your beliefs against the engines of secular academia."

Oliver shook his head and looked back at the Senator. "With all due respect, sir, you don't even know what you're talking about. I gave up my career because I refused to bury my theories, and I'm not sure you'd like half of them."

"However that might be, what concerns me is whether your 'experience' extends to the location and recovery of artifacts."

"It does."

"Might you be willing to recover something for me?"

"If it exists, and the price is right."

The Senator guffawed. He took a gulp from his drink and began to cough, then washed the cough away with another hearty slurp. "It always comes down to that, doesn't it?"

Oliver's voice remained level. "As you astutely pointed out, my stand against the engines of secularism robbed me of a career. Photography pays well, but unsponsored adventure travel is expensive."

"Oh, I understand, my boy. And I am certainly prepared to pay if you can deliver the goods."

"Again, what are you asking me to find?"

"I thought that would be obvious by now. I want to you retrieve the staff of Moses for me."

"I'm not a thief, Senator. If you want the staff from Turkey, go find a burglar to steal it for you. My speciality is tracking down long lost relics, not breaking known artifacts out of museums."

The Senator snorted. "Do you really think there is that much of a distinction?"

Oliver leaned forward in his chair and glared at the Senator. His voice was icy as he spoke. "There is a difference.

The relics I seek out are almost always lost to history. Their very existence as more than plot points in old myths is only believed by a few people. On some rare occasions I've encountered cults that worship and protect the objects, but generally they're hidden away in some decrepit temple or tomb, forgotten by all living people. I bring these objects back to the living. I give them a reason to exist once again."

"The cultural ministries of many nations would disagree."

"Are you this argumentative with everyone, Senator Wheeler?" Oliver asked, settling back in his chair with an exasperated sigh. "Because if you are I would seriously question your ability to govern a nation with nuclear weapons."

"I'm just trying to get the measure of you, kid," the Senator replied. "I need to know the person I send on this mission can be trusted to complete it without causing a diplomatic mess."

"I haven't accepted any mission yet, because you haven't explained yourself, but I assure you that I will not cause any mess. Now why don't you stop jerking me around and tell me why you think the staff of Moses is real, and what it has to to with me."

The Senator eyed Oliver over his drink of a moment, apparently considering his words. Oliver was growing increasingly tense. His father had shown no support for his research in the last decade and this was a hell of a way to start. Maybe he should just leave. He had dealt with prickly collectors and power-mad curators, but nobody he had dealt with in the last ten years had intentionally aggravated him like the Senator was. Something about the grey-haired politician rubbed Oliver the wrong way.

Senator Wheeler took another sip from his glass and set it down on the table. He leaned forward, looking Oliver in the eyes, and said, "The facts are these, kid. I've long been interested in biblical relics. A colleague in the State Department recently informed me that several previously unrecorded scrolls had been stolen from the Egyptian state museum during the recent upheavals in that country. These scrolls showed up on the antiquities black market a month ago. The description that accompanies them says they describe a battle between the Egyptians and the Hittites that ended when the Egyptians captured a magic staff from their enemies."

"That's all?" Oliver asked in a skeptical tone.

"No. Normally the State Department wouldn't have gotten involved in simple antiquity theft, but my colleague started hearing rumors from his contacts within the Egyptian state security community, or what was left of it after the government fell. It seems that one of the ousted officials from the Egyptian state security service has been making waves in the underground artifact trade, intimating that he will personally execute anyone who is foolish enough to buy this particular scroll. Of course, that drew the attention of my colleagues, who identified the official and passed word of him on to me."

The Senator paused and looked at Oliver, as if waiting for him to ask for more of the story. Oliver waited, not wanting to give him the satisfaction of asking for him to continue. If the Senator wanted him to travel to Egypt and track down a relic for him then he would have to stop playing games. A minute passed in awkward silence as Oliver studied the cut of Senator Wheeler's suit and Oliver's father slowly rattled the ice in his glass before the Senator sighed and continued.

"My colleague in the State Department learned that the official was one Rais Karim, former chief of the Egyptian official secrets bureau. Is the name familiar to you?"

Oliver shook his head. "Should it be?"

"I didn't expect you to know him, but it would not have surprised me since you are both in the same business. To the best of our knowledge, Mr. Karim was a member of an element within the Egyptian security establishment responsible for protecting, shall we say, genuine relics. Not just mummies that have been slowly turning to dust over the centuries, but fragments of the past that are deemed unsafe for public knowledge. You might say he managed the Egyptian Area 51."

"We both know that Area 51 is nothing more than a secret weapon testing facility," Oliver interjected.

"Alright, metaphorically speaking."

"So let me see if I'm getting this right. The Egyptian people rebel and throw out half the government. During the chaos a scroll is lost that might describe the fate of a magic staff, which you believe to be the Staff of Moses. And you think all this is real because a deposed Egyptian bureaucrat is trying to get his hands on the scroll?"

"That about sums it up."

"Sounds like a stretch to me," Oliver replied. He didn't say what he was thinking, however. He hadn't exactly told the truth when asked if he recognized the name of Rais Karim. He had heard the name many times before. Indeed, he had counted himself fortunate that his quest for shards of the mysterious mechanism had never lead him to Egypt, in large part because of the reputation of Rais Karim in the relic hunting community.

The world of relic hunting was not especially large and, even if people tended to hide behind pseudonyms, word of their actions tended to leak out. Even a few of Oliver's adventures had begun to circulate around the internet, albeit without his name attached, as other seekers put together the same clues he had and made their way to the hiding places of relics he had retrieved, only to find evidence of them being recently recovered. Oliver knew that there was still a wealth of genuine relics in Egypt, but he had long avoided that region because rumor had it that the secret police were actively protecting many of Egypt's relics, or at least safeguarding the best clues that might lead to them. And who could blame them, he thought, after the Egyptologists of the early twentieth century shipped half of the country's history to England and America. Rais Karim was said to be the chief of Egypt's relic protection forces, and there was more than one story of him personally interrogating would-be relic thieves who got to close to the genuine article.

"Tell me where I come in to this."

"I want that staff, and it looks like that scroll is the best clue out there at the moment."

"Obviously. But why do you want me?"

The Senator sighed, his face suddenly drooping into a mask of exhaustion. "As you so adroitly pointed out, I am running for President. The rest of my party might have self destructed, but I still have a good shot. If I can get that staff however..." His voice trailed off and Oliver thought for a moment that he looked genuinely embarrassed.

"Do you know what powers are ascribed to the staff, Oliver?"

"As I recall, Moses used the staff to call down plagues and draw water from rocks. It is also said to have turned into a snake once, but a literal reading would indicate that it was actually Aaron's staff was used for that bit of magic."

The Senator nodded. "Those are the popular miracles ascribed to Moses and his staff, yes. But there are others in legends and between the lines of the biblical account. At one time the Israelites went into battle and Moses held his staff up in his arms for a whole day. So long as his arms were raised, the battle went in favor of his people. Consider also the man himself. According to Exodus and the Midrash, Moses was a timid man with a weak speaking voice in the years following his flight from Egypt to Midian. But when God blessed him and showed him the fantastic properties of his staff, Moses grew in confidence and the children of Israel followed him."

"Does this have anything to do with your campaign?" Oliver asked.

"Yes. And no." The Senator looked uncomfortable again. "Look, this isn't something I can easily explain. On one level I know it is ridiculous, perhaps even a bit blasphemous, but something makes me think that if I have the Staff of Moses in my possession it might somehow grant me that edge in charisma. It might give me the boost I need to win this election. And even if it doesn't, you of all people must understand the impulse to own a piece of sacred history."

"I understand," Oliver replied. "Even if I think that you're just a bit cracked for believing that a relic that channeled the power of God over three thousand years ago in the Middle East could help you win an election in America this year."

Senator Wheeler shrugged. "What can I say. I believe it will."

"What's in this for me?"

"How does fifty thousand sound?"

"Dollars?"

"Of course. One of my nephews will purchase some shares in your father's horses at a higher than usual price, and he will forward the money to you as a gift. Everything completely legal."

Oliver looked inquiringly at his father, who nodded back at him.

"I assume you have a little more information than you've told me. I mean, if you want me to track down this staff for you, I need more than your word that there is a scroll somewhere in Egypt that says something."

The Senator nodded and reached beside his chair for a briefcase Oliver had not noticed before. He pulled the briefcase onto his lap and clicked it open. He pulled out a manila envelope and passed it to Oliver across the table. "Consider this a downpayment. The remainder will be transferred to your father when you complete the job."

"I don't return deposits."

"Understandable in your line of work."

"Egypt isn't the safest place right now. I'll need some help with getting a few weapons into the country."

"Of course. Give your father whatever you need, up to about this big." He outlined the form of a small travel bag in the air with his hands. "Then let him know what hotel you'll be staying at, and I will ensure it is delivered. We have diplomatic packages going back and forth several times a week, so there should be no difficulty in including your equipment."

Oliver stood and extended his hand to the Senator. "I appreciate that you called on me for this. I'll do my best."

The Senator shut his briefcase, stood to shake his hand and replied, "Certainly, my boy. When I mentioned the staff to your father he assured me that you were the man for this job. When can you leave for Egypt?"

"I've literally just returned from Iceland. I need a day or two to rest and gather supplies for the desert, then I'll be on my way."

"Take a room at a hotel in Cairo. Leave the address with your father and I'll ensure your supplies are delivered promptly, along with all the information my people in Egypt have on the scrolls that are up for sale. How long do you anticipate this taking?"

"That will depend on what I find when I get there. Do you tweet sir?"

"Tweet?"

"Microblogging. I sometimes use a secure account to take notes and share my progress with clients."

"Oh, yes. I have someone on my staff who manages all that social stuff, but I never touch it myself."

"Then you'd better arrange a prepaid cell phone for us to talk on. Buy it with cash and send the number to my hotel."

The Senator nodded, but he was clearly uncomfortable with Oliver telling him what to do.

"Thank you, Senator. I'll do my best. Now if you don't mind, I need to have a word with my father, I haven't seen him since before I left for Iceland." Olive gestured to the door and smiled.

"Before I go, just one thing." The Senator said, holding up a hand.

"What?"

He placed the hand on Oliver's shoulder and gripped it tightly. He looked into Oliver's eyes and said, "If you screw me on this, or breathe a word of what I've asked of you to the media, you'll never fly again. It's not hard. One word to the right agency and your only way off this continent will be with a private sailboat." His voice was calm, and slightly slurred from the whiskey, but there was gravity to it.

Oliver met the Senator's gaze without blinking. He waited, not trusting his voice because he was genuinely afraid now, certain he could out-stare the politician. His muscles tensed as he mentally went through the steps it would take to remove the Senator's fingers from his shoulder and snap them one by one.

Senator Wheeler blinked first. He stepped away from Oliver, nodded past him to his father, and pulled the heavy door open. Ted the Secret Service agent pulled the door shut without a word as the Senator stomped up the steps.

Oliver turned to his father and exploded, "What was that? You hardly say a word to me for six months, then all of a sudden, you're the proud father showing me off to a Presidential candidate?"

Oliver's father rubbed his pointy chin, took another sip of his whiskey, and gave a slight shrug. "I'm sorry Oliver. I know that this won't mean terribly much, but I do feel bad about that. I just wanted to try and make it up to you. I thought this would help."

"And the chance to show off to a candidate had nothing to do with it?"

"Nothing."

Oliver relaxed a little. He was still upset, and didn't believe his father's denial of any political motivations, but willing to listen. "Well, it's good to see you again, Dad."

"Likewise, son. I'll be frank. I still wish you'd at least toned it down a little when your career started to look rocky, but you've still managed to make something of yourself over the last few years, and I am proud of that."

Mr. Lucas stepped forward and offered his hand to Oliver who, after only a brief hesitation, reached out and shook it. Their hands clasped tightly and Oliver looked his father straight in the eye and held his gaze until the older man blinked and broke his grip. He clapped Oliver on the arm and grinned.

"You want to stick around for a drink? I think Gwen might have some of those beers in the fridge."

Oliver shook his head. "Maybe when I get back. I'm still dehydrated from the flight and it looks like I'll be boarding another before the week is out."

Michael Lucas nodded and led his son through the heavy door and up the stairs. At the top he pressed a comically large red button set into the wall and waited for the false wall to swing up and out of their way. Once in the closet, they paused briefly to listen, then opened the door of the broom closet and stepped out into the kitchen. Amber and Gwen were there, sitting opposite one another with a steaming teapot on the table between them. Amber was in the middle of explaining her opinion on a recent live metal album to Gwen, who appeared a bit dazed at the younger woman's blithe summary of the band's onstage antics. Michael swept in and rescued her with a request to see how the gardens were growing since he had last been at the inn.

Amber recognized her uncle's gesture and stood to hug him goodbye before grabbing Oliver's hand and leading him out the door and directly to her car. As they drove away from the inn he filled her in on the encounter in the bunker. She expressed annoyance at having never seen the underground room then lapsed into silence for several miles. Oliver rode quietly beside her, contemplating the day's events.

Eventually she spoke, her voice so calm and level that Oliver knew instinctively that she had been composing the sentence for at least a mile, working over exactly how to say it without too much emotion. "Oliver are you sure you want to take this job?"

Oliver looked at her and sighed, his breath coming out long and slow. Then he spoke. "No. I don't trust the man as far as you could throw him."

Amber couldn't help giggling a little at that remark, but quickly became serious again. "Then why are you taking it?"

"Because... What if? Amber, what if this is real? What if I actually have the chance to get my hands on a real piece of biblical history? So far everything I've managed to track down has been from the scattered remnants of fallen civilizations and dead religions. This might be my chance to find something that half the world would recognize as a genuine relic."

"Except that they'll never get to see it."

"Well, yes. Except for that." One side of Oliver's mouth turned up in an ironic smile. "But it would still feel good."

"Until the Senator turns on you."

Oliver knew she was right. He had been thinking along those same lines ever since the door had closed on Senator

Wheeler back at the inn, but the urge to find out exactly what he was dealing with was too strong.

"I'm going through with it," he said.

Amber knew that tone and knew better than to try and talk Oliver out of his decision, so she just took a deep breath then said, "Do you want me to keep the mechanism fragment for you while you're gone?"

Oliver nodded. "I've got the others locked up in bank vaults across the country. If you could put this on in a safety deposit box somewhere around here, I'd appreciate it."

"If you won't listen to my advice and get out of this game, the least I can do is lend you a hand."

Oliver nodded and settled back into his seat. He closed his eyes and began running through a list of what he might need to pack for his latest adventure.

Chapter Four

Five days later, Oliver was once again aboard a plane winging in for a landing at a large international airport. This time, however, it was Charles de Gaulle airport, fifteen kilometers north-east of Paris, France. While his ultimate destination was an expensive hotel in the center of Cairo, paid for with his advance from the Senator, Oliver needed to make a brief stopover in France first. If all went well, he would only be in Paris for a night or two before carrying on to Egypt and he would have secured a valuable asset for his mission.

Oliver had an insatiable appetite for adventure and an unshakable belief that he was right in his personal quest, but he had a definite weak spot in his understanding of ancient Egyptian languages and writing systems. He could read nearly a dozen ancient languages of Europe, South America, and Asia fluently, and could at least stagger his way through taxi instructions and hotel conversations in most major cities across the globe, but his studies had never taken him in the direction of learning to read the dead languages of ancient Egypt. He had, in fact, intentionally avoided studying Egypt any more than was necessary on the theory that the entire region had been picked clean by grave robbers and amateur archaeologists in the first half of the twentieth century and was therefore unlikely to hide any fragments of the mechanism.

That was why he had taken this detour to the City of Light. His cousin Amber was not the only person fully versed in his theories who still believed that Oliver wasn't completely insane. There was also a certain spunky art historian named Diana Jordan. She and Oliver had dated for a few months during his graduate studies, but their relationship had imploded after Oliver took off to South America with Amber and didn't return for two months. She had also believed that arcane truths lay hidden behind the myths of the ancient world and so they had kept up a lively friendship over the years, sustained in large part by their mutual interest in discovering those truths.

Unlike Oliver, Diana had been willing to keep her more exotic theories to herself and focus her official research on comparatively mundane aspects of ancient art, albeit with a distinctly punk/goth twist. Her graduate thesis had been on the relationship between ancient depictions of gods and heroes and the modern view of them in underground pop art. She had graduated and taken a string of research and instillation development positions at museums across the country until a year ago, when she had won a two-year grant to study the Egyptian artifacts stored at the Louvre in Paris.

The plane landed at Charles de Gaulle airport early in the morning and Oliver made his way through French immigration without incident. He had brought nothing but a shoulder bag with a change of clothes and a few essentials, so there was no need for him to wait for baggage to unload from the plane. He skipped the taxi line and went directly to the train terminal, where he boarded the RER train to Paris.

The train carried him as far as Gare du Nord, where Oliver purchased a stack of metro slips from a vending machine and hopped on line five to Gare de l'Est. There he switched to line seven and joined the press of commuters traveling into central Paris. Oliver had visited Paris twice before and come to love the speed and efficiency of the city's metro system. He especially loved the, increasingly few, conjunctions between the modern metro stations, with their gleaming steel and glass, and the networks of old metro tunnels, both terrifying and beautiful in their profusion of shattered tiles and dripping walls. He left the final train and made his way to the surface at the Palais Royal station, which was built under a wide plaza directly across the street from the north wing of the Louvre.

Oliver knew that most tourists approached the Louvre from the west, walking across the crowded pavement to admire the statuary and fountains of the grand courtyard. There they joined a lengthy queue to enter the museum through the twisting lines of escalators under the enormous glass pyramid in the center of the courtyard. That path was fine to take once, for the grandeur of the experience, but Oliver had quickly determined that he preferred actually being in the Louvre to baking in the hot sun of the courtyard.

If Diana had been with him, Oliver would have used one of the employee entrances, but he hadn't told her that he was coming, so he would have to make his own way into the museum. Fortunately, he knew a path nearly as direct as the employee entrance. The plaza that Palais Royal was directly across from had a side entrance that, while far less photogenic, was almost never blockaded by crowds of tourists because all the maps marked it as nothing more than the entrance to an underground mall.

Oliver pushed through the heavy glass doors and rode the escalator down to the food court. His body insisted that it was nearly three in the afternoon, and Oliver had intentionally fasted and forced himself to sleep onboard the airplane in an effort to get himself synched to Parisian time as quickly as possible. He paused briefly at a vending machine to purchase a two-day Louvre museum pass, then strode to the food court and secured a sandwich and miniature cup of strong coffee from one of the vendors.

He settled in a booth and enjoyed his breakfast, watching people stroll by with shopping bags in hand. The crowds at this entrance to the Louvre primarily consisted of shoppers passing through on their way to an expensive underground shopping mall built under the plaza of the Louvre. Most of the people Oliver saw were here to shop, and the fact that a left turn at the Apple store and a step through a security checkpoint would bring them into the central atrium of the Louvre museum probably didn't even cross their minds.

His meal finished, Oliver strode the short distance to the checkpoint, waited for his bag to come through the X-ray machine, and continued into the museum proper.

He went straight through the reception area, up the central set of steps and past a booth where his ticket was stamped by a suited museum employee. He continued through the moodily lit Sully access corridor, went up a narrow set of stairs, turned left past a miniature sphinx, and turned into an alcove. Oliver glanced around. Seeing nobody around, he pulled out his phone and checked a note he had made on his last visit, then pressed a button set discreetly into the wall. A panel slid up, revealing a number pad. He punched in a number he had seen Diana use several months before when she took him on a tour of her new office in the bowels of the Louvre.

The number still worked. The wood panelling beside the number pad split and slid open to reveal an elevator. Oliver stepped into the car and pressed the button marked "2", then leaned back against the wall and ordered his phone to call Diana.

Diana answered on the fourth ring, "Oliver, this is unexpected."

"Hey Diana, you at the office today?"

"You know I am. This fellowship is up in three months and I don't want to waste a minute."

The elevator door slid open and Oliver stepped out into a small sitting area with halls leading off in three directions. He turned right and began walking down a hallway lined with cramped offices. The carpet here had once been a pale blue, but had worn thin and accreted a beige track down the middle. The walls were a faded eggshell tone, blending to a darker tan near the ceiling from decades of nicotine stains before smoking had been banned in the office.

"Funny you should put it that way," he replied. "I need you to waste about a week, maybe two."

"On what?"

Thirty feet down the hall, a door opened and a man stepped out, a stack of files crammed under one arm.

Oliver switched to French and kept walking, nodding perfunctorily at the man as they squeezed past one another. "I'm going to Egypt on a job, and I need someone who can handle hieratic and demotic scripts. You know I'm lousy at anything Egyptian beyond simple hieroglyphs."

"That's what you get for calling Egyptology 'over-done' and 'so twentieth century colonialist.' Incidentally, why the French?"

"Didn't want to draw too much attention to myself. Frankly, I'm surprised I got this far."

"Attention? Oliver, what are you up to?" Diana's voice slipped into a whisper and Oliver knew he had her hooked. If only he hadn't disappeared for two months without warning, they probably would have been perfect for one another.

"Just this," he replied, then ended the call and knocked on Diana's office door.

He heard a muffled string of expletives from beyond the door and smiled, slipping his phone into a pocket and leaning casually against the doorframe. The door opened and Diana faced him, eyes bright with anger and laughter at once.

"How did you get in here?" she demanded.

Diana pulled Olive into her cramped office, stuck her head out the door to ensure the hallway was clear, then slammed the door shut and leaned against it.

Oliver took in the cluttered space that Diana had been assigned in the warren of offices underneath the Louvre. Her desk was piled high with books and printed photographs, intermingled with scraps of paper covered in Diana's precise, but minuscule, scrawl. The walls were plastered with prints of paintings and bas-relief carvings, except for the wall behind her desk, which was dominated by a whiteboard covered in the colorful circles and lines of an extensive idea map. Oliver spotted the phrases "reborn hero", "overthrown deity", and "zombies", scrawled along several lines drawn between the titles of several popular comic books and strings of letters and numbers that he took to be entries from the museum collection catalog.

Diana stepped away from the door and plopped down on the edge of her desk. She crossed her arms and glared at Oliver. "Seriously, how?"

"I used the elevator. This place really should change security codes more often."

"I'm impressed you still remembered."

Oliver shrugged. "You know me, Diana. I caught it when you brought me through last year and saved the code to my phone before I forgot. No special memory tricks here."

Diana smiled a bit, then stepped forward and wrapped Oliver in an enthusiastic hug. Oliver responded in kind, enjoying the moment before releasing Diana to once again perch herself on the edge of her cluttered desk. He would always remember the summer abroad they had spent together in England. Her hair had been short back then, trimmed almost boyishly tight and dyed pitch black. They had spent nearly two weeks backpacking through the countryside to remote historical sites where they passed hours debating which elements of local legends were based on true events. Now her hair was longer, down to her collar, and the black had been accented with twin streaks of florescent blue. She was dressed simply in charcoal wool pants and a white men's dress shirt, open a couple of buttons at the collar to show off a patch of olive skin below her throat.

"I always liked how you could find your way into places, Oliver," Diana said, looking up at him from her perch at the end of her desk. "You said something about needing a translator for an Egyptian job."

"That's right. I've got a client who swears that he's got contacts in Egypt who have stumbled on a relic of historical significance. He wants it for himself. Thinks that it will give him some sort of advantage in his campaign for President."

"You're joking."

"Wish I was. Old contact of my father, a Senator Wheeler. He's one of the few candidates whose campaign hasn't imploded in the last few weeks, but there are some questions about his old buddies in military contracting business, so even his campaign is on shaky legs."

"How can you help him? Your specialty is relics from ancient religions and magic, with a dash of global conspiracy theory now and then."

Oliver shrugged and pushed his hands into his pockets and leaned one shoulder against the flimsy office door. "Seems the honorable Senator has a strong hunch that the genuine Staff of Moses is within his grasp, and that it might still bestow a dose of magical charisma upon the owner."

"Really?"

"He's a true believer. Though I suspect what he truly believes in is his own importance."

Diana laughed. "Alright, I see where you fit in, but what's this got to do with me?"

"Like I said, this is Moses's staff and my contact is in Egypt. I'm familiar enough with the bible and Egyptian mythology, but you know I'm lousy at interpreting hieroglyphs and scripts."

"You're right about being bad at the scripts."

"You know it. So, I need someone to come with me who knows those particular dead languages, isn't afraid of a little dirt, and won't tie me up and call the loony bin for going after a relic from biblical times. As I recall, you fit all of those requirements."

Diana pondered Oliver's invitation for a moment. He hoped that she would say yes, not only because he enjoyed traveling with Diana, but because if she didn't, he would be forced to find a local translator. That wouldn't be difficult, even in the chaos of post-revolution Egypt, but finding a translator who would stick with him in tight places could prove more difficult.

Diana launched herself from the desk with a giddy shout and leapt into Oliver's arms. He just managed to catch her as she wrapped her legs around his waist and planted an enthusiastic kiss on his cheek.

"Do you really think the staff is real?" she asked, clasping his head between her hands and gazing directly into his eyes.

Oliver nodded.

"And you're not just here in some ill-conceived attempt to win me back?"

Oliver shook his head. "We had a good time together, Diana, but I know as well as you that it'd never last. We work a lot better as friends."

Diana unclasped her legs and swung back to her feet, already pulling Oliver towards the door. He followed without protest and allowed her to spin him out into the hall as if they were dancing and she had the lead.

Diana locked her office and took Oliver's hand again. "Come on, I want to show you something."

"What?"

"Something that will explain why I'm willing to come with you on this crazy quest."

She led him down the corridor, past dozens of doors which Oliver assumed opened into cramped offices similar to Diana's. Eventually they turned a corner and came to another small lobby featuring more worn sofas and doors to restrooms, emergency stairs, and an elevator. Diana pressed the call button and the elevator opened immediately. They rode it back up to the public area of the Louvre.

Diana led Oliver around the imposing circular walls of the medieval Louvre, still preserved here in the basement level of the museum, and up a set of stairs in to the ground floor of the museum. Glancing out through the old glass panes, Oliver saw the distorted image of a group of tourists wandering through the enclosed space of the central courtyard. They continued up the worn marble stairs for two flights until Diana stopped their ascent at the first floor and gestured for Oliver to take in the collection of Greek bronzes marching into the distance of the hall before them.

"It's through here. You know, most people come to the Louvre and head straight for the Mona Lisa, maybe run past the Greek and Egyptian collections, then just head out to visit the Eiffel Tower. They don't take the time to really explore this place and appreciate its beauty."

Oliver nodded in agreement, then shrugged and replied, "True, but you've got to admit that this place is huge. It probably intimidates your average tourist."

"Oh, I get that, believe me. When I arrived I spent almost two weeks of evenings and most of my weekends exploring. Even after a year and a half I haven't done everything justice. Eventually I had to just surrender myself to the enormity of this place and say, 'Diana, you're in Paris. Get out and see the rest of the city now and then.'"

She gestured up at the ceiling of the round room in which they stood. "Part of the problem," Diana continued, "is that the Louvre itself is a work of art. Look here."

Overhead, the naked form of a muscular Icarus plunged to his death amidst a cloud of singed feathers. His father reached out towards him piteously, helpless to save his prideful son from plummeting into the sea. The painting was as richly detailed and vibrantly colored as any that Oliver had ever seen, but it was not a framed canvas hanging on the wall. This work of art appeared to be painted directly onto the ceiling of the room in which they stood.

"That's The Fall of Icarus, painted in 1819 by Merry-Joseph Blondel." Diana explained. "A lovely bit of Greco-Roman mythology, as imagined by an European two thousand years after the story was told."

"I know the myth." Oliver acknowledged.

"My point isn't to refresh your understanding of childhood stories, but to point out the beauty this building. Many museums hold classic art. Some museums, the Pyramids of Giza or the childhood homes of Civil War generals come to mind, are actually the object on display themselves, even if they aren't all they pretty to look at. But this building melds the two so completely that the structure itself is a work of art."

Oliver nodded and patted Diana on the shoulder, understanding her passion.

"But this isn't what I need to show you."

Diana grabbed Oliver's hand again and pulled him out of the round room and through a several long galleries filled with Egyptian artifacts. They stopped in a room lined with ornately carved and painted wooden sarcophagi and Diana gestured for Oliver to look up at the ceiling.

Above them was a scene out of a horror movie. At the far right stood a man in red robes and a striped headdress, gazing sternly into the distance as he supported a dazed woman, bare breasts pressed against him, with one arm. With his other arm he held a golden staff, with which he was fending off a hoard of gaunt fiends and fire-breathing hellhounds. The monsters crowded forward, clutching at the heels of the helpless woman and gazing malevolently at the man in red as clouds of foul smoke billowed up at their backs, but were repelled from her as if by an invisible wall.

"That's Egypt Saved by Joseph." Diana explained. "Painted by Abel de Pujol in 1827."

"Looks pretty terrifying." Oliver commented, walking around the room with his neck craned upward to inspect the work from different angles.

"Of course. If you believe the official story about the painting, Pujol was hired to paint this room with a biblical scene to accent the Egyptian artifacts that King Charles X intended to display in here. The plan was to focus on the story of Joseph saving the Pharaoh and his people from starvation, rather than the more popular Exodus account, since the king felt that a painting of Moses would not have been entirely appropriate to a room dedicated to honoring the might of Egypt."

"That makes sense. Though I wouldn't be surprised if he was also uncomfortable with the idea of a painting of slaves overthrowing their ruler with the support of a wrathful god."

"True. But getting back to the facts, think about the story of Joseph. How did he save Egypt?"

Oliver paused for a moment to ensure he had the facts in order. He was certainly familiar with the story, but for the last few months, he had been immersed in Icelandic folklore and he wanted to be sure he didn't mix up the details.

"As I recall, Joseph was sold into slavery by his brothers because they were jealous of his father's favor. The slavers brought him to Egypt, where he quickly rose to a trusted position in his master's house, only to be thrown into prison when he pissed off his master's wife by rejecting her advances."

Oliver looked at Diana to ensure he was keeping the story straight. Diana nodded and waited for him to continue.

"In prison he correctly foretold the fates of two other prisoners. One was executed, just as he predicted, while the other was restored to his position in the Pharaoh's court. A while later the Pharaoh started having bad dreams and the freed prisoner suggested that he call on Joseph to tell him what they meant. Joseph interpreted the dreams correctly, saving Egypt and winning himself a place as the Pharaoh's chief aid."

"Decent summary, but there are two important things you left out."

Oliver gazed up at the painted ceiling and pondered the scene for a moment. Diana was right, something was missing from his story, and from the painting above their heads.

"I don't remember there being anything about demons or hellhounds in the biblical account, Apocrypha, or what little I've read of contemporary Egyptian accounts."

"The Egyptian evidence is sketchy at best for the entire period, but nothing that can be linked to the likely biblical Pharaohs mentions such creatures. The only place you're likely to find them is in folk tales of the period."

"As I recall, Joseph is said to have saved Egypt from a predicted famine by also predicting a time of plenty that would precede the famine, during which he proposed that the Pharaoh should stockpile grain to be distributed when the famine struck."

Diana nodded and gestured at the ceiling. "You're exactly right. Those monsters are completely out of place. The title and artistic style of the painting indicates that it is supposed to depict Joseph literally defending Egypt from the threats that Pharaoh dreamed about, but if that were the case he should be pushing back a few withered husks of grain and a herd of starving cows. You could almost argue that the human figures are gaunt enough to represent the famine, but that then theory is ruined by the hellhound over there on the left edge of the mural."

Oliver strode over a wooden bench set under one of the room's wide windows and sat, crossing his legs and leaning back to further examine the painting.

"So what's your theory on this?" He asked.

"Pujul was an artist who spent much of his life working here in Paris. When I saw this painting a little over a year ago the differences between the title and the content were just too deep to be ignored, so I started digging for more information about his life and the story of this work. It turns out that Abel de Pujul had a younger brother named Gabriel. Gabriel didn't become an artist. Being the younger brother and unable to depend on an inheritance he needed to find a career that would provide a steady income, so he borrowed money from his brother to purchase a commission into the French Army."

Diana gestured up at the painting and continued. "Reading what I could find of Abel's letters and journals, I discovered references to creatures like what you see up there. Those all trace back to stories that Gabriel told Abel after returning from Napoleon's Egyptian campaign."

"What does that have to do with hellhounds and... whatever you call those hungry fiends up there?" Oliver inquired.

"Napoleon spent about four years in Egypt. That time was marked equally by fantastic discoveries and bloody battles against both the British and native Egyptian forces. We all know about the discovery of the Rosetta Stone, but there were countless other artifacts recovered during that time. Napoleon is also rumored to have sent several ill-fated expeditions up the Nile and out into the desert seeking relics of the Pharaohs. According to one letter that I found, Gabriel de Pujul was the sole survivor of one of those expeditions. The letter is very circumspect, but it had to be, given the amount of censorship that military mail was subject to, but in it he announced his return to France and alludes to seeing his comrades 'taken by fiends of the desert' and quotes heavily from the book of Exodus."

"Couldn't that just be a battle-worn Frenchman getting colorful in his descriptions of native rebels? European soldiers weren't exactly known for their fair portrayals of people they viewed a savages."

"True, but there's one thing I haven't told you yet."

"And that is?"

Diana gestured up at the painted ceiling. "What do you see in Joseph's hand?

Oliver examined the art, then replied, "It looks like some sort of staff."

"Precisely."

"And your point is?"

"Even if we accept that Pujul has set this mural at least seven years into Joseph's rule, when he might have actually held a staff of office and dressed in the fashions of the Egyptian nobility, that staff is all wrong. Egyptian rulers are usually depicted holding straight metal rods topped with the head of a jackal. Joseph's staff in this painting is clearly wood and the head is shaped more like a shepherd's crook. "

Oliver had a feeling that he knew where Diana was going with this. "Are you suggesting that Abel de Pujul intentionally altered the depiction of Joseph in this painting to match his vision of what Gabriel described to him?"

"It fits the timeline. Gabriel was sent back to Paris to serve in a non-combat position soon after surviving that ill-fated mission. There are no more letters between the brothers, but in subsequent years Abel's journal contains frequent notes of meetings between the brothers, alongside sketches that appear to be rough drafts for parts of this painting."

Diana paused and gazed up at the painting for a moment, then turned to Oliver and crossed her arms. She stared until he lowered his head and looked her in the eye.

"Oliver, normally I'd be a bit annoyed at you for suggesting that I drop everything and follow you to Egypt without notice, but this is exactly the chance I have been waiting for. If your employer's scroll turns out to be genuine, then this might be an opportunity to follow Gabriel's trail and learn exactly what he found out there in the desert."

"So you'll come along?"

Chapter Five

Two days later Oliver and Diana checked into adjoining rooms on the nineteenth floor of the Hotel Sofitel Cairo El Gezirah. Diana expressed surprise at the choice of lodging when their taxi pulled up under the carport of the gold-topped pink tower located in the nook of a curve in the Nile. Oliver finished paying the driver, stepped up beside her, and explained that he had received a large advance on this job.

"Besides, we might as well be comfortable for the next few nights. Soon enough, we might be camping in the desert for a week or more."

Diana nodded in agreement and they pushed through the revolving door into the cool air of the hotel lobby.

The clerk at the desk greeted them in flawless English and informed Oliver that two packages had arrived ahead of him. Oliver requested that these be delivered to his room and gestured for Diana to lead the way to the elevator. Once upstairs, he insisted on checking her room before entering his own.

"I'm not helpless, Oliver." Diana complained as he pushed past her into the room.

"Obviously, but when were you last in a fist fight?"

"Eighth grade."

"Well, that puts me in the more experienced category when it comes to dealing with any bastard agents or relic dealers hidden in your closet. We're in-country now, Diana. Things might get dangerous."

That seemed to upset Diana, so Oliver didn't make any further comments as he pulled an electronic bug sniffer, disguised as a light meter for his camera, out of his carry-on bag. Once he was certain that the room was clear of both electronic surveillance and attackers in waiting, Oliver informed Diana that he was going to get a shower and lay down for a few minutes. She expressed similar plans and they agreed to meet again in an hour.

Oliver locked his door behind him and leaned against it for a moment, taking in the view of the room. It was a perfect mirror of Diana's room next door. Both rooms were decorated in shades of amber and beige, with thick green carpeting on the floor and a single wide window looking out over the curving banks of the Nile. A heavy door set into the adjoining wall could be opened to reveal the flat face of a matching door, allowing easy access between the rooms when both doors were opened. Oliver made a quick check of his room and, convinced he was alone and not under any obvious surveillance, stripped and climbed into a cold shower.

It had probably been a mistake bringing Diana along, he thought as the chilly water pounded against his skin. Sure, he needed a translator and he was certain that she was the most competent Egyptian linguist he could trust. For that matter, she was perhaps the only one he could trust if the story about the staff turned out to be true. He was also reasonably sure that she could hold her own if things got rough, which was important. Three years ago, he had allowed a girlfriend to travel with him on a simple photo expedition, assuming that anyone who fell for an outdoorsman and expressed interest in traveling to exotic places would be at least as competent as Diana or his cousin Amber, and that was been a disaster. The relationship had come to an abrupt end when, two days into the jungles of India, his girlfriend had announced that she was taking one of their guides and returning to the city with or without Oliver.

No, it wasn't concern for Diana's linguistic skills or survival skills that had given Oliver a niggling sense of unease, which had grown into a raging headache in the last hour. It was a growing worry that he had gotten in over his head on this job and was now involving someone he cared about. Senator Wheeler hadn't even been vague in his threat to interfere with Oliver's livelihood should he suspect that Oliver had betrayed him. That was disturbing, but Oliver had ways of getting around the no-fly list if matters became desperate. But if the Senator decided to interfere with Diana's ability to travel and work internationally, Oliver would feel terribly guilty and have no ready means of remedying her situation.

Oliver stepped out of the shower, toweled his hair dry, and wrapped the towel around his waist. He shaved in the boggy bathroom mirror, then stepped out into the main room. He stood for a moment, gazing out the window at the lazy waters of the Nile far below. Boats darted past, splitting the sun-specked surface of the water with their wakes. After a few moments of contemplation, he tossed his towel over a chair and pulled on underwear and a pair of brown khakis from his bag.

He settled into a chair by the window and focused on breathing slowly and contemplating the ramifications of his decision to take this job for a few minutes.

"Alright, enough of that," he muttered.

Oliver rolled out of the chair and spent the next ten minutes exercising to work out the kinks in his muscles and clear his head. Then he stood and began unpacking his suitcase. He wanted the room to appear as normal as possible, just in case it was checked by Egyptian or American security. Fortunately, many of the trappings of his legitimate role as an adventure photographer aligned nicely with the needs of a rogue relic hunter.

His exercises were interrupted by a knock on the door separating his room from Diana's. Oliver sprang to his feet and turned the bolt. Diana stepped into the room, glanced briefly at Oliver's bare chest, and strode over to the oak table in front of the broad window, where she fell into a chair and regarded him critically.

"I get the feeling that you don't thoroughly trust your employer." Diana said.

Oliver left the door between their rooms open and stepped over to the closet to pull out a lightweight button-up shirt. "I trust him to act in his best interests, which might not always line up with ours."

"How so?"

"I don't like people treating relics as if they are some sort of cosmic vending machine. Just because something channeled divine power four thousand years ago, or was the focus of belief for an entire nation, that doesn't mean that it is still going to be effective in the present day. And if a relic does still possess power, why should that power be used for personal gain?"

"Understandable. So why did you take this job?"

Oliver studied Diana for a moment, trying to figure out how he could explain his concerns without appearing weak. Finally he turned and gazed out the window at the glistening waters of the Nile flowing past the gleaming towers of the city, and out beyond to where the sand dunes stretched into the distance.

"What's the most intimidating position you've ever found yourself in?" He asked her.

She pondered the question for a moment, then responded, "My thesis board. They were pretty brutal in questioning some of the connections I drew between comics and ancient mythology."

"I know that feeling. You might recall that a similar event cost me my career. Now imagine that times about ten and you might have half an idea what it's like to be standing face to face with a man who has a serious chance of becoming the President of the United States and he's threatening to ruin you. If I fail here and Wheeler decides it was my fault... we both might be in a world of trouble."

"You don't really think he'd exploit his position for a personal vendetta?"

"What do you think this whole job is? Wheeler is a powerful man using his influence to get what he wants, damn the rules."

"You're not a big fan of rules yourself, as I recall."

Oliver had to smile at that. "True, but as hypocritical as I might sound right now, I've got this notion that people who are in powerful places have a responsibility to not abuse their power."

"So why are you helping him?"

"I don't know that I had much of a choice. Senator Wheeler is a powerful man. I couldn't risk him going after me. All it would take is one call to the TSA and I'd be unable to fly for months, maybe years. I couldn't even prove it was him. Just a mistake. A simple mixup of names on the no fly list, happens all the time."

Oliver stepped up to Diana's chair and rested his hands on her shoulders as he spoke intently. "Diana, I'm this close. Just a few more pieces and I might be able to finish assembling the mechanism, then I'll understand why so many ancient cultures refer to it. Why inexplicable technologies cropped up across the globe. I need to know, Diana. I can't afford to be trapped in the United States indefinitely. And if he targets you too..."

She looked at him closely, studying Oliver's expression with an intensity normally reserved for faded paintings and eroded glyphs. Finally she said, "Don't worry about me, Oliver. If things go bad there's plenty of work for me in the States." She studied him a moment longer, then put her hand on his cheek. "You might be afraid Oliver, but I see in your eyes that you're hungry for this. You want to find that staff, don't you."

Oliver released her shoulders and fell back onto the bed. "You know me too well, Diana. I don't know if I can give it to the Senator, but I absolutely want to find it."

"Then stop fretting. We'll find it if we can, then we'll deal with the Senator."

There was a knock at the door.

Oliver rolled off the bed and went to squint through the peep-hole. A uniformed hotel employee stood in the hall, one hand resting on the handle of a hard-shelled black rolling suitcase. A small briefcase rested at his feet. Oliver recognized the large case as the one he had delivered to his father to be sent over in the diplomatic mail. He opened the door.

"Delivery for Mr. Oliver," the man stated.

"That's me."

The man rolled the suitcase into Oliver's room and asked where he would like it left. Oliver told him to toss it on the bed, then fished a few crumpled bills out of his pocket for a tip and hurried the man back out into the hall.

"Is your door locked?" he asked Diana.

She nodded.

"Alright, now we can get started."

Oliver stepped over to the bed and grabbed the briefcase first. He didn't recognize it, but considering its arrival alongside his bag of toys he had a good idea who the briefcase was from. It was a fairly generic business unit with a small name plate set under the handle, Oliver's name scrawled across it, and a simple three-dial combination lock set into the left latch. He put the briefcase on the table and slipped the paper tag out of the name plate and examined it.

"From our friend in Washington," he said.

The back of the paper bore a simple message: *The date of our meeting.*

Oliver slipped the paper tag back into place and spun the dials of the combination to the day and month of his meeting with the Senator, just over a week ago. The lock clicked open and Oliver opened the case to find several stacks of Egyptian currency and a manilla envelope. Oliver unwound the string on the envelop and dumped its contents out on the table: A simple flip-shell cell phone, three poorly lit photographs of what appeared to be an ancient manuscript, a printout from an internet forum, and a hand-written note.

The note was written in blocky capital letters that could have been penned by the senator, one of his aids, or a dexterous kindergartener. It said, "CALL RAIS. HE WILL WANT TO MEET IN PUBLIC. GOOD LUCK. CONTACT ME AT NUMBER BELOW WHEN DONE." Under the words were the ten digits of a phone number.

Oliver slid the photographs over to Diana and glanced over the printout. It appeared to be a message from a private internet forum Oliver was familiar with from his years of relic hunting. It had been posted during his time in Iceland, otherwise he would probably have seen it himself before the Senator and his lackeys noticed. The post described a scroll from the private archives of the Egyptian state museum, now for sale for an unspecified sum to persons capable of meeting in Cairo to collect it. Three images, printouts of which Diana was now examining, were attached to the post.

If the Senator hadn't brought this job to him, Oliver would have thought the entire posting a scam. He and the other regulars on the forum might operate in a shadow world where myths and conspiracy theories were treated as truth, but a posting like this reeked of either rank amateurism or falsehood. A small string of text along the top of the printout informed Oliver that the comment thread on this post had been locked by one of the forum moderators only days after going up to contain the verbal war that had erupted between the regular board members, most of who believed the post to be a hoax, and the increasingly hostile original poster.

Oliver shook his head and suppressed an urge to laugh at the situation. "Well, at least we'll get a couple nights in a nice hotel and I'll go home with a couple thousand dollars in my pocket."

Diana looked up from the photo she had been examining. "It's definitely hieratic, but so far I'm not seeing anything especially noteworthy."

"So it's at least a real scroll?"

"I can't tell from these, but if it is a complete hoax, then someone went to the effort of tracking down photos of a genuine Egyptian artifact."

Oliver nodded and slid the printout across the table to Diana.

He flipped the phone open. It was powered off, so he held the red button and waited while it cycled through a slow boot-up accompanied by brightly colored Arabic script dancing across the screen. When the menus finally loaded he was relieved to see that the phone interface was set to english. Oliver could read and speak enough arabic to get by in street conversations, but his vocabulary didn't extend to technical terms. He thumbed his way through several menu options until he came to the address book, which contained only one entry: RAIS. Apparently Senator Wheeler's contacts in Egypt had managed to track down the man's phone number.

"Anything I should know about those photos before I call Rais Karim?"

Diana shook her head. She put down the photograph and retreated into her hotel room without saying anything. Oliver could tell from her expression that she was slipping into her studious mode and would soon be content to ignore him for hours unless he was contributing something useful to her work. He watched her walk away, then turned to the window and pressed the green button on his phone.

The screen changed to indicate that his call was being connected and Oliver held the phone to his ear.

"Hello?" said a man speaking in Arabic.

Oliver slipped his mind into that language and replied, "Hello. My name is Oliver. A mutual friend suggested you might like to meet for coffee and discuss the intersection of biblical archaeology with modern politics."

Rais, if that's who Oliver was speaking with, paused for a moment before responding. Finally he spoke, "Such topics are of interest to me."

"I am unfamiliar with Cairo. Perhaps you could suggest someplace near my hotel? I am staying at the Sofitel, on the riverbank."

"There is a coffee bar there on the grounds of your hotel. I will be there within the hour. Tell the concierge your name and that you are expecting a guest so that I can find you."

"Excellent. I'll be waiting."

Oliver clapped the phone shut and flipped it over in his palm. He removed the battery and set the phone and its battery on the table. He had spent years avoiding Egypt so as to never enter Rais Karim's crosshairs and now, in the course of less than a minute's conversation he had not only spoken to the legendary hunter of tomb raiders, but arranged to have a drink with him.

Diana returned with a large document magnifier and a notepad. She settled into her seat again and eyed the disassembled phone. "I take it your conversation went well?"

"We're meeting downstairs in an hour."

Diana nodded and turned back to the photographs. She placed one under the document magnifier and began scribbling on her notepad.

Oliver decided to leave Diana to her work. He pulled his smartphone from his pocket and set it on the table beside a stack of Egyptian currency. He then pulled the large hard cased suitcase up onto the bed and dialed in the combination. The suitcase popped open and Oliver removed a small black zippered case, a small handgun, and two clips of ammunition. He set these on the bed and relocked the suitcase, taking care to flip the tumblers of the locks several times before lifting the case and setting it against the wall beside the bed. He stepped over to the closet and pulled a dark grey field vest off a hanger, then returned to the bed to gather up the items he had drawn from the suitcase and deposit them on the table.

Diana glanced up from the photographs. She looked from the gun to Oliver, then back again for an instant before returning her gaze to the photos.

"Expecting trouble?" She asked, not looking up again from the lens of the document magnifier.

"Not today, but I'm not taking any chances on this job."

Oliver lifted the gun and checked that the chamber was empty. It was a small Glock, rigged for concealed carry with a thin, but rugged, belt clip grafted onto the side of the slide. He checked the ammo clips and slipped one into place in the gun, racking the slide back and letting it forward to chamber a round. The other clip he slipped into the inner pocket of his vest, alongside a case holding several blank SD cards. He reached an arm around and slipped the gun inside his pants, clipping it to the waistband at the small of his back.

He opened the black zipper case and extracted a sliver of metal. He pulled his smart phone out of its case and used the metal sliver to pop out the SIM tray, then swapped the SIM for one of the half dozen SIMs in the case. These were a collection of active chips from local carriers, as well as international carriers that had good coverage in Egypt. It could get expensive, purchasing prepaid data from all around the world, but Oliver preferred to use local cellular accounts when he was out on a job. Doing this didn't guarantee security or connectivity, but it cut the risks. Even if a rival managed to identify one of his travel accounts, which he never used while at home and had purchased with cash, they would be unlikely to get a full picture of his movements by tracking the phone because he switched cards so often. He also wasn't especially concerned about his communications being tapped because he insisted on using fully encrypted services for all communication while on the job.

Communicating with a client generally worked something like this: If the client needed to share a file with Oliver they would simply drop the file into a shared folder, which would then ping Oliver's phone through an encrypted connection wherever he was in the world and no matter what SIM card he had installed. Oliver could then pull up the file and view it on his phone, posting a reply if necessary. For faster, albeit less secure, messaging they could also send direct message to one of Oliver's private Twitter accounts. That message would ping his phone and he would reply with another direct message.

Of course, all of these means of communication could be intercepted by a seriously motivated hacker or a strongly worded court order, but Oliver wasn't concerned about that. The services he used had worked hard in recent years to close security holes and when hacks did occur they were generally traceable to a celebrity or politician using a weak password. As for federal orders to crack a Dropbox or open the feed of a Twitter account, there was nothing Oliver could do to protect himself that wouldn't be painfully restrictive and scare away his clients, who tended to not be the most tech savvy people. It was easy to give an artifact collector the login details of a temporary account, then block them after the job was over. It was a lot harder to convince them to run a full-disk encryption package and communicate exclusively through 1024-bit encrypted protocols.

Oliver inserted the SIM and waited for his phone to authenticate to the network. Once the connection had been established he launched his Twitter client and posted a brief update to his private feed:

Made it to Egypt. About to meet contact re: scrolls.

Posting his movements on the internet, even to a private Twitter feed, was a calculated risk. Oliver had long since weighed the danger of someone hacking into his account against the value of keeping Amber and, when she wasn't traveling with him, Diana tuned in to his actions. Back in the United States Amber would be checking his feed at least once a day to track his progress. If he failed to post at least once in twenty-four hours she would attempt to contact him. If he didn't reply or post again within another twenty-four hours she would assume he was in trouble and contact someone to look for him. All of Oliver's posts were tagged with a GPS coordinate, which could give any rescue party a useful starting point. Hardly a failsafe emergency plan, but better than freezing to death on a remote glacier.

Oliver slipped his phone into a pocket and moved to look over Diana's shoulder.

"Figure out what these are yet?" he asked.

Diana nodded and passed him her notepad without looking away from the document magnifier.

The notepad was covered in scrawled translation notes, some crossed out and re-written as Diana revised her translation based on context clues found further along in the document. Some words were surrounded with question marks to indicate that Diana was uncertain of the translation. In the worst of these cases the words were simply replaced by boxed in comments like, "verb related to worship" and "reference to unnamed person or group." Oliver had made similar notes himself when studying scrolls and inscriptions, and the sight of Diana working hard to translate the photos filled him with relief that he had brought her along. If she was struggling with some of these references, Oliver knew he would have been utterly lost in the nuances of the ancient Egyptian script.

The portions of the script that Diana had already translated told the story of a band of Hittite raiders attacking an Egyptian village. The narrator was obviously Egyptian, his story punctuated with appeals to the gods for intervention and colorful descriptions of the Hittites as barbaric half-men who deserved to be eviscerated by the just wrath of a vengeful Pharaoh. The narrator waxed poetic here, praising the Pharaoh for building vast cities and providing copious support to the priests of Ra. So mighty was the Pharaoh that he had fought back scourges that afflicted his predecessors, who were mighty in themselves but had fallen to the wrath of a foreign god. The Hittite raiders appeared to be overcoming the villages with the aid of that same god that the Pharaoh had previously confounded, so he called upon all of his priests to ascertain the source of the enemy's power.

"This sounds promising," Oliver said, laying the notepad on the desk beside Diana, who immediately began scribbling on it again.

After a moment Diana paused and leaned back from the the document magnifier on the desk. She stretched and cracked her fingers, then picked up the pad and read from it, "And so, in the twenty-seventh year of his reign, on the advice of his most trusted and glorious priest of Ra, Amneth, the Pharaoh sent his most worthy general and a contingent of three thousand men to drive back the Hittites and capture the source of their unholy power."

"I think we're on to something here," Diana said. "The references to a foreign god are not specific and I haven't been able to find the name of the Pharaoh, but I've heard of Amneth before and the timeline fits."

"How so?"

"Egyptologists haven't been able to precisely match the biblical story of the Hebrew Exodus with any particular pharaoh. Guesses range from Dudimose, which would put the Exodus at around 1695BCE, to Ramesses II, which would put the date closer to 1212, so anything in that range would make the story in this scroll believable."

Oliver whistled. "That's a pretty wide range of possible times for such a major event."

"You're a mythological historian, Oliver. This shouldn't come as a surprise."

"You know that I didn't focus on Egypt. That's why I brought you along."

"Anyway, the popular perception is that Moses led the Hebrews out of Egypt from under the thumb of Ramesses II, since that's the name used in most movies about the Exodus, but there are lots of issues with the order of events in Canaan if you move the time that late. Some rabbinic interpretations of history point more towards Horemheb as the Pharaoh of the Exodus, which would place it around 1313BCE. That's 34 years before the rise of Ramesses II. That date also fixes some of the Canaanite timeline issues. Additionally, this passage I've just translated mentions the Pharaoh overcoming struggles faced by his predecessors which were caused by a foreign god, which sounds like a good match to the stories of Moses and the plagues. Finally, we have this name: Amneth. That really helps narrow down the date of this particular scroll. Amneth was a priest of Ra during the reign of Ramesses II, which would match the story suggested in this passage with both the rabbinical timeline and the likely window of historic possibility."

Oliver nodded his head and began to speculate aloud. "So if we assume that Moses carried the staff out of Egypt with them in 1313, then spent about 40 years wandering around the desert before settling in Canaan, then add a few years for the staff to be capture or lost or otherwise passed around and end up in the hands of the Hittites, that brings us to around 1265BCE. Does that date line up with anything in the timeline of Ramesses II?"

"It actually does. A few years later, around 1258BCE, Ramesses II made a treaty with King Hattusili III of the Hittites to end all wars between their empires. After that treaty, Ramesses stopped engaging in wars north of Egypt and turned his attention west and south."

"So maybe the Pharaoh's troops were successful in capturing the staff from the Hittites, which led the them giving up any efforts to fight Egypt."

"It's a possibility. I'll need to see more of the scroll to know."

Oliver checked his watch and stood. "Let's get down to the coffee bar. Rais Karim should be arriving in a little while and I want you in place to overhear our conversation. If all goes well he will be able to get us access to the actual scrolls and you'll be able to get the rest of this story. Hopefully we'll find a clue that will lead us to the staff."

Diana pushed her chair back from the table and strode wordlessly to her room, returning a moment later with a messenger bag and a large hat. Oliver double checked that his gun was concealed and shrugged on his photo vest, then grabbed a camera from the bag on his bed and slung it around his neck.

Chapter Six

They slipped out of the room, leaving a "Do Not Disturb" sign hanging from both of their doorknobs, and boarded the elevator. As the car descended, Oliver explained the plan to Diana.

He would go into the coffee shop, tell the concierge he was waiting for a friend, and get a seat near the window. Diana would follow him in a few minutes later and sit someplace where she could overhear, or at least watch, whatever went on at Oliver's table. If possible Diana would use her phone to record the meeting. Afterwards they would compare notes and, hopefully, be on their way to see the scroll.

"Why don't we just sit together?" Diana asked as the elevator dinged to a stop at the ground floor.

"Because I want someone else's perspective on what's happening. Does Rais look nervous? Is he alone? Has he just made a hand signal I couldn't see and now a dozen armed guards are about to storm into the room?"

Diana nodded and waved to him casually, as if they had merely been making casual conversation on the elevator, then strode off across the lobby towards the coffee bar at the far end.

Oliver followed more slowly, pleased with how quickly Diana had slipped into the subterfuge. He stopped at the front desk and waited for the concierge to finish telling a couple dressed in Hawaiian shirts how to sign up for a pyramid tour. When the suited man turned to Oliver, he told him his name and explained that he was expecting a colleague to meet him in the coffee bar.

As he turned away from the desk Oliver surveyed the room and saw nobody who appeared to be watching him, so he hurried into the coffee bar and selected a comfortable chair by the large glass windows. A waiter arrived and offered Oliver the lunch menu, but he declined it and asked for a simple cup of whatever coffee the waiter recommended, as well as an appetizer of his choosing. Oliver wasn't particular about his coffee. He liked it for the bitter taste, which he had always found bracing when facing a long day or stressful situation, and its efficient means of delivering caffeine to his system. He was not especially picky about the brand or method of brewing, so long as the resulting coffee was strong. The waiter returned a moment later with a small cup of coffee so strong and thick that Oliver could feel the weight of it as it slid down his throat, as well as a tray of pita bread cut into squares and topped with hummus and assorted leafy and meaty garnishes. Oliver thanked the waiter and settled in to admire the view out the window.

The bright waters of the Nile river curved past only a few hundred feet from the base of the hotel and the busy streets and skyline of Cairo stretched off into the distance on the far bank. Oliver had never been to Cairo before and had, for some reason he now found ridiculous, half expected to see the pyramids or desert dunes from the windows of the hotel, but this wasn't the case. The Cairo he could see out the window was a large modern city and the hotel was situated right in the heart of it.

Still, there was something disconcerting about the cityscape. After pondering this for about five minutes, sipping his coffee and munching on pita bread the while, Oliver thought he had put his finger on it.

Cairo was a modern city in an ancient land. The feeling that had risen up in Oliver when he looked out upon the city was the same feeling he got in London, or Paris, or any other modernized city that had grown up in the shell of a much older place. It was a feeling he rarely got in American cities. For all the grandeur and excitement of the big cities of America, there was always the subtle sense than nothing you looked at was older than a couple centuries. Here though, in the lands that had been occupied by city-building civilizations for a thousand years or more, the roots of human habitation twisted deep into the landscape.

A voice broke into his reverie. "Deep thoughts for a sunny afternoon, Mr. Lucas?"

Oliver looked away from the window to see Rais Karim lowering himself into a chair across the table from him. He was a man of middle age with wisps of thinning white hair combed across his brown scalp, wrinkles creasing his face, and a large belly straining the buttons of his pale blue shirt under a khaki blazer. Oliver had heard rumors of Rais Karim for several years, vague whispers about a man who lead Egypt's secret relic agency with an indomitable will and a strong aim towards retrieving every mystical relic that had ever been stolen from his homeland, but he had never so much as seen a photo of the man.

Oliver inclined his head towards the city beyond the windows. "I was just contemplating the history of your nation, Mr. Karim. My homeland has nothing so glorious or long-lived."

"I'm sure you don't completely believe that. A man in your line of work cannot be ignorant of the cultural achievements of the Native Americans."

When Karim spoke it was with an accent that Oliver found odd and difficult to place. He suspected it to be some combination of his native Egyptian with a soft inflection of British, but he could not be sure.

He considered Karim's words briefly before replying. "Certainly, but we have no remnants of their society so vast, or thoroughly integrated into modern life, as that city out there." He gestured with his coffee cup towards the expanse out the window.

Karim chuckled and waved a waiter over to take his order. Once the waiter had departed he continued, "A valid point. My ancestors forged an impressive testament to their engineering and civic prowess that has stood the test of time. However, I am under the impression that you did not travel to Cairo to discuss the relative merits of our national histories."

"As I mentioned on the phone, I have an interest in Biblical archaeology. Specifically, I am looking for information regarding an object from the story of the Hebrew Exodus. Certain parties who are mutual acquaintances of ours have asked me to look into the matter."

"Those parties wouldn't happen to be connected to the American embassy here in Cairo, would they?"

"No specifics, but I'm not going to lie to you, Rais. I'm an American and so is my client."

Rais sighed deeply and turned to gaze out the window. Oliver waited in silence for him to decide he was ready to speak. A waiter arrived, left a cup of thick black coffee and a small plate of cookies beside Rais's elbow, and departed without speaking. Eventually, Rais sighed deeply and looked away from the window. He lifted his coffee cup and took a quiet sip as he looked Oliver over.

"How did you come to hear my name?" Rais asked.

"My client has contacts in the American embassy. Word reached those contacts that you had lost your post in the government and were making, shall we say, more noise than is usually advisable about a scroll that was misplaced during the recent revolution. My client is interested in the contents of that scroll but not eager for a public outcry, so he hired me to come here and track down that scroll. He provided me with your name and phone number."

"I presume he also wished you to retrieve whatever relics might be mentioned in this elusive scroll?"

"Perhaps, if they exist."

"And what leads your client to believe that I will aid him in this effort? I don't know you, Mr. Lucas, but if you truly are the sort of person who might be hired to track down a relic I imagine that you have heard of me." Rais paused and let his statement hang in the air as a question.

Oliver took the bait. "Of course. I'm especially aware of your hatred towards the British for looting so many of Egypt's treasures over the past two hundred years, and your efforts to punish native grave robbers. That's why I've often counted myself fortunate that I had little involvement in Egyptology, but then this little adventure came up..."

"So what makes you think that I will help you?" He leaned forward and fixed Oliver with a gaze that could have set ancient scrolls ablaze. "What makes you think I won't shoot you in the knees, drag you into a little room, and work you over with hot pliers until you beg for the privilege of never setting foot in Egypt again?"

Oliver didn't even glance away. He raised a corner of his mouth in a crooked smile and replied, "I think you'll help me because you were once a man entrusted with the protection of objects that your government might just prefer not exist in this modern age. Then, after decades of service, you were tossed out into the cold when the government was overthrown. For all I know you didn't even get your pension. My guess is that you are still so dedicated to protecting relics that you're even willing to let foreigners get involved, so long as they are the right type."

"Very perceptive, Mr. Lucas, but not entirely correct."

Oliver raised his eyebrows and took a sip of his coffee, waiting for Rais to continue.

The deposed Egyptian agent slammed his coffee cup down heavily on the table. He appeared about to stand and storm away from the table, but then reconsidered it and leaned forward, placing his elbows on the table and pressing his hands together with his fingertips pointed at Oliver.

"I am looking for something that went missing, but it is not the scroll itself for which I am concerned. The scroll points the way to several unspoiled tombs which, if one is inclined to believe in such things, contain relics of incredible power. Specifically, the staff used by Moses to call down plagues and perform miracles in the story of the Hebrew Exodus, as well as magical weapons that the Pharaoh used to raise the Hittite dead to fight against their own comrades.

"If I were still in my position within the ministry of defense I would have been able to recover the scroll weeks ago without a word of the operation reaching curious ears, but now that I am on the outside things are more... difficult."

"How did the scroll get out of whatever archive you were keeping it locked up in?"

"Did you hear about the staff of the National Museum banding together to protect it from looters when my country's government collapsed last summer?"

Oliver nodded.

"Well, those stories weren't completely true. Oh, the National Museum was protected from looters, and the staff are to be commended for their efforts, but all the news reports got the motivation wrong. It wasn't a couple bricks thrown through windows by angry youth or greedy treasure dealers.

"My agency had a vault in the basement of the National Museum. A room specially dedicated to protecting items that need to be kept secret, but also preserved. When the government lost control of the Egyptian army the guards at that vault were among those who abandoned their posts. I've since managed to track down those men and speak to several of them. They had no idea what was in the vault, only that they had been assigned guard duty by a government official, that would be me, who their commanding officers had publicly disavowed on the radio and television, so they walked away from their posts and went home.

"I've spoken to all of the museum staff, and everyone who was working in the museum that night tells a story that agrees: Late in the night a museum security guard was found dead by one of the cleaning staff. The other guards investigated and found that the man's neck had been broken and his body left in a dark nook near the secure vault, which had been cut open with a plasma torch and emptied. He must have stumbled across whoever broke into the vault as they were carrying the relics from the vault to their vehicles. The police were unable to respond, being rather tied up trying to keep the protesters contained, so the guards called in the museum director and staff to arrange the now legendary defense of the museum."

"And you don't know who these looters were?" Oliver inquired.

"Mr. Lucas, you need to remember that at the time I was practically under house arrest by the military. They had just switched sides in the conflict and I was among those who they listed as corrupt officials who were to be deposed."

"Of course. I mean now. Do you now know who raided the relic vault?"

"Yes. I initially suspected a foreign power. Nothing else was taken and, were it not for the dead guard, I doubt that anyone would have noticed the theft until the revolution wound down a few weeks later. That vault was used exclusively for top secret relics. Nobody from the museum was able to see so much as the outer door without passing through military security, so the staff was in the habit of avoiding that hall. Who else but another nation would have the intelligence resources to know that we stored relics in that particular vault?"

"Organized crime?"

"Also a possibility that I investigated, but no. My investigation suggested that the raid was conducted by a private military contractor based in the United States, one Leonidas Security. Someone within this company must have learned of the vault. They raided it, carried off the relics, and are now starting to sell them off on the black market."

Oliver thought about that for a moment. If the vault had been cracked by a gang of organized criminals or tomb robbers he wouldn't have been surprised, but to learn that a private military contractor was involved brought in new concerns. You could generally count on criminal gangs to be brutal, but not do anything terribly overt. The occasional mutilated body might surface and once in a while a politician would admit to taking bribes, which would throw a wrench in the criminal workings for a few weeks, but in the long run organized crime was a slow burning fuse that only rarely burst into highly visible actions. Oliver's experience had taught him that the treasure hunting game, like organized crime, was occasionally brutal and highly visible, but for the most part the players did their best to stay below the radar. If you made too much noise about a find collectors would be scared away from purchasing your goods, and even a hint of impropriety lingering around an object would drive away the museums. But private military contractors were a different animal all together, one which Oliver had always been cautious to avoid. You never knew where you stood with a PMC. They were made up of private citizens, so overt crimes were rare, but there were few actions that couldn't be covered up under the excuse of, "defending a client's assets." Toss in the fact that just about every government in the world had ties to private military contractors and the possibility of dangerous complications grew a hundredfold.

Rais cleared his throat and Oliver realized that he had been quiet for a long while. He smiled nervously and took a sip from his cup. The coffee had grown cool and he grimaced as he choked it down.

"I sense you are uncomfortable with what I have just told you." Rais said.

"I'm just not a fan of private security agencies."

"Do you have some experience with these companies?"

"Not personally, but I've known people who crossed them in the past. The stories aren't pleasant."

"No worse than what you may have heard about me, I imagine."

Oliver chuckled darkly and waved the waiter over to order a second cup of coffee. He waited until the waiter had gone before saying, "Can you arrange a meeting with the individuals selling the scroll?"

Raid inclined his head in agreement. "Of course. I had not yet done so myself because my funds have become somewhat limited since returning to private life last year. My contacts in the market tell me that they asking the exorbitant price of five hundred thousand American dollars for the scroll."

"Give me a day to check with my employer. I'm not sure if I can secure that much money, but I'll try."

Rais rose and brushed the wrinkles from his shirt. "I will make contact, using your name of course. If matters turn out poorly it would give me great pleasure to watch a grave robber like yourself be caught up in the tumult."

Oliver stood and offered Rais his hand. The older man hesitated a moment, then reached out and took Oliver's hand in his own. Oliver looked him in the eye as they shook hands and replied, "I would expect nothing more of you."

Rais released Oliver's hand and turned away. He strode out of the coffee shop without looking back.

The waiter returned with Oliver's fresh cup of coffee. Oliver told him that he would have no further orders and asked for the bill to be charged to his room. He returned his gaze to the scene outside the window and sipped his coffee contemplatively.

The price quoted by Rais Karim was beyond Oliver's means. He had tracked down and recovered dozens of ancient treasures over the last decade, but he had made surprisingly little profit for his efforts. Part of that was because he did not sell everything he recovered. His private quest to recover the shards of the mechanism had consumed tens of thousands of dollars, only some of which had been reimbursed by selling photos he had taken on the expeditions. His client list was short and consisted primarily of wealthy lovers of history and rich socialites who wanted something rare and exclusive for their private collection. These clients paid well, but frequently in gifts that could be justified on their tax returns and did little to add to Oliver's bank account balance. Oliver's parents were wealthy, but beyond accepting their offer to pay for college both Amber and he had assiduously avoided taking any money from them since graduating from high school. He would indeed contact the Senator and attempt to arrange funds, but he didn't think that the man would be willing, or able, to pay the price Rais Karim had quoted.

This could, Oliver realized, be his escape from the net that the Senator had cast. If the Senator was unwilling to put up half a million dollars for the scroll, then Oliver would have the perfect excuse for backing out of this little expedition before the Senator's grip on him grew any tighter. He couldn't be blamed for the the actions of a third party who had stolen the scroll and set their price for it before Oliver even came into the picture, so there was no risk that the Senator would seek revenge. If the Senator pulled the plug on this mission then Oliver would have done his best and, while he wouldn't get the complete payment, he should be able to walk away with his livelihood, reputation, and a couple thousand dollars to spare.

But did Oliver really want to give up?

He sipped at his coffee and watched boats cruise up and down the rippling water of the Nile. The longer he sat there, the more Oliver felt the grip of an adventure closing around him like the coils of a python. He had spent the last decade searching for clues to uncover a conspiracy of global proportions stretching back centuries into the past. When that quest had destroyed his career he had turned to treasure hunting and adventure photography as a means of supporting his personal quest. Over the years he had come to love the danger of traveling to long lost places and tracking down forgotten relics. It went against his nature to turn his back on an adventure like this just because a new complication had arisen.

He finished his coffee, pulled out his phone, and used a virtual phone app to send a text to the burner cell phone number that Senator Wheeler had provided in the briefcase:

Complication. ~$500k *to recover first objective.*

He followed that with:

Call via Skype ASAP. Username: lucasacquisitions. Do not use phone.

He checked that the Skype app was running on his phone and he was logged in under the appropriate account, then stood and strode out of the café, glancing towards where Diana sat at the bar and jerking his head for her to follow.

When they were aboard the elevator he quickly filled her in on what had passed between him and Rais Karim in the coffee bar.

"I didn't hear much of the conversation, but I'm pretty sure your man was alone." She replied when he was finished. "None of the people who entered the bar before him left after he did."

"The question is whether he is more or less dangerous for working alone."

Diana nodded quietly.

The elevator stopped at their floor and the doors slid open just as his phone started to buzz. He pulled it out of his pocket and saw it was a Skype call coming in over the hotel's wifi. Oliver didn't recognize the username, a string of letters and numbers that could just as well have held special meaning for someone or have been pounded out on a keyboard as the Senator fumbled through creating an account in under five minutes. Oliver was impressed that the response had come so quickly. He tapped the answer key and held the phone to his head.

"Oliver here."

"Is this a secure line?" The voice on the other end wasn't the Senator. Probably some aid tasked with watching the Senator's phone when he was unable to carry it, Oliver thought.

"As secure as you can get in Egypt. Public key crypto end to end, though you never know if Microsoft has bowed to political pressure and given the NSA or locals here a backdoor."

The voice hesitated, then replied, "I'll take that to mean yes. Please hold."

Oliver pulled his keycard from his pocket and ran it through the reader on his room's door. The little LED above the handle winked to green and he pushed the door open. He glanced quickly about the room, saw that everything was as he had left it, then stepped aside and waved Diana into the room.

The Senator's voice came through his phone as he pushed the door shut and turned the lock. "Oliver, boy, this you?"

"Sure is, Senator. I take it you got my message?"

"Yes. What's this horse shit about a half million? You trying to squeeze more cash out of me?"

"No sir." Oliver responded.

He went on to give Senator Wheeler an abbreviated version of the story that Rais Karim had told him in the coffee shop downstairs. When he reached the part about the mercenaries breaking into the vault, then putting the contents up for sale on the open black market, Oliver could have sworn that he heard a sharp intake of breath echo across the data packets from the other end of the connection.

"I don't have to tell you that this is disappointing, kid."

"I'm sure it is. Will you be sending the money?"

"Hell no! I just had to release my tax returns from the last fifteen years to the press to prove to them that I'm not some sort of crook. There's no way I can hide a transfer of that magnitude."

"I understand."

"There's no way you can snatch the scrolls from the mercenaries and keep going after the staff?"

"That sort of thing is far from my line of work, Senator. You hired me because I'm experienced at solving ancient riddles and tracking down artifacts hidden in caves full of ancient traps. I'm not prepared to get into a shootout with a private army."

"Of course, of course..." The Senator was silent for several moments. Oliver let him stew and took the time to unzip his boots and kick them off. After nearly a minute the Senator said, "This is most disappointing"

"Understandably so, sir."

"So I take it you're coming home now?"

Oliver replied immediately, keeping his tone level and businesslike, lest the Senator catch the lie in his voice. "Not right away. An old friend of mine is in town doing some research. I think I'll spend some time with her, maybe go on a tour of the pyramids, then come back in a few days."

"Keep your head down. If you do happen upon a way to track down that staff, be sure to contact me."

"Thank you, sir."

There was a loud "boink" and the connection went dead.

Oliver looked at the phone in his hand. He had just made the first move of a dangerous game. If it went well he would find the staff and be able to keep it for himself. If not, then the Senator was guaranteed to track him down and put his head on a stake.

"What exactly am I supposed to be researching?"

Oliver turned to see Diana laying face down on his bed, bare feet sticking up behind her, pert chin supported on interlaced fingers. Oliver smiled and placed his phone on the table before sinking into one of the chairs by the window. He drummed his fingers on the table a few times, then said, "Promise you won't get angry?"

"I'll do nothing of the sort."

"Then at least promise that if you don't like what I'm about to do you'll say so. This could be dangerous and I don't want you to even leave the hotel unless you're sure you can handle it."

Diana smiled and rolled herself into a seated position on the bed. "I'm all in on this adventure, Oliver. Now tell me the plan."

So he went ahead and explained his plan. Diana was initially skeptical. She pointed out several holes, some of which Oliver had already anticipated and accepted as necessary risks, which he was grateful to her for spotting. They sussed out the details over the next couple hours, playing through all possible failure points and coming to the conclusion that it was their best option, assuming that they didn't want to give up on the scroll.

"Are you sure you want to go through with this?" Oliver asked her that evening as they rode the elevator down to the lobby where a taxi was waiting to take them to a traditional Egyptian restaurant the concierge had recommend. "You could stay here in the hotel and I could just bring you the images."

Diana grinned impishly and looked up at him through the lenses and thick glass frames of her newly fitted glasses. "And let you have all the fun?"

Chapter Seven

Rais Karim called early the next morning as Oliver and Diana sat together on the balcony of Diana's room eating breakfast. Oliver slipped his smartphone from a vest pocket and stabbed blindly at the device's blank screen with his thumb a few times before he realized that the ringing phone was the cheap clamshell model laying on the table. Before he could correct his mistake Diana had dropped her fork and grabbed the phone from its place between their breakfast plates.

"Oliver's phone." She chirped.

Oliver was briefly annoyed, but not surprised. Diana had agreed to his plan, even insisted on taking a more active role in it, and now she wanted to demonstrate to the other players that she had entered the game.

Listening to their conversation while he finished his breakfast, Oliver was impressed at how quickly Diana slipped into the role of international treasure hunter, going toe to toe with a brutal intelligence agent and holding her ground. She explained that she was an antiquities expert Oliver had hired to authenticate and, if necessary, translate the scroll. From what he could hear, Oliver got the impression that Rais Karim was not happy with this plan. He heard Karim shouting that he had personally seen the scroll before it was stolen from and been privy to expert analysis that proved its authenticity. That was, after all, why it had been in the secret vault in the first place. Diana pointed out that she and Oliver didn't question his integrity, only that of the mercenaries, who had already proven themselves untrustworthy in putting the scrolls up for sale in the first place. That seemed to calm Rais and, after about five minutes of tense discussion, Diana ended the call and tossed the phone onto the table.

"He's a tenacious old bird." She said.

"You don't rise to power in a secret military agency without being tenacious." Oliver replied.

Diana shrugged in agreement and explained that Rais was getting in contact with the sellers to confirm the meeting location and inform them that she would be coming along to examine the scrolls prior to purchase.

According to the agreement they had worked out, Diana would be present at the meeting to authenticate the scroll. She would require access to it in a clean environment where they would not be disturbed, so that she could view the scroll and confirm that it was written in the proper dialect of ancient Hieratic script. Once that was done, Oliver would contact their employer and arrange for a transfer of funds. If she wasn't satisfied with the scroll's authenticity the deal would be off, but they would, of course, make no mention of the failed transaction to any other potential buyers.

"Now we just hope that they don't overreact and kill us when we don't buy the scroll." Diana said.

"They won't. The market for illegal antiquities is hot, but these are military contractors, not professional relic dealers. Go back a few years and they would have probably never double-crossed their employer. This whole mess probably started just because Egypt is filled with buyers hoping to exploit the chaos of a major change in governance and these mercenaries thought they could sell a couple of the items in the vault without getting caught."

Diana nodded and chewed on the last of her breakfast thoughtfully. Oliver had the distinct impression that something was on her mind, and he thought he had a decent guess what it might be. "You're worried what the Senator will do if word of this meeting gets back to him."

Diana nodded.

"Even if he hears about it, I'll just say I wanted to get a look at the scroll for curiosity's sake. There's no way he'll find out about the recorder unless one of us tells him."

"I hope you're right."

Oliver grinned and reached for the phone, which had started to rattle across the surface of the table as it rang. Before opening it he caught Diana's eye and nodded, "I'm right. Everything will work out fine."

Oliver answered the phone. Rais Karim sounded surprised to be speaking to Oliver again as he said, "The meeting is arranged."

"When and where?"

"One hour. There's an antiquities dealer on Al Maqases in the El-Gamaleya district. It is the only one on the street and not far from a popular souk, so you should have no difficulty finding it."

"Will you be there?"

"Certainly not. I want as little to do with those bastards as possible. Verify the scroll, buy it, and get the hell out of my country, Mr. Lucas."

The phone went dead.

Oliver looked at the phone in his hand bemusedly, then stood from his chair and tossed the phone onto the table.

"We're on." He said.

He pulled his handgun from his waistband and checked that it was loaded with around chambered. He didn't like carrying the weapon into meetings, but the way Oliver saw it, this meeting would either go quickly and without incident or rapidly unravel into the sort of situation in which he and

Diana might have to shoot their way out and make for the nearest airport.

"Bring your passport and some cash, just in case we have to run."

"Do you think this will turn dangerous?"

Oliver slipped the gun back into his belt and shrugged on a tan blazer that almost, but not quite, matched his khaki pants. "I don't think so. My gut tells me that Karim and the mercenaries don't want any trouble, since he isn't officially involved with national security anymore. If he weren't trying to lay low I think that those contractors would already have been found dead in the street."

"How do you think he'll react to the plan?"

"Probably be angry. Maybe track us down and argue the authenticity of the scroll with us after the meeting, but I don't think he'll get violent. Again, he's not official anymore."

"Alright. Give me five minutes to get ready and I'll meet you in the hall."

Oliver took that as a hint to leave and hopped over the railing between their balconies, then slipped into his own room to make some final preparations of his own.

They rode the elevator down to the lobby and the concierge immediately pointed them towards the taxi that Oliver had ordered from his room phone. Oliver gave the taxi driver a slip of paper with the address of the antique dealer and they settled back for the ride through the crowded streets.

The streets of Cairo were crowded, despite the early hour. The narrow streets were hopelessly packed, especially in the places where there were no sidewalks and the vehicles had to compete with pedestrians and animals. A wide selection of cars from the past fifty years were jammed bumper to bumper as they crept through streets that twisted at odd angles between buildings that had stood in this city since before

Oliver's homeland had been settled by European colonists. The pedestrians were likewise a brightly colored mix of business people and youths in Western-style dress, men and women wearing all manners of traditional clothing, traditional being defined as everything from long robes to pants and shirts that differed from their Western counterparts only in the pattern of their cut, and obvious tourists in loud shirts toting large cameras. The main avenues had been widened and paved over with tar. These weren't crowded so terribly. The side streets, however, were still paved in an assortment of cobblestone and brick and were so narrow that the taxi's mirrors occasionally scraped against the stone of buildings on either side.

Oliver briefly considered paying the taxi driver, getting out, and ordering his phone to give him walking directions to the meeting place, but he restrained himself. Instead he took advantage of the drive to pull out his phone and post several tweets informing Amber of their plans. The final message said, *Sellers are supposedly from Leonidas Security, keep in mind if things go bad.* He switched to a web browser and tried to track down information about Leonidas Security, but could find nothing but the bare facts that it was a private security contractor headquartered in Arlington, Virginia. The corporate website did little to explain what, exactly, the company did to secure its clients, and offered no contact information. Apparently if you were to sort of person who might need Leonidas Security's services, they would contact you.

Forty-five minutes after leaving the hotel the taxi deposited them in front of a dusty stone building with windows of thick, possibly bullet proof, glass under a wide green awning. Faded gold Arabic lettering scrawled across the awning. Oliver's command of written Arabic was more shaky than the spoken language, but he got the impression that the text proclaimed this to be a bookshop specializing in antiquities. Diana confirmed this and went to look in through the window while Oliver paid the driver and offered him a generous tip to remain parked in front of the shop until they returned. The driver agreed to this proposal and spun the volume of his radio up a bit before levering his seat back.

"Crowded street. Several people browsing in the shop. Looks like they plan on letting us out of here alive." Diana remarked as Oliver stepped up to the window.

"The customers could be working with the mercenaries, but I agree with you. They probably picked this place to make the deal appear legitimate. Place like this you probably see someone walking in or out with a scroll a couple times a month."

Oliver opened the door and waved for Diana to enter ahead of him. He glanced out at the street one more time, satisfying himself that the crowds were thick enough that even a mercenary turned black market antiquity dealer would hesitate to shoot them if the deal fell through, then he followed Diana into the shop.

The walls of the shop were stacked high with bookshelves filled with codexes bound leather and cloth. Tall glass fronted display cases held an assortment of scrolls, some partially unrolled to display the writing on their aged surfaces, others shrouded in heavy cloth to protect them from the light. Scattered throughout the middle of the shop were a variety of glass topped display cases, some of older vintage with oiled wood sides and other, newer models, with sleek metal frames and built in humidity control units. These cabinets contained more delicate books, their spines and covers cracked with age, scraps of parchment held flat under thick plates of glass tinted to block ultraviolet rays, and rolled up scrolls, some sealed in tubes with tightly fitted caps at the end, each with a paper placard beside it describing the contents of the scroll in Arabic,

English, and French. There were no price tags apparent and Oliver knew without looking that none of these books would have a price penciled in at the top corner of the cover page. To every appearance this was a legitimate, and serious, antique dealership.

The proprietor was a short man with a thin fringe of gray hair around the back and sides of his scalp. When Oliver entered the store he was perched on a tall stool behind the counter discussing a leather-bound codex with a customer in a rapid flow of Arabic. Oliver listened to their conversation as he took in the contents of a display case near the door. The proprietor was pointing out the merits of the book and recounting its chain of ownership back to the private library for which it was ordered three hundred years before, while the customer pointed out the flaws in the binding, scuffs on the case, and general ignobility of the original owner. After a few moments they appeared to reach a mutually satisfactory assessment of the book's value. Hands were shaken, money exchange, and the book lovingly wrapped in a strip of white cotton before being sealed in a waterproof bag. The purchaser slipped the book into an inner pocket of his jacket and shook the proprietor's hand again before stepping out into the street.

The proprietor turned to Oliver and eyed him for a moment before asking, "How may I help you?" in a crisp British accent.

"That obvious, is it?" Oliver asked.

"I suppose you could have been from the continent, but English seemed more likely than Arabic."

Oliver strode over to the counter and offered his hand to the man. "Oliver Lucas." He spoke in Arabic, saying, "I could have handled your language, but you probably would rather I didn't." Then he switched to English and continued, "My associate over there is fluent in the languages of Egypt, but I only enough to get in and out of trouble."

The man nodded took Oliver's hand and replied in English. "Nasir Saab, owner of this emporium of knowledge. You don't speak so terribly, though your accent is obviously American. How may I be of service?"

Oliver gestured to a scroll in a nearby display case. "We were given instructions to meet someone here. I don't know their name, but they are probably also American and ought to be carrying a scroll."

Nasir's eyes darkened and he leaned forward to place both hands firmly on the polished wood countertop. Oliver got the distinct impression that the man might be willing to engage in black market dealing, but considered it unnecessary to extend the same level of politeness to those who participated in such deals. Nasir cleared his throat haughtily and nodded his head towards a door at the back of the shop.

"I believe you will find your man in my clean room. Go back there and knock on the door so you don't surprise him, then I will ring you in."

Oliver didn't allow Nasir's shift in attitude to put him off. He slapped the counter, grinned, and strode to the door the man had indicated. Diana followed, her face serious.

Oliver knocked on the door then put his hand on the knob. It resisted for a second, then he heard a faint buzzing sound and the knob turned in his hand. He stepped into the room and found himself looking down the barrel of a large handgun.

Oliver managed not to flinch, barely. He was in good shape and not afraid of a fair fight, but he had no illusions about being a blindingly fast martial artist. The instant he saw the gun he ruled out any possibility of fighting, or running, and determined to play cool. He looked straight down the length of the gun and locked eyes with the man holding it across the sights.

When he spoke, Oliver's voice was soft, but firm. "This is no way to launch a business relationship. May I suggest you lower that gun and we try this again?"

The gunman's brown eyes narrowed. He appeared to consider Oliver's words for a moment before another voice burst in, "Frank, put that damn thing down. We're here to deal, not fight."

"What if this joker is armed?" Frank replied. His eyes never strayed from what Oliver imagined to be a spot somewhere just above the bridge of his nose.

"Frank, huh?" Oliver asked.

The eyes flickered briefly, but the man said nothing.

Oliver continued, "As it happens, Frank, I am armed. But I have better sense than to go pulling my gun in a respectable bookshop on a crowded street in downtown Cairo. I'm here to inspect a product for my client. If you're not here to show it to me, I'll just turn around, go back to my hotel, and none of this will have ever happened. If you are looking to sell me something, then I'd suggest you get that gun out of my face before I cancel the deal on principle."

The other voice came again. "We're here to deal. Frank here is just a bit jumpy. This isn't his usual line. Right, Frank?"

Frank nodded slowly. He continued to gaze at Oliver for a moment, then lowered the gun to a holster strapped to his thigh and stepped back to lean against the wall with his burly arms crossed in front of his chest.

Oliver looked to the center of the room and saw the other speaker. He was as tall and muscled as Frank, but he did not immediately appear to be armed. Like his taciturn colleague, this man was dressed in desert camouflage and sported a military-style buzzed haircut. A patch on his left shoulder bore the embroidered image of a shield crossed with a spear. The words Leonidas Security were stitched around the shield. He stood behind a large glass and steel work table on which rested a short tube that Oliver guessed held the scroll they had come to inspect.

The speaker reached across the table and offered his hand to Oliver. "Sorry for that, I hope it won't impact our negotiations. Your contact told me that I should call you Oliver, is that right?"

"That's right. And you are?"

"Call me Kyle."

Oliver shook Kyle's hand and gestured back to the door. Diana had ducked back into the shop when she saw the gun, but now that it was no longer pointed in her general direction she squared her shoulders and made her entrance into the room. "This is Diana. She'll verify the authenticity of the object and determine if it is worth my employer's money."

Diana held out her hand and Kyle shook it without comment. She turned her head and gave Frank an icy glare. He returned it without blinking until Diana finally broke and turned back to Oliver and Kyle.

"Is this the artifact?" Diana asked, affecting a French accent and waving an open hand towards the tubular case on the table.

"It is." Kyle replied. He put one hand on the tube and looked from Oliver to Diana and back again. "But before I open it, how do I know you're worth dealing with?"

Oliver had been afraid of this. It was clear to him that these men were amateurs at the black market artifact trade. Had he been conducting this deal he would have taken one of two routes: Preferably, he wouldn't have even agreed to the meeting unless he was reasonably certain that his customer was reliable, usually by means of a personal recommendation from a past customer or trusted contact in the business. In that case he would display the artifact in a secure location and hand it over upon confirmation of the payment being wired to one several island nation bank accounts. If a recommendation wasn't possible, as happened from time to time in his trade, he would have requested that they bring a downpayment of somewhere around fifty percent of the asking price, which he would hold while they examined the object. If all went well, they would pay him the rest and he would allow them to take the object from the room. If it didn't, he would return the money and keep whatever artifact was under negotiation. This was all a delicate dance, of course, and often conducted with firearms visible and an armed guard at the door, but such negotiations had rarely failed to yield satisfactory results for both sides.

But these guys weren't following either method. They were dancing along a dangerous path along the middle: Threatening Oliver with a gun and demanding some evidence of his credibility, even after accepting the recommendation of Rais Karim and setting up this meeting. That made them unpredictable, and Oliver didn't like dealing with unpredictable people, especially when he was planning to double-cross them.

"I assume you know the man who contacted you on my behalf?" Oliver asked.

Kyle nodded.

"And he explained the situation to you?"

"He did."

"So what is the problem?"

"The problem is that I need to know that I'll be paid for my product. That burnt out bureaucrat has been nosing around for weeks, trying to get his hands on this scroll. How do I know you're not going to try and snatch this thing and get it back to him without paying?"

Oliver rolled his eyes and half turned to Diana, holding his hands out palm up as if to say, "What am I supposed to do with these guys?"

Diana picked up on his attitude and played her part perfectly. She stepped forward and leaned across the table, her eyes burning with contempt.

"You are an idiot!" she said with quiet force. "You think only with your guns, so I'll put it in simple macho terms: If we try to screw you and run away with the scroll, then obviously you'll shoot us. We are people of business. We think about money. If we bring money, what is to stop you gun men from shooting us and taking it? Nothing! Of course we didn't bring any money."

Kyle appeared confused by this sudden outburst. Frank remained impassive.

Oliver put one hand on Diana's shoulder as if trying to calm her. He looked Kyle in the eye and said, "The lady has a point, Kyle. From what our mutual acquaintance told me about the provenience of this scroll, we have more to be worried about than you. But I want this deal to work out, so let me tell you something."

Oliver patted a pocket on his vest and continued, "I've got a phone right here. If Diana is satisfied that this is the scroll my client is looking for, I'll make a call right away and arrange payment. I assume you have an account prepared to accept payment?"

"Yes."

"Alright. So let's all stop strutting around here and get down to business. That alright with you?"

Kyle appeared to ponder this for a moment, then nodded thoughtfully. He picked up the case and flipped a latch, then pulled the end off the tube. He set the end cap on the table, reached inside the tube, and pulled gently at a cotton-wrapped bundle inside. The bundle came out smoothly and he laid it on the table before stepping back, still holding the tube.

"There you go. That's the scroll crazy old Karim said you wanted a look at. Price is half a million, American."

"The price is whatever it is worth." Diana remarked, pulling a plastic baggy containing a pair of plastic gloves from her pocket. She donned the gloves and reached up to click on a lamp and pull it closer on its adjustable boom arm. Then Diana unwrapped the cotton cloth from around the scroll. It came away easily. The cotton cloth was obviously of recent vintage. Oliver guessed that it had been wrapped around the scroll by technicians in Karim's agency when they had entered the scroll into their archive.

Diana adjusted her glasses and peered closely at the scroll, now exposed and laying on its modern wrappings. She tweaked the angle of the lamp and looked at the scroll from several angles before announcing, "This scroll appears to be in incredibly good condition. Just from looking at it, I'd say it is made from a very fine vellum, which is unusual but good from a preservation standpoint. Many Egyptian scrolls are papyrus or leather, neither of which hold up very well over centuries, but vellum lasts a good deal longer if it is properly protected."

She looked at Kyle and asked, "Are you the one who took the photographs we saw?"

"Yes. I didn't use a flash. Saw something online about how that might damage the material and cause the letters to fade."

"Over time, that is possible. Was it difficult for you to open?"

"Nope. Was actually surprised how quick it all went, but I figured that the museum's archaeologists had done something to treat it."

Diana touched a gloved finger to the edge of the scroll. Oliver knew she was violating just about every rule of preservation that had been drilled into her during her training. The gloves were about the only element of this situation that were standard protocol, but they needed a look at the contents of the scroll. If a few flakes fell away from the edges as they examined it, that wouldn't be Oliver's problem, even if it might send modern preservationists into conniptions had they been there to watch the procedure.

The thin material bent slightly at Diana's touch. She drew her finger back and Oliver thought he saw a spark of surprise in her eyes. Then she reached out and grasped the wooden grip at the end of the wound vellum. She pulled slowly, unwinding the translucent material and getting her first glimpse of the neat rows of lettering scribed upon the inner surface. The farther Diana unrolled the scroll, the bolder she grew. She began twisting the carved wooden handle of the main scroll body, allowing more of the vellum to roll out across the tabletop. This continued until she had unwound about three feet of the material and was gazing at the entirety of the scroll.

The vellum was a buttery white-yellow, so close to its original appearance that Oliver immediately knew they were dealing with either a true relic or a clumsy forgery. No scroll that was even three hundred years old, let alone three thousand, had any business being so well-preserved. But Rais Karim had been insistent that this scroll was a genuine relic which had been under the protection of his agency until only a few weeks before, so to Oliver's mind that left only one option: The scroll had been preserved using some form of magic. He had seen that before with relics, but he knew of no way to test for it scientifically.

Diana turned her head slowly from side to side, examining the tight rows of hieratic script and brushing her fingers across the surface of the vellum. After a few moments of this she pulled the adjustable lamp closer and bent over the scroll, using the lamp's built-in magnifying lens to examine the scroll more closely. She huffed and pulled back a lock of her black hair that had fallen in front of her eyes, then began fumbling in her large purse for the document magnifier she had used to examine the photographs of the scroll in Oliver's hotel room. She bent close over the scroll, holding the glass and plastic body of the magnifier within millimeters of the surface, but never allowing the device to touch the ancient material.

After nearly five minutes of examination, during which Oliver and the other men remained awkwardly silent and exchanged as few glances as possible, Diana straightened and exclaimed, "Gentlemen, I hate to break this to you, but you've been had."

Kyle gave her a puzzled look.

Diana gestured to the object rolled out on the table. "There is no way I can advise Oliver's client to purchase this. It's such an obvious forgery that the very fact you tried to sell it to us makes you look like fools."

Kyle's face flushed a deep red and the muscles in his thick neck began to bulge. His right fist tightened and he appeared ready to launch himself across the table and punch Diana. Frank stepped forward, keeping one hand on the the grip of his gun as he caught Kyle's eye. Kyle swallowed and shook his head slightly. Frank nodded and stepped back.

Kyle stepped forward and gripped the edge of the table. As he spoke each word came out crisply and laden with venom. "What. The hell. Are. You. Saying?"

Diana beckoned for Oliver to come closer, then waved her hand across the scroll, inviting the men to examine it. "Just look at it, the vellum is still supple. It unrolled without a single crack. That alone is so suspicious that I had to spend extra time examining this to try and find what made you think this scroll was genuine. Honestly, the only thing I could find that appears genuine is the hieratic. The symbol structure and what I read of the grammar is spot on, but that doesn't make up for the fact that the ink is as fresh as if it had been written a few days ago. I will also give you that the vellum and ink both appear to have been manufactured using ancient techniques.

If you use my glass to examine the ink, for example, you'll see small particles trapped within it. Those are the result of grinding the ink components with a stone mortise and pestle and putting them directly into an inkwell, rather than processing them further to remove all but the finest pigments. That is consistent with the manufacturing process used in ancient Egypt, but the object as a whole is certainly not five thousand years old."

"My client will not be happy to hear about this," Oliver growled, trying to transform the growing excitement he felt into a tone of frustration. "He has already spent a great deal to send us here."

Kyle pounded a fist on the table and shouted, "How could this happen? I was with the team that recovered this scroll. It comes from a collection that was supposed to be of unquestionable authenticity."

Oliver shrugged. "You are the seller, Kyle. My client and I merely heard from our mutual associate, Mr. Karim, that this item had become available. We know what collection it came from, so either the contents of the vault were switched before you reached them, or someone in your organization is trying to double cross you. I'd suggest you check your sources, as I am about to do.

"Diana." Oliver gestured towards the door.

Diana adjusted her glasses, collected her document magnifier from the table, and walked out the door. Oliver followed her, hoping that he wouldn't feel a bullet burrowing into his spine as they walked away. He had barely pulled the door shut behind them when he heard the sound of glass cracking and Kyle's voice screaming obscenities. Frank's voice joined in, his tone defensive, but by then Oliver was too far away to make out any words.

"You may wish to screen the people who use your back room more carefully, I think they just broke something in there," Oliver quipped as he strode past Nasir Saab, who was standing behind his counter staring open-mouthed at the door to the room Oliver had just exited.

Chapter Eight

Rais Karim was waiting for them in the lobby of the hotel when they arrived. Oliver spotted him through the wide glass windows, sitting in one of the comfortable chairs and obviously pretending to read a magazine.

He jumped up, throwing down the magazine, and accosted Oliver as he pushed his way through the revolving door. "We need to speak. In private."

Oliver motioned for Rais to follow them and the three of them stepped into the elevator together. Oliver intentionally moved in front of the control panel after pressing the button for the top floor. He didn't expect that Rais Karim would try to stop the elevator, didn't even know if that actually worked outside of movies, but figured it was worth avoiding the issue. He figured that he could also press the button for the next floor if he and Diana needed to make a quick exit. Diana stood beside Oliver with her arm around behind his back as if they were lovers. Oliver initially thought this odd, but his confusion was ended when he felt her fingers slip around the grip of the gun in his waistband.

"The meeting did not go as planned." Rais said, his tone cold.

"This should not come as a complete surprise to a man with your history."

"Not an hour ago I was sitting in my favorite café enjoying a cup of coffee and my morning newspaper, hoping to hear that you had secured the scroll for your rich American client and gotten it out of the hands of those mercenary bastards. Then I got a call. It was from one of those very same bastards. He said that your expert," he spared a vitriolic glance for Diana before looking back to Oliver and continuing, "called the scroll a forgery and advised you not to purchase it."

"What's he planning to do?" Oliver asked, affecting a disinterested tone.

"I do not know. Given the sort of man he is, I imagine he might have already torn the scroll to bits or set it on fire in a rage."

"Good. Then your secrets are safe."

Rais Karim appeared to be gathering himself for a scream, or possibly even to throw a punch, when the elevator dinged to a stop and the doors opened. A young Japanese woman dressed in exercise shorts and a sports bra stepped aboard. Oliver stepped aside to allow her access to the elevator controls. She tapped the already glowing button for the roof and leaned against the wall beside Diana tapping a tennis racket against her knee. Oliver didn't think it prudent to obviously block the panel with this woman in the elevator, so he remained standing a few feet from it as the elevator doors closed and the car began to ascend again.

Oliver turned away from the woman and addressed Rais in a calm tone, as if they were discussing an everyday business deal, "Anyway, I highly doubt that the supplier is going to act on any of the documents on his possession, assuming they haven't been shredded already. That was your goal, wasn't it? To ensure that your business assets remained guarded?"

Karim scowled at Oliver, but managed to engage with his charade. "You are not entirely wrong, but I would have preferred that the documents be preserved intact. I did not seek their destruction."

"Business can be unpredictable. The deal would have fallen through anyway. My client balked at the share price."

Karim glowered at Oliver, breathing slowly and deeply.

Oliver wondered if the old spy was about to attack him, despite the presence of a witness. He had no idea whether the young woman in tennis attire could understand English, but given her dress and presence in a hotel that catered to westerners, he had thought it prudent to speak metaphorically. He was actually grateful for her presence, as it seemed to have turned Rais Karim's rage inwards.

Rais muttered something unintelligible and stepped forward to press the button of the floor they were approaching. The elevator dinged to a stop almost immediately and he stepped off.

Before the doors closed he turned back and said, "I hope this brings our business to a close, Mr. Oliver. If I have anything to say about it you will never again attempt to purchase stock on the Egyptian market."

"Fortunate for me you are no longer involved with that business then, isn't it?"

The doors slid shut on Karim's face as it shifted to an expression of unmitigated hatred.

"Bad business deal?" the tennis woman asked. She spoke in English, only softly accented.

"You could say that," Diana replied for Oliver.

The woman nodded and said, "I've been there."

Oliver smiled wistfully, but did not say anything. The three of them rode in silence until they reached the rooftop tennis courts. There the woman waved to several friends and set off at an easy jog to join them on the court while Oliver and Diana settled in at the rooftop bar and ordered drinks.

They killed nearly an hour sipping their drinks and discussing the meeting at the book shop in low tones. Oliver wanted to give Rais Karim time to cool off and leave the hotel, just in case he had harbored any thought of waiting for them at another floor or tracking down their room number to continue their discussion. Diana quickly caught on that they would not be leaving in a hurry and joined enthusiastically in the discussion.

As they reached the end of rehashing the encounter in the bookshop, Diana took a long sip from her drink, then turned to Oliver and said, "I'm telling you Oliver, if Rais and your Senator buddy hadn't vouched for it, I would have truly believed that the scroll I saw today was a forgery. A truly spectacular example of ancient Egyptian style manufacture, to be sure, but a complete fake less than a century old. I've handled paperback books from the 1900s that were more brittle than that scroll. What do you think the explanation could be?"

"There is the obvious explanation that the scroll is a fake, but I'm not inclined to go with that. There is little motivation to fake an artifact in every detail of authentic construction, ink chemistry, and content unless you also artificially age it. So if we throw that line of thought right out the window it leaves us with the simple result that this scroll is the genuine article, just remarkably well preserved."

"But what could protect it so well? I've handled scrolls and works of art that were sealed in clay jars, hidden in temples, buried in mud, you name it. None of them were even close to that well-preserved. Most scrolls in museums have never been opened or were examined over the course of months, even years, of painstaking preservation efforts. And here I am, sipping a coke and recalling just..." Diana swept her arms apart, "...rolling open a five thousand year old scroll."

Oliver took a sip of his drink and grinned, but didn't reply.

Diana laughed aloud and shook her head. "This isn't your first time encountering something like this, is it?"

Oliver shook his head and slipped Diana a wicked smile.

"Is it always this exciting?"

"Yep. I still remember my first genuine relic."

"That's the one your uncle brought back from South America, right? The one that got you started on all of this tomb raiding business."

"Precisely. Although I still think I'd have been a legitimate historian if my doctoral board hadn't taken such a dim view of me pursuing the truth on the university's dime and reputation."

Diana nodded gravely and lapsed into silence for a while.

That made Olive feel bad. He hadn't meant to shut down their conversation by bringing up the past. His disgraceful fall from the halls of academia was far enough in the past that it hardly bothered him any more. He had spent about six months sulking and posting venomous rants on the internet, but then he had found the second of the metal fragments and it had rekindled his desire to search for the truth, damn the consequences or obstacles. That was when he had taken up adventure photography as a cover and a means of earning a living, and he had never looked back.

"It's alright, Diana," he said when it became apparent that she wasn't going to speak again without prompting.

She looked up at him. Her eyes seemed to search his for a moment, as if questioning whether he was honestly alright with her bringing up his past. He nodded and said, "I've seen many genuine relics in the last decade. There's no way of knowing for sure without following the clues, in the case of documents, or attempting to use them, if they are objects of power, but you develop a feeling. These things are special. They aren't completely part of the natural world anymore and something about them just... feels right."

"I was afraid to say it," Diana replied. "It's not like my fingers tingled when I touched it or anything silly like that, but I just knew that that scroll was different from any I had touched before. I got this feeling in my head..."

"Sounds about right. I wish I'd been able to touch it myself. My guess is that long ago the scroll was blessed in such a way that it doesn't age or, at the very least, ages at a far slower timescale than the rest of our world."

"Is that really possible?"

"I've seen it a few times before. Armor that never rusted. Bits of food left in temples that are still fresh after hundreds of years."

"But that's..." She broke off.

"Afraid to say it?"

Diana nodded.

"Go ahead. You already believe me about the conspiracy, why not take it one more step?"

Diana drained her soda and set the glass on the bar. She looked out across the rooftop and watched the hotel guests lifting weights, playing tennis, or simply sunning themselves. From this height she could just make out the sands of the surrounding desert across the rooftops and through the smog of modern Cairo. It seemed a ridiculous thing to contemplate but if there was one place to accept such a thing it was here, in this place where the ancient and modern continued to coexist and likely would for centuries to come.

She turned back to Oliver, who handed her a freshly filled glass of coke.

"So?" he asked her. She didn't need to ask to what he referred.

"Is it... Is it some sort of magic?"

"You might call it that. I honestly don't have a real explanation for it yet, but that word is as good as any."

"But magic is... well, it's just magic. It's made up."

"What about miracles?"

"Well, sure. You don't grow up the daughter of a Pentecostal minister and not encounter more than your fair share of them."

"So you believe in miracles, but not magic?"

Diana sighed. "I've spent the last fifteen years dissecting myths to see where they intersect with modern culture, Oliver. My rational mind treats all of that as stories told down the ages to explain things mankind didn't have the science to understand, but I have to admit that my heart still has a soft spot for dad's faith healings."

"That's my point. Part of your mind insists that everything you grew up believing is completely true, even as another tries to examine it under cold hard light of rationality. No matter how much you fight it, there is some part of your soul that clings to the faith that those miracles you learned about in Sunday school and saw in church were real. What I need you to do, Diana, is realize that those parts of your psyche don't have to be in conflict. I don't have it all figured out yet, but the longer I spend in this line of work the more I'm convinced that this world is filled with secrets that we may never be able to explain as anything but 'magic.' I'm starting to think that's where my quest is leading me: to unlock some sort of secret about how all of this works."

Oliver sat back, realizing that he had leaned ever closer to Diana throughout this speech as he whispered it to her intently. He knew that he would have been waving his arms and nearly shouting with excitement, had they not been sitting in such a public place.

"So you're calling this a quest now?"

"A bit too melodramatic?"

"Just a little."

Oliver laughed. "Sorry. I just don't get much opportunity to explain it to people. The point is that yes, I do think that scroll is protected by something that you might as well call magic."

"Do you think Kyle and Frank would even have been able to destroy it?"

"Probably. I've seen a lot of relics over the ages and none were invulnerable. In my experience, the protection tends to be specific. The scroll probably doesn't age like you'd expect. Maybe it resisted mold and insects, but I strongly doubt that it would survive a bullet or being tossed into a fire."

"I felt bad telling them it was a fake. Everything in me wanted to take that thing back to a museum and see it preserved forever. And now... Oliver, I just as good as ordered the destruction of a piece of history."

"Sometimes that's necessary, Diana. We needed the information on the scroll and there was no way we could afford to purchase it. Besides, if Rais and the Senator are right about the scroll leading to the staff of Moses, the greater good might be to destroy the scroll so that nobody else can find the staff. Speaking of which..."

Oliver flicked a finger at Diana's glasses. She grinned again and reached up to take them off her face and examine them.

"I felt like a regular spy wearing these. Can't wait to see what they captured."

Oliver stood and took Diana by the arm, leading her towards the elevators.

"Rais is probably gone by now. Let's get you to work on the translation."

Chapter Nine

Back in Oliver's hotel room, Oliver showed Diana how to download the video captured by the small camera embedded in the frame of the glasses. As soon as the file transferred she began stepping through the video frame by frame to translate the hieratic script written on the scroll. The process of translation turned out to be quite tedious, as Diana typed partial translations of each line of the scroll into a word processor, then went back and applied what she had learned from the later portions of the text to revise her translation of earlier portions.

After an hour of tedious work, occasionally interrupted by turning to yell at Oliver for breathing down her neck as he read each translated line over her shoulder, Diana shoved her chair back and jumped to her feet.

"Enough, Oliver," she shouted. "Leave me alone or do your own damn translation."

Oliver shrugged and flashed her a playful grin. "You know I can't read a word of hieratic."

"Then that settles it," Diana muttered. She grabbed the laptop from the table and stormed through the doorway into her room, slamming the door shut behind her.

Left alone, Oliver quickly began to fidget. Normally he would have been the one doing the translation, experiencing the wonder of uncovering an ancient secret line by line, but his ignorance of ancient Egyptian languages meant that he could do nothing but wait. Rather than letting his mind run wild with the possibilities of what secrets might be hidden in the inscrutable lines of text on the scroll, he clicked the television on and tuned it to a channel showing a soccer match between South Africa and Ethiopia. Needing something to keep his hands busy, Oliver unlocked the large case of supplies that Senator Wheeler had shipped over through diplomatic mail.

The majority of the supplies consisted of survival gear, with a few weapons, a generous supply of ammunition, and some of his spare camera gear filling the remaining space. He had correctly assumed that Diana would not have any camping equipment of her own, so he had packed extra supplies as well as a second backpack for her to use.

Oliver pulled the spare backpack out now and began filling it with the necessities for a trek of several days in the desert. This occupied him for a good while as he attempted to pack the bag in such a way that Diana would be able to find whatever she needed without delay. Once the bag was filled he lifted it and judged that it might be too heavy for her. Diana was not a weak woman, but she was still smaller than Oliver and not accustomed to trekking through the desert. So he went back through the bag and dithered over every piece of equipment until he was certain that he had cut the bag down to the bare minimum that he felt safe giving her for several days among the dunes.

Glancing at the clock on the bedside table, Oliver was frustrated to see that he had not even expended an hour packing and repacking Diana's bag. He pulled his own backpack out of the case and double-checked the contents. He checked the charge on the spare camera batteries, freshly formatted each of the memory cards for the camera, and ensured that the spare magazines for his gun were fully loaded. Unfortunately, Oliver was so well practiced preparing for adventures into remote places that within another hour he had completed all possible preparations and was once again left with nothing to do but wait for Diana to finish her translation.

He sighed deeply and settled down on the bed to watch the remainder of the soccer match, doing his best to not think about the lines of ancient writing scrawled across Diana's computer screen, giving up their secrets one at a time as Diana worked her way through the scroll.

Oliver started to wakefulness at the sound of a lock clicking in the darkness. He reached out and grasped the grip of the gun that he had set on the bedside table, then rolled off the bed. He glanced at the clock and balcony doors as he rolled. 9:35 at night. He knelt beside the bed and sighted down the gun barrel at the door to the hallway. Nobody opened it, so he turned his attention to the door into Diana's room. It pulled open and he saw Diana's body silhouetted in the light from her room spilling through the open door and her face lit up in the glow of her laptop.

Oliver relaxed and stood, setting the back on the bedside table and rubbing his eyes with on hand.

"Must have fallen asleep," Oliver yawned. "Did you finish?"

Diana nodded and strolled across the dark room to deposit her laptop on the table. Oliver took that to mean that she had, so he flicked the bedside lamp on and joined Diana at the table.

Diana looked at him with bloodshot eyes and yawned as she settled into a chair. "Is this what you always do on an adventure? Take naps and let other people do the hard work for you?"

Oliver shrugged and smiled back at her. "Nope. Generally I'm all alone and don't get nearly enough sleep until I get back home."

Diana nodded and yawned again. She stretched and pulled her feet up under her in the chair, then waved at her laptop. "I've got a rough translation finished. Still needs a lot of polish, but I'm pretty sure it's accurate."

Oliver stepped up the the table and settled down in front of the computer. His eyes were still a little bleary from sleep, so it took a moment for them to adjust to reading the screen. The open document consisted of several pages with neatly organized rows of text. Each line of the text was labeled with a number which, at a glance, Oliver saw corresponded to bright red numbers that had been added before each line of the original scroll in a series of screen captures. As she said, Diana's translation was far from perfect, with many words and phrases still bracketed and colored to indicate that there were only an approximate translation of the original intended meaning of the text. Occasionally a word, or even an entire line, had been replaced with bracketed question marks to indicate a place where Diana had been unable to make any sense of the text.

The first three columns were merely a refinement of the translation that Diana had produced yesterday, working from the photographs supplied by the Senator's contacts at the American Embassy. A few minor details had been filled in, especially at the bottom of each column where the text had been cut off in the photos, but the overall story remained the same.

From the fourth column onward the translated narrative was entirely fresh to Oliver, and the story revealed in Diana's translation certainly captured Oliver's attention.

According to the scroll, Pharaoh's army had advanced across the desert in bronze chariots pulled by the strongest horses in the entire land. Led by the Pharaoh's most trusted general, Sephor, the army stormed through the lands that had been conquered by the Hittite raiders, utterly destroying the forces left behind by the heathen invaders. Every Hittite man they encountered was killed and hundreds of woman and children were taken as slaves to be set to work rebuilding the ravaged lands.

All of this was described in such a triumphant tone that Oliver couldn't help wondering if the campaign had actually been a terrifying slog of bloody battles and high casualties for the army of Egypt. He looked up to ask Diana if Egyptian historians were as prone to rhetorical spin as their European counterparts, but her chin had fallen on her chest and she was snoring softly. Oliver went back to reading her translation.

The Egyptian army's advance was unchecked for nearly a month until one day they came to rest at the western ridge of a deep valley. Encamped across from them, arrayed in a line that stretched as far as the eye could see, was a vast army of Hittites, come to recapture the lands they had stolen and sweep into the Egyptian homelands. Throughout the night, messengers ran back and forth between these armies, the generals of each demanding that the other surrender and offer up a tenth of their troops as a sacrifice to the god of the opposing forces before delivering the remainder of their men to be slaves.

The battle began as the sun rose, sending its first beams of light coursing down the floor of the valley. The Egyptian chariots led the charge. So brightly was the bronze of their chariots polished that the sun reflected back off it with renewed brilliance, blinding the first wave of Hittites that they encountered. These were trampled under the feet of the horses and the Egyptian soldiers, emboldened by this obvious sign of Ra's blessing on their cause, fought with a bravery unequaled in the world since that day.

Throughout the day the armies of Egypt and the Hittites continued to clash in that valley of glorious death. Not only were the Egyptians outnumbered more than ten to one, but the Hittite sorcerers continually rained down death upon them in the form of bloody rain, hail, and flies.

General Sephor knew this to be the work of the unholy relic that the great priest Amneth had uncovered and he feared for the fate of his army. He therefore kept one eye out for the source of these plagues, even as he led his men from the heart of the battle. Late in the day he discovered it in a group of three Hittite sorcerers, all standing around a staff of carved olive wood, which hovered in the air between them. These men dared not touch the staff itself, but continually made gestures and prayers towards it, as if the staff could hear them and be bent to their will.

The sorcerers were protected by a force of thirty men ringed about them, but Sephor, the Pharaoh's most worthy general, took it upon himself to charge the group and capture this powerful relic for the glory of his Pharaoh and the salvation of his army. Single handedly, he slew each of the thirty guards, though swarms of flies surrounded him and bloody hail pounded down upon his head. Boils broke out upon his flesh, but that did not prevent him from slaying the first of the three sorcerers. Fleas sprang from the ground and covered his flesh, but he slew the second of the sorcerers without hesitation. And though he fought blindly through a sudden and complete darkness, while still beset by all of the previous afflictions, Sephor slew the third and final sorcerer with a mighty thrust from his sword. He then turned and took the staff in his own hands and commanded it to turn back every plague it had unleashed upon his men.

Liberated from the afflictions of the staff, the Egyptian army quickly annihilated what remained of the Hittite forces and turned back to Egypt to deliver the newly captured staff to the Pharaoh.

Upon receiving the staff from his most trusted general, the Pharaoh recognized it as that which had afflicted his benighted predecessor in the hands of the Hebrew Moses. He rejoiced at its capture and praised his most worthy general above all others in the land. The Pharaoh then ordered that a temple be constructed to the west of his capital in which the staff would be kept under the guard of Amneth, the priest who had scried the source of the Hittites' unholy power. In that place the gods of Egypt would be perpetually worshipped in thanksgiving for granting Sephor victory over the foreign gods. He further ordered that Sephor be granted a vast tract of land upriver of the capitol, on which to build his estate.

The final lines of the scroll described how the Pharaoh, in his wisdom and mercy, sent messengers to the Hittites and their heathen king and offered a treaty of peace between the two nations. He would retain possession of the staff and all liberated lands, and, as an offering of life to the gods, the Pharaoh would spare the Hittites the death and humiliation of being enslaved. This offer was accepted and still stood as one of the many accomplishments of his, the greatest of all the Pharaohs.

Diana's translation might have been rough, but Oliver was impressed at how quickly she had completed it. The story of Sephor's victory over the Hittites was replete with hyperbolic descriptions, honorifics, and metaphors, but she had managed to not only translate the essential meaning of it in a mere few hours, but make it intelligible to someone like Oliver, who had purposefully neglected his Egyptian studies in favor of steeping himself in the legends of lands that had been less picked over by the first wave of professional archaeologists over a hundred years before he was born. He was familiar with the broad outlines of the land's history, but couldn't have told you the difference between Seth and Horus or where exactly one dynasty ended and another began. Despite his professed ignorance, Oliver had no difficulty following the narrative of the scroll.

Now that he knew the legend, Oliver would need to begin piecing it together with the known history of Egypt to determine what truth might exist behind the fantastical story. Many historians he knew would begin by discounting the magical elements of the scroll's narrative and instead focus on clues that they considered more "reliable", such as the names of the trusted priest and worthy general, description of the battlefield, and numbers of troops. Oliver, however, was more interested in the elements of the story that related seemingly magical events. In this case he was especially pleased because they were not merely random events that occurred to the hero of the story, but specific plagues ascribed to the manipulation of a magical object. Moreover, these events matched with the Biblical account of the plagues that the Hebrew god had rained down the the Egyptians.

The remarkable similarities between the magic of the staff described in the scroll and the events in the book of Exodus were exactly the sort of convergence of myths that Oliver looked for when tracking down a relic. The obvious explanation was that the scroll was a forgery, written to take advantage of the Exodus story, but Rais Karim had sworn that the scroll had been reliably dated by his agency while it was in their possession. This assertion, when combined with the clearly unnatural lack of aging of the material, served to make Oliver fairly confident that the scroll was as old as the legend seemed to indicate.

Oliver stood and stretched, then stepped over to Diana and shook her awake. She came around slowly, but responded enthusiastically to Oliver's suggestion of a late dinner. They pulled on shoes and rode the elevator in silence, Diana still rubbing her eyes to wake up and Oliver contemplating what he had read. After they had settled into their seats in the hotel restaurant and ordered dinner, Oliver summarized his thoughts on why the story in the scroll seemed reliable. Diana listened to him, occasionally interjecting comments on how the linguistic makeup of the narrative supported Oliver's theory.

Their main courses arrived and Diana and Oliver both fell silent again for a few minutes as they focused on eating. Neither of them had eaten a proper meal since breakfast, so Oliver was content to wait until after dinner to continue their conversation.

After several minutes Diana got a quizzical expression on her face and began tapping her fork gently against her plate. She took a sip of wine and asked, "How would the Hittites have gained control of the staff?"

Oliver looked up from his plate and chewed his food thoughtfully, nodding a little.

"Think of it," Diana continued. "The staff was an important relic for the Hebrews as they came out of Egypt and began conquering Canaan. Wouldn't they have preserved it?"

"You know Egyptian and Biblical archaeology better than I," Oliver replied.

"Yes. I'm just thinking out loud here." Diana paused to chew a mouthful of her dinner, her face contemplative. After a moment she said, "Now that I think about it, there is no actual mention of Moses's staff in the Bible after his death. Some commentaries claim that it was passed down through kings of Israel, but there is no clear description of its fate until the staff supposedly surfaced in the possession of Sultan Selim I in the sixteenth century."

"I know. I mentioned that to Senator Wheeler when he hired me, but we both agreed that it was unlikely that the Sultan's staff was the genuine article. Egypt and the Holy Land had already been raked over by Christian and Muslim armies several times over by then, so something as significant as a genuine relic of Moses would probably have been carted off to the Vatican or a sultan's palace long before then."

"Exactly. So what would cause the genuine staff to disappear from the Biblical account and never again surface?"

"I've got a theory on that," Oliver responded. He chewed a couple mouthfuls and sipped his wine before continuing. "The narrative you translated indicated that the staff was in the possession of a massive Hittite army, which used the staff to rain down plagues on the Egyptians."

"Yes, but remember that the narrative is almost certainly embellished. There is no archaeological evidence for such an event occurring and the descriptions in the text are so overwhelmingly heroic that I'd wager that the scribe charged with writing down the official account made some rather drastic changes."

"Of course. He had to make the Pharaoh's army look good. It happened all the time in official histories, but there is usually some kernel of truth behind it all." Oliver paused dramatically and waited for Diana to sigh and wave for him to go on. He grinned and continued, "Here's my theory: There are mentions of the Hittites throughout the Old Testament. They are described as being one of the few civilizations that the nation of Israel was unable to conquer and there are also mentions of Hittite generals serving alongside the army of Israel under various kings. So what if the army described in the scroll consisted of a joint Hittite and Israelite force, and the 'Hittite sorcerers' were actually Hebrew priests?"

Diana pondered this for a moment before replying, "It would explain the presence of the staff at the battle."

"And its disappearance from history."

"But this is all conjecture, Oliver. How does it help us actually track down the location of the staff?"

"That's where my speciality comes into play. I've got a hunch that if we cross reference the narrative in the scroll with what you were telling me in Paris about that painter's brother..."

"Gabriel de Pujul."

"Gabriel, right. What if his army unit somehow stumbled onto the trail of the staff? The scroll makes reference to the staff being placed in a temple that will be 'eternally guarded' against all invaders. Some of the horrors that Gabriel described to his brother might have been those guardians."

"Or merely the ravings of a lunatic, driven mad by the desert, or war, or syphilis."

Oliver smiled crookedly at Diana and leaned back in his chair, waiting for her to get his point.

"Okay. I get it. You're pointedly not saying that I accepted a scroll being magically preserved for thousands of years just this afternoon, so why not take another step and believe that the monsters Gabriel encountered might be real."

Oliver nodded.

"So what's our next step?"

Oliver leaned forward and picked up his fork. "Let's finish our dinner and get a good night's sleep. In the morning we'll go over the translation some more and compare it to your notes on Pujul's letters and journal."

Oliver woke the next morning to find Diana already hunched over her laptop at the table in his room. After a quick shower and a call to room service for some breakfast he joined her and together they dug into the mountain of reading that lay before them. Diana had brought scans of the entirety of Pujul's published letters, as well as his journals and that of his brother, on her laptop. Oliver transferred a copy to his own computer and together they worked throughout the morning and late into the night, stopping only to rest their eyes and enjoy lunch and dinner at restaurants in the hotel.

As he pulled up yet another scanned letter, written in a precise but old fashioned French script, Oliver reflected that this was the element of relic hunting that you never saw in movies: The tedious slog through hundreds of pages of documents written in multiple languages. The dozens of pages of notes, half of them scratched out after being contradicted or surpassed by later discoveries. The careful comparisons of maps produced at various points throughout history. All of this had been made far easier by computers, which allowed Oliver and Diana to keep hundreds of reference works on their laptops as PDFs, to say nothing of online access to the collections of entire libraries. Still, this particular adventure didn't come with a convenient treasure map, but with a series of vague clues and coincidences.

They continued in this fashion for several more days. Oliver was relieved that Diana didn't complain about the work, but wasn't especially surprised. She was, in fact, even more accustomed to the slog of academic research than Oliver, who had admittedly grown sloppy in the decade since his fall from academia. She still carefully documented every source and kept neat notes, as if she was preparing to write a thesis. Oliver hadn't even tried to publish anything in years, so he tended to let his ideas run together and mix in his mind, on the theory that he would recognize patterns and connection in the sheer mass of data pouring into his mind.

Midway through the afternoon of the fourth day, Oliver stood up, cracked his knuckles, and pushed the lid of Diana's laptop shut on her fingers. She jumped back in her chair and glared at Oliver.

"What gives?"

"It's time to go."

"What are you talking about?"

"I think I've got the location of Sephor's estate."

Oliver spun his own laptop around and showed Diana an annotated image of a map, with a small red circle located in the desert south of a large lake.

"What's that?"

"Gabriel's last few entries before the journal breaks off describe his army unit moving along the west bank of a large freshwater lake. They go fishing every night and enjoy eating their catch as, how did he put it, 'the heavenly orb poured out its blood upon the waters.' No shock that there was an artist in his family."

Diana rubbed her eyes and yawned, then stood and went over to look out the window. She spoke while gazing out across the river. "I've read that passage before. It's the last entry before he stopped writing for nearly a month. The next one comes around the same time that he sent a letter to his brother in France, describing his services to Napoleon."

"And it's also the last entry that doesn't have at least some reference to his recurring nightmares or the terrors of the desert."

"So you think that you've found where he was when he wrote this?"

Oliver nodded and tapped the red circle on the screen of his laptop. "Yep. I compared the pace they seemed to be keeping, according to the journal entries, with the description of the property with which Sephor was rewarded for capturing the staff. There is an ancient estate there that was explored by archaeologists about twenty years ago, but they abandoned it when their leader and one of the crew disappeared without a trace."

"So why didn't your predecessors find any clues to the staff?"

"I don't know, but if this isn't Sephor's estate, we might as well pack up and head home. It's the closest match we have to the location that Gabriel Pujul may have explored, so I say we give it a shot."

Diana appeared to ponder this for a moment. She stepped away from the window and pulled Oliver's computer over in front of her, then began examining his notes.

Oliver waited quietly. He was certain she would be happy to go along with him, but knew better than to press her. He figured that Diana would probably be sulky about him finding the correlation between Gabriel's journal, the scroll, and the archaeological dig maps first, but soon enough the thrill of exploring an ancient ruin would overcome that. She was just as accustomed to working alone as he was and, to be honest, he would have been a little jealous too if she had made the connection first.

After several minutes of double-checking his work, Diana nodded and leaned back in her seat. "Alright, it makes sense. When do we leave?"

Chapter Ten

That afternoon, Oliver secured a single small room at an inexpensive tourist hotel down the street from the Sofitel and stashed what supplies they weren't bringing along in a locked case in the closet. He booked the hotel room for a week and scattered several bits of laundry and surplus camera gear about the room to make it appear to all but the most observant maid that they were occupying the room. If all went well, Oliver expected them to be back within four or five days. They spent one last night enjoying the fine food and comfortable lodgings of the Hotel Sofitel, then checked out early the next morning.

By seven-thirty, they were in a rented Range Rover streaking up the Cairo Aswan Road with the Nile on their left and a wide strip of fertile farmland stretching away to the west on their right. They followed that road for about three hours, though the time seemed to pass quickly as Oliver regaled Diana with stories about his latest efforts at tracking down the mysterious shards of metal that had become his obsession. For her part, Diana provided Oliver with a detailed summary of the book she was writing based on her research at the Louvre.

Soon enough they arrived at Faiyum, the nearest large city to the expected location of Sephor's estate. There they refueled the Range Rover, including filling several extra containers in the cargo bed with gasoline, and purchased a freshly cooked lunch. Once they had finished eating and their legs were no longer cramped, they climbed back in the Range Rover and headed south west along a regional highway with

Diana at the wheel, following a path that Oliver had plotted into the GPS.

This course would take them through several small towns along the wide loop of highway that encircled Al Fayyum Lake. They followed this loop to its southernmost point, skirting the southern edge of the long lake, then drove off the side of the road and headed out across the desert. Oliver had already loaded maps of the region, supposedly updated within the last two years, into a GPS app on his phone. They also had a collection of printed maps ranging from the hand-drawn work of the archaeologists who had first discovered the site to which they were traveling to a topographic map of the desert. Determining where to look for Sephor's estate had been difficult, but now that they had selected a location, traveling to it, even across the desert, was proving to be a simple exercise in following the paths worked out by the archaeological expedition that first discovered the site twenty years before.

As Diana drove, Oliver pulled out his phone and posted several updates to his secure tweet stream, letting Amber know where they were and giving instructions on where to find them if they didn't get back online within three days. She replied almost immediately, wishing them good luck and joking about his prospects of rekindling a romance with Diana in the desiccated remains of an ancient Egyptian temple. He ignored her jokes and slipped the phone into his pocket.

According to the maps they had examined, the distance from their highway turn-off to the dig site was only about a hundred miles. Their route, however, turned out to be far from a straight line. According to the notes that the previous archeological team had submitted to their university sponsors, the best route would take nearly an hundred and fifty miles of twisting along canyon ledges and around rock piles. That had been twenty years ago, however, and as they drove Oliver had to continually seek out new paths through the shifting sands as

Diana came across insurmountable sand dunes and unmarked gullies formed by the flash floods that occurred whenever the rare, but violent, rain storms struck this region. All told, it took nearly six hours for them to arrive at the the mouth of the canyon that he had marked as the likely location of Sephor's estate.

They drove through the mouth of the canyon and parked the Range Rover in the shadow of a rocky wall. Looking out through the window, Oliver could see a long wall of mud brick, about twenty feet high, encircling a compound of ancient stone and brick buildings of obviously Egyptian design. The wall was breached in two places. The first was at the gate house, where stone towers rose on either side of a wide gateway. The gate had long ago given way to time and Oliver could see a paved courtyard within the gateway. The second breach was in a place where the wall had collapsed above and around a dry stream bed.

"Think this is the place?" Diana asked, drumming her fingers on the steering wheel.

Oliver shrugged. "Only one way to find out. There's still some daylight left. Let's go take a look."

They climbed out of the car and both spent several moments stretching before Diana opened the back of the Range Rover and pulled out the spare fuel canisters and her backpack. She deposited the canisters beside the car and checked that the vapor locks were functioning before standing up and shrugging her bag on over her shoulders.

Meanwhile, Oliver pulled his own bag from the car and slipped it on. He checked the water tube that peeked out through a hole in the bag and ran up to a clip on his shoulder strap, verifying that he could draw water from the rubber bladder stowed in a zipper pocket within the pack. He reached back and worked the zipper along the bottom side that would let him slip his hand into the bag and pull out his camera.

Even if this little expedition didn't work out on the relic hunting front, he might be able to get a few photos that he could sell to National Geographic or a travel website. Finally, Oliver pulled his Glock out of the side pocket of the pack and pulled the slide back part way to verify that there was no round in the chamber before clipping the gun to his waistband.

"Expecting trouble?" Diana asked, stepping back from the car and pushing the door shut behind her. She had the GPS in her hands and was tapping the screen, saving the coordinates of their vehicle.

"Not expecting, but preparing. You remember that time Amber and I went to South America?"

"Your first time in the field."

"That's right. One thing I'll never forget about that little jaunt is that I was completely unarmed most of the time, and that's a big part of the reason Amber and I barely got out alive."

Diana nodded and slipped the GPS into her bag, then adjusted her own water tube. She turned to face down the canyon and said, "I don't see anyone else here."

"Nobody alive." Oliver agreed.

Diana gave him a surprised look, then shrugged and started to walk toward the wall.

They hiked down the canyon, keeping to the shadow of the high wall as much as possible while navigating the wash of boulders and heaped-up sand strewn along the floor of the canyon. According to the archaeological reports that Oliver had read, the canyon was thought to have once been the site of a small oasis, with a winding stream running out from a small lake at the end of the canyon. An unknown nobleman, who Oliver hoped would turn out to be Sephor, had built his estate around the oasis. The estate had thrived for an unknown period of time, the size of the central house and its numerous outbuildings was testament to that, but eventually the oasis spring had dried up and the estate had been abandoned. The site had only been excavated by a single crew of archaeologists, since being discovered on satellite scans thirty years before, and that team had spent less than a month at the site before rumors of a curse and lack of funding drove them away. Nobody had conducted a serious investigation of the site in the nearly twenty years since.

A ten minute hike along the dry stream brought them to the broken segment of the wall. Shards of metal poked out of the sand near the wall, remnants of an iron grid that had once prevented anyone from sneaking into the estate through the tunnel under the wall where the stream flowed out. Through the gap they could see the paved surface of the courtyard, still visible in places where the archaeologists had dug away the drifts of sand. Statues of men and animals were placed throughout the courtyard, some standing and others toppled into broken humps, their bases surrounded in drifts of sand. Inside the walls the stream bed became a brick-lined depression in the sand, meandering back and forth across the courtyard, occasionally widening into areas that must once have been calm pools of water, before it disappeared around the corner of the house at the far end of the yard.

"So, I know where I'd begin if we were preparing a proper excavation, but what does my favorite grave robber suggest in moments like this?" Diana quipped as they stood on either side of the broken down wall.

Oliver kicked at a small stone with his toe, then bent down and hefted it in one hand. "Generally I've got a better idea of what I'm looking for before I go in. In this case, however, we don't have much to go on. We don't really even know for sure that this is the right place."

"So, what then?"

Oliver tossed the stone through the gap in the wall and watched it skip across the sand and clatter to a stop against the shoulder of a shattered statue.

He waited, listening.

After a minute or more passed with no sign of movement beyond the wall, Oliver stepped carefully over the rusted iron grid and toppled stones to stand within the walls. He held up a hand for Diana to wait where she stood outside the wall.

After another minute of quiet observation, Oliver turned to Diana and said,   "Let's head in while its still light out and get some photos of the place, especially any wall carvings or mosaics. It's too late to do much exploration, but we can at least get a head start on translating anything we find."

He turned back towards the house and began walking across the courtyard, pausing every few feet to listen. He heard nothing but the sound of their breathing and the crunch of sand beneath Diana's boots as she followed him. Oliver didn't expect to encounter any traps here in the courtyard, but it never hurt to be cautious. The archaeological team that had discovered this site twenty years ago had spent two weeks mapping out the exterior of the estate in detail and carefully examining several unusual piles of bones and weaponry scattered throughout the courtyard, but they had only just begun exploring the interior of the buildings when their leader disappeared.

The official report stated that Dr. Herbert Yancy, leader of the team, abandoned the expedition and eloped with a young graduate assistant. Without his leadership, the team abandoned the site. Oliver couldn't prove that the story was false, but it struck him as odd that the missing professor and his lady were never seen again by any of their family or colleagues. Nobody from the expedition ever returned to the site and in the years since, the site had been all but forgotten.

To Oliver, these circumstances raised the possibility that maybe, just maybe, the team had encountered some form of defense, be it mechanical or supernatural, when they entered the main house. He didn't want to alarm Diana over what was little more than a hunch, but as he moved across the courtyard, Oliver was resolved to proceed cautiously and be prepared for any threat that might arise.

They approached the carved stone walls of the central house and paused for a moment to inspect the pillars that stood on either side of the yawning front door. These supported a heavy slab of cut stone that served to shade main entrance of the building. Diana took Oliver's camera and enthused over the intricacy of the carvings on the pillars, as he edged closer to the doorway and inspected the structure for any sign of traps. Finding no sign of dangerous mechanisms, Oliver turned to look back across the courtyard they had just crossed. He could imagine what it must have been like to stand here in the shade and gaze out down the length of the canyon five thousand years ago. The stream would have poured through the paved channel in the courtyard, filling at least five pools with fresh water and irrigating the raised beds that lined portions of the channel. Standing here it would be possible to see anyone coming from several kilometers away and send word for the servants, or house guard, to prepare an appropriate reception.

Turning his back on the view, Oliver saw that Diana had already entered the house and had pulled a powerful flashlight out of her backpack and clicked it on. She played her beam along the floor, checking for any desert creatures that might have entered the room to hiding from the sun, but there didn't appear to be any living thing in this place except for Oliver and Diana. That was a little unusual and he was about to remark on the absence of snakes and scorpions when Diana suddenly sucked in a deep breath and froze, staring at something that was blocked from his view by the edge of the doorway.

"Oliver..." she whispered, but he had heard her inhalation and was already hurrying towards her, his gun drawn and held at his side.

"What is it?"

Diana slipped her flashlight beam sideways, revealing the thing that had made her gasp.

It was a human skull. The desiccated flesh was drawn tightly across the bone, revealing grinning teeth between the dry lips and shriveled stalks hanging from the holes of its eyes.

She moved the flashlight slowly past the skull to a lumpy pile of rags covered in dust and sand a few feet away from the skull. After looking at them for a few seconds, Oliver realized that the pile consisted of a body, the dry skin and muscles shriveled tight around the bones, still wrapped in the tattered remains of modern work clothes. The body lay just outside a black doorway that appeared to open into a long corridor leading deeper into the house.

Oliver pulled out his own flashlight and approached the body cautiously, playing his flashlight beam around the room to search for any sign of a trap that might have killed the person. The room in which they stood was about thirty feet wide and half as deep. At the midpoint of the outer wall was the open doorway through which they had entered. He noted the large brass hinges, still projecting from the stonework even though the doors they had once held must have crumbled millennia ago, as well as several stone and brass lamp fixtures jutting out from the wall around the interior of the room. Several pieces of furniture, desks, stools, and daybeds intricately carved from wood and banded in bright lines of silver and brass, rested against the walls around the perimeter of the room. Directly across from the front doors, against the interior wall, was a carved stone altar. It was flanked by inlayed carvings of Egyptian gods, which Oliver recognized but could not immediately identify. Hieroglyphic symbols were engraved in the wall above the altar, a dozen or more lines of stylized creatures and household objects running down the wall between the two household deities. Two doorways were set into the inner wall of the room, leading deeper into the house. It was outside one of these doorways that the skeleton lay.

Oliver put an arm around Diana's shoulders. "You ok?" He asked.

She shivered briefly under his touch, then nodded firmly and replied, "Yes. It just surprised me. It's not like I haven't seen plenty of skeletons in the museum, I've just never stumbled across one like this before."

Oliver grinned and squeezed Diana against himself briefly before dropping his arm and stepping over to the corpse. "It doesn't look as if it's been disturbed by anything. The fabric of the clothing is worn, but it's not chewed through by mice or bugs. Even the skin and flesh don't seem to have decomposed. It's just had all the moisture sucked out of it, almost like a mummy."

"There's no telling how long it's been here I guess."

"Probably not. I hear that a few weeks in the desert could turn just about any body into a mummy that would take expert analysis to distinguish from the old ones."

"That's true. One of my advisors at the Louvre was involved in an experiment like that."

Oliver nudged the sleeve of the robe with the toe of his hiking boot. It shifted up and he chuckled. "Well, whoever this guy was, he's not ancient. He's wearing a Casio."

He pointed with his toe to the black plastic band of the watch, still encircling the withered skin and dry bone of the body's left wrist. Diana smiled at the incongruity of the situation, then crossed her arms and shivered again.

"Sure you're alright?"

"Really, Oliver. You don't have to play all chivalrous with me. I... I was just wondering why the head is so far from the body."

Oliver flicked his flashlight back and forth between the body and its head. "No idea, but it's worth being careful. I doubt that there are any traps here in the common rooms of a house, but you never know what smugglers or soldiers might have added over the years."

"I wonder who he was."

Oliver nodded, but didn't say anything. He had been wondering that himself and was beginning to wonder if this might be the missing Dr. Yancy. But if the professor had died here, so close the entrance of the house, why had the rest of the team left his body here and reported that he had run off with his assistant?

He stepped to the side of the doorway and shone his light around the frame, inspecting for any sign of hidden blades, trip lines, or garrote wires. Oliver had evaded his own fare share of such traps over the last decade, but the relic hunting community was small and everyone in it knew of someone who had been killed by a trap while exploring some ancient temple or tomb. Oliver didn't see any signs of traps in the doorway or as far down the corridor as his flashlight could show him. This only increased his unease, however.

A bright flash popped at the edge of his vision and Oliver spun to see Diana standing in front of the altar, snapping photos of the hieroglyphs and household gods. Calm down. He told himself. You're the one whose been investigating tombs for a decade, shake it off like she did.

"Odd combination, this." Diana said, gesturing with the camera Oliver had loaned her at the two relief carvings of Egyptian deities.

"How so?" Oliver asked. "I'm familiar enough with Egyptian mythology to recognize names, but I couldn't point out any of the gods in a lineup."

Diana rolled her eyes and gestured to the statue on the left of the altar depicting a man with a long beard holding a crooked staff and a stylized whip. "This is an image of Osiris, the Egyptian god of the afterlife. It's a common enough feature in homes from the seventh dynasty onward that even the poor Egyptians would commonly have a small statuette of him on their family altar at home. The odd thing is the pairing of deities."

She pointed at the statue on the right of the alter, which depicted a dog-faced creature with long pointed ears sprouting from the top of its head. "This is Setesh, the Egyptian god of chaos and darkness. According to Egyptian mythology, Setesh was the mortal enemy of his brother Osiris. In some myths he even kills his own brother, leading to epic adventures in which his nephew Horus hunts Setesh down to exact revenge for the death of his father."

Oliver moved to where he could see the two statues and examine the hieroglyphs between them. He couldn't read the symbols, but the placement and pictographic tone of the engravings didn't give him any sense of enmity between the two statues. They were of equal height, except for Setesh's ears, which reached almost to the stone ceiling of the room.

"Do these hieroglyphs give any indication of why these two are set side by side?"

Diana slipped her camera back into the side pocket of her backpack and stepped forward to scrutinize the engravings. Her lips moved quietly as her eyes darted down the rows of symbols.

Oliver waited patiently, glancing around occasionally to verify that they were still alone. The sun, fiery red with the dust of the desert, was visible through the doorway. It rested just above the edge of the canyon. Oliver estimated that they had about twenty more minutes before the sun dipped below the ridge and the entire canyon fell into shadow. That should be enough time for them to explore one of the hallways and still make it back to the car before nightfall. They both carried flashlights, but the desert night could grow cold and as a rule, Oliver preferred to explore unknown places during the day. Most folktales and myths were just stories made up by superstitious people who didn't understand the world around them, but Oliver's short career as a relic hunter had taught him to maintain a healthy respect for legends about nighttime terrors.

"Most of this is fairly typical stuff for a household altar." Diana said. "From here to here," she gestured from the top right of the engravings to a point about half way down the center, "the glyphs call upon each of the gods and ask them to guard the house and its occupants." Diana stabbed her finger at a place in the middle of the engraving and continued, "But here things get interesting. The glyphs describe the boundaries of the household and give specific instructions for all who might invade the home to have their heads removed from their bodies and souls fed to Setesh's minions. Then these last two lines seem to have been intended as a description of those who may command the guardians of the house, as well as listing of the estate's most treasured property, but as you can see, the stone is cracked mid-way down the last line."

Oliver stepped closer and noticed that Diana was right. Not only was the stone cracked, but it looked as if whole chunks of the stone had been chipped away.

"It almost looks like someone took a chisel to those glyphs." He commented.

"It's hard to tell after more than three thousand years, but the damage certainly is highly localized. It reminds me of the erasures carried out by Horemheb and his successors when they decided to reform the Egyptian religion and remove all mention of the sun god Aten from monuments."

Oliver took Diana's hand and pulled her towards the dark passage outside which the skeleton lay. "It's going to get dark soon. Let's take a look down this hall then get back to the car for the night. Stay close to me."

Diana squeezed his hand and followed. She didn't show any consternation as they edged around the body and paused, standing over the withered legs, long enough for Oliver to double-check the doorway. After a moment he turned and flashed Diana a grin, then stepped into the hall.

Nothing happened.

Diana giggled nervously. Oliver clipped his gun to his belt and took another step down the dark hall.

They walked down the hall to the first doorway, which was set into the right side of the hallway. They looked in through this door and saw a large room with faded paintings of battle scenes splashed across the walls. It was dimly illuminated by a red light streaming in through small windows set high in the southern wall. The walls were lined with wooden furniture, the largest of which was a large bed, complete with linen coverings, located on the eastern wall between two relief carvings of women holding baskets of bread and flowers.

"This site is amazingly well preserved." Diana commented, her voice filled with awe. She pointed at the furniture. "From the construction, I'd say that is probably the original furniture, but that should be impossible. Even if no insects got to it, it should have dry rotted and collapsed over the millennia, but nothing in here looks older than a few centuries."

Oliver didn't say anything, but he nodded and thought carefully about what Diana had said. He'd seen sites this well-preserved over the years, especially when a magic artifact was preserved within the site, but rarely had once been so accessible to visitors. It was as if this place had been completely forgotten for thousands of years, visited briefly by the ill-fated archaeological expedition twenty years before, and remained untouched since.

That made him nervous. Even remote temples and graves were often booby trapped to keep out invaders, but he had yet to see anything like that here.

They turned from the ornately decorated chamber and stepped across the hall to a doorway set in the left wall. This opened into an expansive room with four statues of proud-faced Egyptians placed around a central area with an inlayed mosaic floor. A large chair of finely carved alabaster, its arm rests carved in the shape of snarling dogs, stood on a raised dais between the statues near the eastern wall. Shining his light around the edges of the room Oliver could see a doorway directly opposite the one in which they stood and another behind the stone chair.

"This was probably the main hall." Diana pondered. She shone her light onto the faces of the statues, pausing to examine each. "I don't recognize any of these as Pharaohs, so my guess is that these represent the owner of this estate and his family. They would have been placed here to watch over guests as they waited for the master of the house to make his grand entrance, probably from the door behind the throne."

Oliver nodded, recognizing the layout from innumerable castles and mead halls he had explored or studied. The basic configuration of any such room didn't vary much from culture to culture. No matter who owned an estate like this, they always had the urge to build a room in which they could sit higher than those who came to them with business offers, petitions for aid, or grievances against their neighbors.

Diana stepped back from the door and continued down the hall with Oliver at her side. They could now see the end of the hall, where it turned to the right and presumably continued for some unknown distance. A dozen or so feet beyond the entrance to the main hall, another doorway was set into the right wall of the corridor. Diana stepped towards it, but froze as Oliver grabbed her left bicep and yanked her back against him.

She spun to face him, confusion and anger playing across her face in the light of their flashlights, but Oliver held a finger to his mouth and shushed her question before it even came out. He listened intently for the sound that had set his hairs on end.

The hall was completely silent for a dozen heartbeats. Diana opened her mouth to ask Oliver what he was about when the sound came again. It was a low scuffling and creaking, like a bundle of dry sticks rubbing against each other as they were dragged across the stone floor.

Oliver pushed Diana back down the hallway in the direction of the front hall and drew his gun. He checked that there was a round in the chamber, then raised the flashlight and gun in a two handed grip pointed down the hall. The light revealed nothing but the finely cut stone of the walls and a thin layer of sand strewn smoothly across the floor. He began backing down the hall, pushing Diana behind him.

The sound came again, louder this time and clearly emanating from around the corner at the end of the hall. Oliver pushed a shoulder into Diana's chest, urging her to move more quickly.

Oliver and Diana were just passing the entrance to the room with the bed when the scuffling, scraping sound came again. This time it was accompanied by the appearance of something at the end of the hall. The beam of Oliver's flashlight played over and past it for an instant, then he snapped the light back onto the thing.

It was a skeleton, standing upright with a bronze short sword griped in one bony hand, reflecting the beam of Oliver's flashlight back at them from its wickedly sharp edge. The empty sockets of the skeleton's skull glowed with a pale blue light that seemed to trace wisps of glowing smoke through the darkness as it turned to face them. The scraping and clattering sound came again as the skeleton turned slowly and placed its bony foot upon the stone floor of the hall.

"Get to the car. Now!" Oliver growled.

He steadied his aim and pulled the trigger. The gunshot was deafeningly loud in the narrow stone corridor. The skeleton jerked back as the mass of the 9mm hollow point round slammed into its ribcage with shattering force, sending out a burst of fragmented bone to dance in the flashlight beam. Blue smoke surged out from the shards of bone and the ribcage shuddered as if ready to collapse forward, then steadied and held firm. Then the skeleton raised its sword and opened its jaws and charged.

To her credit, Diana immediately turned and ran for the exit. Oliver fired one more shot at the advancing skeleton and took off after her, the shot whizzing past the creature's empty jaw and caroming off the stones behind it. As Oliver turned he saw Diana lurch into an awkward tumble as she tripped over the body of the beheaded man. She righted herself, spouting profanities and slapping fragments of bone and flakes of dry skin from her clothes, and ran for the door to the outside.

Oliver spun back towards the skeleton and dropped into a controlled fall, landing on his backpack and sliding through the scattered remnants of the headless man as he fired three more shots towards the advancing skeleton. Two missed it, whizzing through the empty spaces where its flesh should have been, but the third struck the monster in the collar bone and knocked it off balance. The skeleton spun wildly, lost its footing, and slammed into the wall of the corridor with a mighty clatter of bone and metal.

Oliver rolled to his feet and ran, following Diana down the wide steps of the house and across the courtyard. They ignored the winding path through the pools and raised gardens, electing to make a straight dash across the stones and drifts of sand to the yawning opening they had entered through. Oliver didn't dare look back until they had hurtled through the gap in the wall.

Once they had passed the wall Oliver spun to face the courtyard, praying that the skeleton was not right behind him, preparing to slice his head off. The skeleton was still behind them, clattering and scraping across the stone and sand of the courtyard in the fading light of day. Its left arm dangled at an strange angle from the shattered collar bone, but it still clenched the age worn sword in the bones of its right fist. The creature moved quickly, but did not leap across the brick lined waterways and through the dry pools as Oliver and Diana had. Instead it followed a slower path, crossing the dry stream only on the ancient stone bridges.

Oliver glanced back to see that Diana had slowed in her retreat and was also watching the skeleton's progress across the courtyard, her mouth hanging open in complete shock. He darted up to her and gave Diana a push in the direction of the Range Rover. "Go! Get the car running!" he shouted.

She closed her jaw with a snap and turned, running again.

Oliver continued to move towards the car also, but at a slower pace, stepping slowly backwards across the rocky terrain and always keeping one eye on the skeleton.

The skeleton advanced past the gap in the wall and disappeared from view. Oliver continued to move back, not trusting that the creature wouldn't realize its mistake and come hurtling out towards him through the breach in the wall. It didn't. Glancing back and forth along the wall as he retreated,

Oliver saw the skeleton appear in the opening where the gates had once stood. It saw him and roared again, dashing forward for a dozen feet before coming to a sudden stop in the midst of the gateway, as if the gate had still been standing and the skeleton had run up against it. The fiend continued to glare menacingly at Oliver and make unsubtle flourishes and jabs with its sword, but it came no closer. Oliver watched it for a moment or two until he was certain that the skeleton was not going to pass the invisible barrier where the estate gates had once stood, then he turned and loped up to the already running car.

"Please tell me we weren't just chased out of an ancient Egyptian mansion by a skeleton with a sword." Diana said as Oliver climbed into the passenger seat.

"Can't do that."

"Let's get the hell out of here." She muttered.

She reached for the gearshift, but Oliver got his hand on it first and said, "Wait. Just look at the thing, it's not going past the wall."

Diana slapped Oliver's hand away from the gearshift and glared at him, but he met her gaze levelly and nodded out the windshield at the gateway of the estate. Diana sighed and looked out her window to see that Oliver was correct. The skeleton's bleached bones seemed to glow a soft red in the fading sunset, with occasional sparks of something like blue fire darting out from its skull and between the joints as it prowled back and forth in the gap, never crossing the place where the gates had once stood.

"The hieroglyphs above the altar," she whispered. "They described the border of the estate as all that stood within the walls. Do you think that those words were... what, some sort of instruction for magical guardians?"

Oliver nodded. "Probably. I told you, Diana, there are places and things in this world that can only be described as magic. We've just escaped from one of them."

"So what are we going to do now?"

Oliver looked to his gun, which he was still gripping tightly in his right hand. "Let me try something."

Before Diana could stop him, Oliver threw open the car door and jumped out. He strode across the sand towards the gatehouse, ignoring Diana's shouted threats of what she would do to his body if he didn't come back to her immediately. As he approached the empty gateway the skeleton stopped pacing back and forth across the opening and turned to face him. It raised its heavy bronze sword and snapped its jaws together with a terrible clacking sound. Air whistled through its teeth, propelled by invisible lungs and shaped by a tongue that no longer existed, and roared out of its mouth as unintelligible words in a dead language. Oliver stopped less than ten feet away, separated from the fiend by nothing but the rusted shards of metal that had once banded the

"Let's see if this stops you." Oliver muttered. He raised the gun and aimed it directly between the glowing blue holes of the skeleton's skull. He pulled the trigger twice.

The first shot shattered the skull, sending fragments of bone skittering across the sand and stone of the courtyard. The second the bullet ripped through an expanding cloud of blue smoke, scattering it backwards in a glowing spiral that quickly faded to nothingness. A high-pitched screech broke the cooling night air for just a second, then the whole body of the skeleton collapsed into a pile of dusty bones.

Oliver turned and walked back to the car where Diana was glaring furiously at him through the windshield.

"Why did you go out there?" Diana shouted as Oliver slipped back into the passenger seat.

Oliver opened his mouth to reply but found himself unable to articulate as Diana launched herself across the center console, wrapped her arms around his neck, and pressed her lips against his.

Chapter Eleven

Oliver was paralyzed with surprise for a moment, but soon enough he gave in to the kiss and allowed himself to be lost in the experience of it. It had been a long time since he had kissed a woman and Diana was absolutely the type of woman he was attracted to. He closed his eyes and lost himself in the warmth of her lips, dry from the trek through the canyon yet pleasingly soft. When Diana finally pulled back, Oliver reached down to pull the seat lever. He leaned back in the soft cushion and scooted sideways to make room for Diana to lay beside him on the seat. She slid lithely over the center console and pressed herself against him, wrapping one arm tightly around his neck as she pressed her face into his chest. Oliver wrapped both arms around Diana and pulled her closer, enjoying the soft press of her body against his own. She began to shake gently against his chest and spent the next ten minutes alternating between pounding her fists ineffectually against Oliver's back and kissing him on the neck, softly sobbing the while.

Oliver did his best to ignore the soft pressure of her body, knowing that this was nothing more than a momentary outburst. He focused instead on reviewing his concerns of the previous few days, letting each of them melt away and be replaced by a warm thrill at having found the site of Sephor's estate. Working together, they had managed to get a look at the scroll and interpret its contents to uncover this ancient estate. They had shaken off Senator Wheeler's grip on the expedition, and apparently rid themselves of Rais Karim. Most importantly, Oliver no longer felt any guilt about bringing Diana along on this excursion. Her sudden need to be held by another living human was a fairly predictable reaction to encountering an honest to god undeniable sign of magical power, especially one that took the form of a murderous undead skeleton. Oliver was honestly impressed that Diana had not frozen when the skeleton charged at them in the hall. Present tears aside, she had a strong spirit and Oliver was confident that Diana would soon recover and continue to be a valuable asset on this quest.

Eventually, Diana reached a hand up between them and wiped away the tears from her cheeks. She looked into Oliver's eyes for a moment then turned away, blinking back more tears. "Some strong, independent, modern woman I am right now." She quipped, wiping away more tears and pressing her face against Oliver's shirt to dry her cheeks.

"There's nothing wrong with having a good cry. You just survived a literal encounter with death."

"You're not crying. Hell, I was on the brink of collapse and you went back out and shot that thing right in the face."

Oliver smiled and pushed a strand of tear-sodden hair away from Diana's right eye. "Trust me, Diana, this is nothing to be ashamed about. The first time I encountered a magical guardian, I didn't have time to even think about it for three days as Amber and I fought our way out of the jungle. When I finally escaped from the jungle and made it back to civilization, I spent a week waking up screaming with night terrors."

"Really?"

"Complete truth. Only reason I'm not freaking out now is that I've faced dozens of things like that skeleton in the last few years."

Diana sighed and laid her forehead against Oliver's chest. They lay together in silence for a while, until finally she stirred and said, "What comes next?"

Oliver had been pondering that very question and had a response prepared. "Tomorrow we go back in and see if we can find any clues to the location of the staff. Sephor clearly had links to genuine Egyptian magicians, so I think we can assume he really did have something to do with the staff. I wouldn't be surprised if we find some sort of clue to the location of the staff somewhere in his estate."

"But what about the skeletons?"

"You saw what I did to the one that chased us."

"Yes."

"I've got a spare gun and plenty of ammo. How's your aim?"

The next morning, Oliver and Diana crawled out of the Range Rover feeling stiff from a night spent sleeping on car seats, not to mention the tumble Diana had taken running away from the skeleton. The sun was just rising over the eastern rim of the canyon as Oliver stretched his sore muscles and contemplated the layout of Sephor's estate, trying to determine the best plan for exploring it. He went back to the Range Rover and found a pair of binoculars, then pulled a printed map of the exterior of the estate, drawn by the archeological team that had briefly excavated the site, from an exterior flap of his backpack.

That team had consisted of both British and American students participating in a work study program with an Egyptologist named Herbert Yancy. Dr. Yancy was an experienced excavator, known for his meticulous field work, who had grown weary of vying for a place digging in the more famous areas of Egypt, which he considered to be picked over and trampled anyway. Instead, he had elected to investigate this previously unexplored site, which had been recently spotted on commercial satellite imagery. The team spent a mere three weeks at the estate before the disappearance of Dr. Yancy and a female student brought the expedition to a sudden end. Egyptian authorities conducted a cursory investigation, during which one team member made vague mention of a curse, but said no more when pressed for details. All of them unanimously swore that their professor and the missing girl had fallen in love and run off together in the middle of the night. The authorities ruled that there was no evidence of foul play and sent the students home. The story supposedly ended there, but Oliver did find it odd that the aged Egyptologist and his young lover girl had never been seen again.

Before he disappeared, Dr. Yancy and his students had focused on mapping the exterior of the site, cataloging the piles of bones and weaponry that littered the courtyard, and examining the guards' quarters in the gatehouse. They produced the map that Oliver now held, as well as a moderate collection of notes which were remarkable only for their description of how untouched the site appeared to be.

The contents of the notes and map got Oliver thinking. He and Diana had been within the walls of the estate for under an hour before they were attacked by a skeletal guardian. How had the previous team managed to spend nearly three weeks here without being attacked? The only logical explanation Oliver could come up with was based on Dr. Yancy's slow and cautious methods. His team had not even entered the walls of the estate until they had spent two days making measurements of the perimeter wall and photographing the courtyard from a distance. Even after entering the estate, Dr. Yancy had forbidden his students to cross the courtyard until it had been thoroughly swept for artifacts laying under the sands. Once they discovered the piles of bones and weapons, which Oliver now believed to be remnants of skeleton guards which had been destroyed in the past, progress had slowed tremendously as each pile was photographed, described, and cautiously transferred into storage.

Diana stepped up beside Oliver and handed him a metal mess kit cup filled with hot tea. He accepted it with thanks and filled her in on what he had been pondering.

Diana considered what he told her, then replied, "Well, we know that they started lying at some point."

"You're referring to Yancy suddenly abandoning his students in the desert to run off with a woman half his age."

"I never met the man, Oliver, but I did read some of his field notes in the course of my research. He was careful. Quiet. Not the passionate type. He didn't even rage at his workers when they screwed up. Instead, he calmly fixed the problem and didn't rehire people the next year if they didn't learn from their mistakes."

"Maybe Yancy and his supposed lover were killed while mapping out the estate. The other students went in to find them and were chased away by a skeleton."

"Exactly. They don't want to destroy their careers so they make the best of the situation and say that the old man ran off with his student."

"Wouldn't be the first time. I wouldn't be surprised if the body we found yesterday was Yancy." Oliver sipped his tea and examined the map again. He looked back and forth from the map to the estate a few times. "This map describes the courtyard in detail, but it doesn't show any of the building interiors and only covers about half of the private garden in the rear of the house."

Diana pulled the map closer to herself and examined it, then nodded in agreement.

"I bet the skeletons primarily guard the inside of the house and only come out if they are chasing someone." Oliver said, setting his tea down and picking up the binoculars again. "Let's get some breakfast, then see if we can get to the interior yard without provoking another attack."

Oliver only asked Diana if she was sure about coming back into the estate. The look she gave him in reply was so withering that he immediately wrote off any future chivalrous comments or discussion of her strengths as a fighter of undead horrors. For her part, Diana appeared to have fully recovered from the shock of last night and determined to dive headfirst into the messy business of, as she repeatedly called it, "tomb raiding."

"Listen, Diana," Oliver said, as she strapped the holster to her right leg and checked that she could draw her gun with ease. "You're no more Lara than I am Indy. For starters, that gun only has twelve rounds and you've only got two spare clips."

"I'm flattered that the first difference you pointed out was the gun."

Oliver rolled his eyes, pointedly avoiding any comment on her appearance, and shouldered his backpack. "Just be careful. We were lucky last night."

Diana threw Oliver a mock salute and picked up her own bag, then followed him towards the gatehouse.

They paused briefly at the pile of bones that lay in the gateway. Oliver kicked at them a few times, but there didn't appear to be anything remarkable about them now. With no muscle or magic to hold them together, the bones had fallen to the ground in a jumbled heap that gave no indication of having been a fiendish guardian only a few hours before. He unholstered his gun and check that there was a round in the chamber, just in case they had been wrong in assuming that the skeletal guards only cared about the inside of the house.

According to the survey map that Oliver and Diana had examined, the southern wall of the house consisted of an expanse of stone broken only by small windows set high in the wall and the chiseled grooves of lavatory drains. That wall of the house merged smoothly into a low stone wall that ran around the south and east of the central complex. A dry stream bed curved along outside this wall and up into a cleft in the rock, which Dr. Yancy and his team had not explored. On the northern side, the wall of the house ran only half the distance of the western wall before it broke inwards in two zigzags to provide exterior access to a large formal garden. This garden was bordered on the north by low stone dwellings that had not been explored, but had been preliminarily identified as a kitchen or quarters for servants. At the center of the garden stood a building labeled as a chapel. The rear half of the map was roughly sketched, rather than drawn with precisely surveyed lines, and the notes Oliver had read indicated that the private garden had not been thoroughly surveyed before the team abandoned the site.

Moving as silently as they could, Oliver and Diana walked across the wide courtyard, angling their path towards the north side of the house. They paused for a moment at the corner of the house to sip from their hydration packs and listen, but there was no sound but their own breathing and the distant whisper of the wind blowing grains of sand across one another. They continued onward until they reached the corner of the main house.

Peeking around the corner, Oliver saw why the unexplored building at the center of the garden had been labeled as a chapel. It stood on a square platform of stone, seven steps higher than the rest of the garden. The entrance facing the wall of the house was flanked by weathered statues of Osiris and Setesh, which had clearly been carved with great care and detail before millennia of wind, sand, and occasional rain had pitted the smooth stone and blurred the finer details of their clothes and faces. The garden itself must have been a sight to behold when this house had been occupied by the living. Drifts of sand, some of them four to five feet deep, had accumulated against the walls, steps, and terraces, but it was clear that the garden had been carefully landscaped with terraced planting beds, columned porches, and long pools of water.

Oliver felt Diana move up alongside him and heard her gasp in astonishment at the sight of the garden and the chapel. "This is amazing," she whispered. "I've never seen a site so well preserved." She pointed at the porch that ran along the rear of the house and said, "I think those smooth patches under the windows are table tops, buried just under the sand."

"Word of the skeleton guards probably kept looters away until knowledge of this place died out after a few generations. After that... the wild places of this world are good at keeping secrets. Not to mention whatever magic kept the wood from dry rotting."

Diana nodded. She had a puzzled look on her face that Oliver couldn't fully ascribe to the unspoiled condition of the house and surrounding estate. "What are you thinking about?" He asked.

"It's the orientation of the house and chapel. It's all wrong."

Oliver pulled his phone out and looked at the digital compass. As he had expected from the map, he was facing south-east. The garden was on the eastern side of the house, between the house and the rocky wall of the canyon.

Diana saw him looking at the compass and said, "Something caught my eye on the survey map, but I didn't realize what it was until now. The whole complex is laid out wrong."

"You mean it's not secure, or the servants' quarters are too close?"

"No. It's the orientation to the sun. The ancient Egyptians believed positions of the sun represented life and death. That's why those who could afford to lived in cities and palaces on the east side of the Nile, closer to the life-affirming sunrise. They built their tombs and necropolises on the western shore, in the domain of death. Likewise, the homes of the wealthy were rarely built with the doors facing west, and never chapels or temples."

Oliver pondered that for a moment as he looked out across once beautiful garden. His eyes wandered to the chapel with its statues of long dead gods.

"What if Sephor was some sort of death cultist?"

"That's not out of the question. Many ancient Egyptians did gravitate more towards one god or another, even as they paid respect to the entire pantheon."

"Let's check the chapel first. I've got a hunch that we might find some clue there. If that turns up dry, we'll take a look in the main house."

They moved quickly across the uneven stands of the garden, being careful to not twist an ankle on the hillocks of drifted sand surrounding, and sometimes covering, long abandoned plant beds. Oliver moved ahead with his gun drawn while Diana got out her camera and began to take pictures of the garden features, house walls, and the large statues flanking the entrance to the chapel. Oliver knew that he ought to snap some photos as well, if only to try and make some money from this venture, but ever since he had nearly been killed by a golem seven years before, he developed a firm belief in securing a site before going into photographer mode. If that made him more of a relic hunter than a photographer, so be it.

Oliver mounted the stepped base of the chapel at the northern side and approached the chapel door cautiously along the wall. He edged around the weathered base of the statue of Osiris and peered into the dark interior of the chapel. A bright shaft of light slanted down from an opening at the top of the eastern wall and illuminated a stone altar at the center of the chapel. The sand covering the floor around the altar lay in uneven ripples that Oliver recognized as scuff marks from someone walking back and forth across it. Following the marks with his eyes, Oliver thought he could see the marks leading back into the darkened rear corners of the chapel, but the hewn stones of the altar blocked his view and the relative darkness of the chapel interior, compared to the bright sands on which he crouched, made it impossible for him to be sure.

Diana arrived at Oliver's back whispered, "Do you see anything?"

He described the scene within the chapel and pointed to the stone statue of Setesh on the opposite side of the doorway. "It's probably safe to cross over and look from there. Yancy and his students surveyed this half of the garden without being attacked, so if there are any more skeletons here, they probably don't come out into the garden."

Diana nodded and darted across the opening to crouch at the base of the Setesh statue. Oliver watched the shadowy interior of the chapel carefully, but saw no sign of movement within as Diana moved across the doorway.

He slowly got to his feet and said, "I'm going to go take a look around."

Diana held up one finger for him to wait. She slipped her camera into her backpack, pulled out her own gun and nodded back at him.

Oliver straightened and rounded the base of the Osiris statue, then stepped up to the threshold of the chapel entrance. Standing, he could see more clearly that the shallow drifts of sand around the base of the altar had indeed been disturbed, and recently. Short scuff marks circled the altar in concentric rings and led off into the shadows at the back of the chapel, as if someone had circled the altar a few times, walked away, and returned to circle the altar again.

He walked forward slowly, listening carefully for the sound of creaking bones that had preceded the skeleton's appearance in the main house yesterday evening. He heard nothing but the subtle crackle and swoosh of his own footsteps on the sand covered stone floor.

He reached the altar without incident. It was a simple platform of polished stone about four feet high and three feet square at the top, with no decoration except for one line of engraved hieroglyphs running down the center of each face. Oliver couldn't read the hieroglyphs, but some of them reminded him of those above the smaller altar in the front hall. Shallow groves were cut into the surface of the stone and ran out the the edges and down to a channel in the floor, surrounding the altar.

"Can you take a look at these?" he called back to Diana, motioning towards the alter. "I'm going to take a look at the back of the temple."

Diana sprinted up to the altar, nodded and slipped her gun back into the holster on her thigh. She pulled out her camera and began photographing the altar from every angle, already muttering to herself about possible translations of the hieroglyphs.

Oliver took a flashlight out of his pack and clicked it on. He played the beam around the perimeter of the chapel, revealing numerous faded murals painted onto the walls. These depicted various scenes of ancient Egyptians engaged in armed conflict, always led by a tall man carrying a sword. Oliver swept the light towards the back of the chapel and spotted a narrow doorway set in the stone wall. This was flanked by painted relief carvings of Osiris and Setesh and topped by an intricate painting of soldiers armed with spears and short swords following the tall man, but this time the man was holding some sort of rod instead of a sword. Running the beam of his light down to the floor, Oliver saw that the marks in the sand led up to the doorway and disappeared into the dark passage beyond.

Oliver stepped towards the doorway, flashlight and gun raised in front of him. He had a hunch that if this estate held any clue to the location of the guarded temple, it would be here, in a place that seemed to be dedicated to commemorating the accomplishments of Sephor as much as to the worship of any deity. He approached the door cautiously, shifting back and forth as he attempted to get a view of the room beyond, but the passageway was narrow and the wall between so thick that he could only see a narrow sliver of the back wall. This seemed to be painted with yet another battle scene, the colors remarkably vivid in the beam of Oliver's flashlight.

He reached the doorway and smiled because he was finally beginning to get a better view of the mural at the far end, when suddenly his view was obscured by the grinning visage of a skull.

Chapter Twelve

Oliver threw himself back and twisted to the side just in time to dodge a sweeping blow from a long sword. He landed hard and skidded back across the sandy floor. By the time his body came to rest, his gun was up and Oliver had the doorway in his sights. He didn't want to waste bullets firing blindly into the dark corridor, but he was ready to shoot the instant anything came into view.

The creature hurtled out from the dark, rasping out a terrible cry of rage from its parched throat. This was not a skeleton like the one Oliver had destroyed the night before. The thing that emerged from the dark doorway was a tall man with deep olive brown skin that had been darkened and worn by countless days spent fighting under the merciless sun. Long ago he had been dressed in a fine linen kilt supported by a belt of linked copper, but the linen had browned with age and begun to crumble. Now it was little more than a few threadbare scraps dangling from the scuffed copper links and twisting across the creature's body. The thing's head, where it was not bare skull, was covered in a patchwork of short hair, once thick and black but now a matted sandy gray ripped out in ragged patches. It gripped a long iron sword in its right hand, the sun glittering from large chips in the blade.

Oliver gaped as he lay on the stone floor, examining the thing over the sights of his gun. He knew that he should begin shooting and running, but his finger froze on the trigger at the sight of the ghastly slash that crossed the creature's chest, exposing layers of bone and viscera that looked as if they would have glistened and oozed were they not coated in a thick layer of dust and sand. Another wound had ripped away a chunk of the monster's left side, revealing the sagging shape of a tattered heart behind the ragged skin and splintered remains of brittle white ribs.

The creature advanced on Oliver, raising its sword to strike at him again.

Oliver fired.

His shot ripped into the creature's chest and exploded out the back of its body in a cloud of dark red dust. The undead thing jerked back and seemed to stumble, then got its footing and leapt towards Oliver with its mouth open in a cruel scream that sounded like air tearing through the pipes of a shattered organ. Oliver fired again and rolled sideways, stumbling to his feet and nearly tripping over something buried in the sand as the monster's sword hit the stone beside him with a terrible rasping clang and a shower of sparks.

Three more shots echoed through the chapel as Oliver rolled to his feet. He heard the distinct whine of a bullet passing close by his head before it slammed into the stone behind him. Glancing away from the creature, Oliver saw Diana kneeling behind the altar, steadying her aim by resting her gun atop the flat stones. She fired again and this time the bullet hit its intended target, knocking the creature sideways and sending out another cloud of red dust.

Oliver aimed his gun, trying to line up his sights on the fiend's head, but it charged towards him, body swaying with an awkward gait. He dodged to the side to avoid another swipe from the sword, firing into the monster's chest as it swung past him. He gave up on trying to destroy it in a single headshot and instead turned and ran towards the side wall of the chapel. As he ran, Oliver heard more shots booming and assumed that the thing was still chasing him, with Diana trying to slow it down. As much as Oliver appreciated Diana's help, her presence made this situation more difficult. If he had been facing the undead warrior alone, Oliver would have been in grave danger, but able to focus all of his attention on staying out of reach of the monster's sword. With Diana here, he also had to contend with the additional risks of being hit by one of her bullets and the chance that the monster's attention would be drawn to her.

A moment before he reached the wall, Oliver turned to the left and used his right leg to kick off hard against the wall. This launch him into the air and caused him to twist rapidly around to face the pursuing creature. He brought his gun up as he turned, aiming in the direction of where he expected the monster to be. As it turned out, the thing had been even closer than Oliver had expected. Before he could adjust his aim, Oliver slammed into the floor and skidded across the sand, but not before he saw the monster crash headlong into the wall from which he had just pushed off. Oliver raised his gun and fired repeatedly at the monster, pushing it back against the wall with each shot. He heard more shots and assumed that Diana had intuited his tactic and begin firing repeated shots at the monster's back as well.

His trigger clicked on an empty chamber and Oliver saw his slide had locked itself back. He was out of bullets. Two more shots sounded, then Oliver heard a curse from Diana as her magazine emptied as well. He jumped to his feet, ejecting the spent magazine into his left palm. He swapped it for a full spare from the front pocket of his vest and slammed the fresh magazine into his gun.

The monster's body was now riddled with gaps, some large enough that Oliver could see the wall through them. Dark red dust poured from the holes and was blown into a foul smelling cloud by the creature's wild gyrations as it attempted to turn and attack Oliver. Freed from the repeated body slams of hot lead, it managed to spin and swipe out with its sword, as if it had expected Oliver to be right behind it, but Oliver was still a dozen feet away.

Oliver released the slide, chambering a round. Before the monster had time to recover from its wild swing, Oliver aimed at its skull and smoothly pulled the trigger three times. Just as with the skeleton last night, the monster's skull shattered with a harsh shrieking sound and a puff of bluish smoke that seemed to wrinkle the air surrounding it as it drifted away. The headless body collapsed, still spewing the foul red dust as it fell.

Oliver stepped back, keeping his gun aimed at the monster. He kept moving until he felt the solid stone of the altar behind him.

"Do you think it's... dead?" Diana said.

Oliver looked around and saw Diana, still crouching behind the altar. An empty clip lay on the carved stone and she was in the process of inserting another into her gun. He turned back to face the prone body of the monster. The cloud of dust had mostly dispersed, but a faint haze of the foul substance still hung around the shattered remains of the creature's head. It reminded Oliver of the spores of a large powder mushroom, drifting lazily through the air after the mushroom was kicked.

He shrugged out of his backpack and dug in a side flap to find a handkerchief. He tied it around his face and put on a pair of rubber gloves from his first aid kit, then advanced on the body. He knelt on the floor beside the now restful corpse and started to examine it.

What clothes the creature had once worn had deteriorated over the ages, leaving little but a brass belt around its waist and a gold signet ring on the middle finger of its right hand. The deep gash cutting across the monster's chest had been nearly obliterated by the many gunshot wounds dealt to it in the last couple minutes. Oliver slipped a gloved hand inside one of the wounds and pulled back the leathery skin to reveal the remains of the creature's stomach and kidneys, all perfectly preserved and completely dry. It was as if they had been transformed into resin molds of their original forms without withering in the process. He had never seen anything like this before, but assumed that it was the result of whatever magical forces had transformed the once proud soldier into an undead fiend.

"What's all that dust?" Diana asked, coming up behind him.

"I'm not sure, but it was probably his blood. See, all of the organs are in place and undamaged, except where we shot it and here..." He pointed at a deep gash in the lower part of what might have once been the monster's liver. "That's not a gunshot wound. My guess is he was slashed and stabbed several times before being transformed."

"What could cause him to dry out like that?"

"I don't know. Probably some form of magic, combined with the dry air of the desert. My guess is that he was preserved exactly as he was in the moment the magic took hold, except that all of the moisture drained from his body over the next few thousand years."

Diana shivered and looked around suspiciously. "Do you think there are any more?"

Oliver shook his head. "This fiend is different from the skeleton that attacked us last night. I bet that this was once Sephor and he was somehow transformed after being cut with a sword." He pulled the signet ring from the creature's hand and passed it to Diana. "Can you read this?"

She held the ring up so the sunlight shone on the hieroglyphics embossed in the flat surface of the ring. "These symbols look similar to the markings over the household altar we examined yesterday. We can't be sure based on just this, but I wouldn't be surprised if you just killed the corpse of Sephor himself."

Oliver nodded and surveyed the wrecked body of the once great warrior. It seemed a shame for someone who had fought so hard for his pharaoh to end up like this, a shriveled wreck of a creature, destroyed so swiftly after spending millennia trapped in this small chapel. Moments like this gave Oliver pause, causing him to wonder if he should stop in his pursuit of relics, especially the fragments of the mechanism. Some powers he encountered were simply too dangerous and the humans who dared to meddle with them ended up like this. He shook his head, coughed, and turned his mind back to the task at hand.

Oliver got to his feet and looked Diana in the eye. "Are you alright?"

She nodded. "Fine. I was scared for you when I saw that thing try to slice you with its sword, but now that it's gone... it was kind of exciting."

He smiled and slapped her playfully on the shoulder. "That's normal. At least, it's normal for me."

Diana grinned and slipped her gun back into its holster. "Want to get a look in that room?"

Oliver nodded. He stripped off the rubber gloves and stuffed them into a pocket and pulled down the handkerchief covering his nose, then trod back to where his flashlight had fallen and picked it up, wincing as he bent. The first bruises from his wild tumbles across the floor would begin to form in a few minutes and he would have to keep moving or he might stiffen. The day had just begun and there was no point letting pain bring him to a halt now. As he lifted the flashlight, Oliver saw a scrap of tattered blue cloth sticking out from underneath the sand. He paused, remembering how he had tripped while getting back to his feet after Sephor's reanimated corpse had burst out of the doorway.

"Hey, Diana, take a look at this."

He began brushing away the sand, uncovering more of the cloth and the desiccated body that it covered. Diana joined in and they soon had all of the sand cleared away to reveal the body of a man dressed in a red and gray tunic and a blue jacket with tattered gold fringes dangling from pads on each shoulder. The dark blue fabric of soldier's jacket was ripped and stained a deep reddish brown where he had been stabbed right beneath his ribcage.

"That's a French military uniform!" Diana exclaimed.

"Looks like you were right about the expedition."

"I wonder who he is. Gabriel de Pujul listed the expedition members in one of his letters."

Oliver began rifling the dead man's pockets. He found several coins, a handful of tattered wax paper powder cartridges, and a bundle of letters. He passed the letters to Diana and stood, looking towards the dark doorway that Sephor's reanimated corpse had come through.

"The French expedition must have tried to enter the inner sanctum of the chapel, like I was about to." He flicked the flashlight on and wave it towards the dark doorway. "I'm going to head in there."

Diana looked up at Oliver from where she was squatting beside the body of the French soldier, flicking through the folded letters. She shoved the letters in the breast pocket of her shirt and stood.

"I'm coming with you. I don't even know his name yet, but I can look through these later.

"Don't you want to stay here and finish translating the altar inscriptions?" Oliver asked.

"I'm not finished, but from what I've seen so far they appear to be fairly typical temple altar prayers. The only thing unusual about them is that they address both Osiris and

Setesh, so you're probably right about Sephor following a strain of the Egyptian religion that was obsessed with death."

Oliver nodded and strode towards the doorway, shining his flashlight ahead of them and keeping his gun pointed in the same direction, ready to fire the instant anything undead appeared in the beam of light. They slipped through the doorway between the relief carvings of Osiris and Setesh and continued down a corridor barely wide enough for them to walk head-on for about five feet. With each step, Oliver's light revealed more of the brightly colored mural ahead of them.

Finally they stepped out into a chamber about ten feet deep and twenty wide. All four walls and the ceiling were painted in an intricate series of murals. While the paint was faded from exposure to oxygen over thousands of years, its location in this dark chamber had protected it from exposure to the ultraviolet rays of sunlight. That had done much to preserve the paint. As a result, the murals in this room were shockingly vivid compared to those in the main chamber of the chapel, except at the base of the walls, where the murals had been violently chipped away. Two tall bronze lamp stands flanked the doorway and the wall above them was darkened with soot, but not so much that it obscured the flow storytelling in the mural. Two small niches were cut into the stone, one on either end of the chamber, but these appeared to be empty.

Oliver was not particularly experienced reading Egyptian murals, but they followed a similar structure to the Mayan images that he had studied extensively during his first expedition to South America, so he had little difficulty following the general flow of the story. There were no dividing lines between the scenes of the story, and the ancient Egyptian artistic convention of drawing nearly all characters in profile could make it difficult for the inexperienced viewer to identify where one scene ended and another began. However, a carefully observant eye would quickly unlock the key: By watching for the same key characters repeating, as well as images of servants changing their facing direction from left to right and back again, it was possible to identify the key element of each scene, even as the edges merged together into a continuous flow of storytelling.

Each scene in this mural occupied a stretch of wall between two and four feet in length and about a foot high. Following the narrative of the mural from where it began, just to the left of the doorway, Oliver concluded that it retold essentially the same story as the scroll that Diana had translated a few days before. At the center of the wall facing the door was a scene that showed Sephor slaying numerous foes and taking a long shepherd's crook in his hand. Due to its position directly opposite the door, where a little bit of sunlight just managed to cast its destructive glow upon the painted stone, this scene was the most faded, but Oliver could still sense the triumph in Sephor's body language as he took hold of the staff.

"There's something missing, Oliver."

He turned to see Diana examining the niche cut into the north wall of the chamber. Oliver walked over and saw that the niche was set at chest height and surrounded by hieroglyphs carved into the six inches of uncolored stone that surrounded each niche.

"I don't completely understand what's missing. There's not enough context, but these hieroglyphs seem to indicate that key of some sort was stored in this niche. Key isn't really the right word though. Maybe more of a token?"

Oliver put his gun away and pulled out his camera and a wireless remote flash to begin photographing the room. He gestured at the south wall of the room.

"What about that? There's another empty niche there."

Diana went over to examine the hieroglyphs surrounding that niche while Oliver set to work photographing the chamber. Even if the empty niches meant that the clues they sought were long gone, he would almost certain be able sell photos of this place to archaeology magazines. He didn't like the idea of giving up hope, but in the relic hunting business, it paid to be pragmatic. By its very nature, the job required one to accept the existence of things that many people thought mere myth, so there was no sense in deceiving oneself about things that actually were black and white. Oliver had to make money from this adventure somehow.

He began with several establishing shots of the chamber, using the remote flash to get some dramatic light and shadow effects. He then set about photographing each panel of the story, framing his shots carefully so that the entire mural could be digitally reconstructed as a continuous narrative. This took a while and midway through the process Diana announced that she was going back out to finish examining the body of the French soldier. Oliver nodded distractedly and continued working in contemplative silence until he reached the bottom row of the mural. This seemed to elaborate upon the narrative of the scroll a little. Oliver began to grow excited as the painted figures were shown constructing a temple and performing rituals around an altar in an underground chamber, upon which lay the staff that Sephor had captured in battle. The exact nature of these rituals was obscured, however, by numerous shallow marks gouged roughly into the stone.

Oliver had noticed the damage to the mural when they first entered the chamber, but such was common in ancient monuments and he hadn't paid much attention to it. But now, after spending nearly an hour carefully photographing the rest of this remarkably well-preserved mural, the chips and scratches struck Oliver as odd. Unlike so many other ancient sites in Egypt, this place had been left practically untouched in the thousands of years since its original occupants had abandoned it, except for this one patch of vandalism.

"Hey, Diana!" he shouted.

"What?" she called back.

"I may have found something. Can you come take a look?"

Diana popped back into the chamber a few seconds later. Oliver pointed out the marks scratched into the wall and explained why he thought them unusual. Diana crouched down and gazed at the marks for a few moments, running her flashlight back and forth across them.

Finally she looked up at Oliver and said, "It's writing. A form of hieratic."

"Can you read it?"

"Give me a few minutes. Hieratic was essentially cursive to the Egyptians. They used it for personal documents, tribute records, things like that. The flowing nature of the text made it less suitable to stone carving than hieroglyphs, which is why both writing systems persisted in parallel for over a thousand years."

Oliver grinned and gave Diana a "get to the point" look.

She swatted at his leg and continued, "Anyway. I'll need to look this over carefully. It's not only in hieratic, which is more difficult to read than hieroglyphs to begin with, but it looks like it was scratched into the wall with a knife."

Oliver nodded and began packing up his camera equipment. "I'm going to poke around the courtyard and main house while you're busy with this."

"You aren't afraid of the skeletons?"

"I'll mainly look through windows. If I do go in, I'll take it slow and keep my gun out." Oliver bent down and squeezed Diana's shoulder. "I do this for a living. Don't be afraid for me. You though..." He pointed down at the gun on her thigh. "Keep that thing at hand. I'll announce myself before I come through the passage. Keep your ears open and if you hear anything coming that isn't me, shoot it in the head."

Diana nodded solemnly and unholstered her gun. She checked the chamber and put the gun back in the holster. Then she shrugged out of her backpack and pulled out a yellow notepad and a pen. She settled into a position from which she could see both the inscription and the doorway and began sketching out the lines of hieratic on her pad.

Oliver nodded in approval and slipped out through the passage into the main chamber of the chapel. Something felt missing in all of this, but he wasn't quite sure what.

He bent to examine the long dead bodies of the French soldier once more. The soldier had clearly been killed by a sword thrust to his gut. The presence of a French soldier in this tomb would have been utterly inexplicable were it not for the clue Diana had provided in the form of Gabriel de Pujul's half-mad letters to his artist brother. He had been part of an expedition sent to scout the desert and ascertain the hostility of native tribes living around the desert lakes. Somehow, they had blundered into this place and, if the descriptions that inspired Abel de Pujul were to be taken at face value, continued on to a place where the staff of Moses was hidden.

Oliver picked up Sephor's sword and began poking it through the larger drifts of sand throughout the chapel. It only took him a few minutes to find the next body. All told, there were seven uniformed corpses of French soldiers scattered throughout the chapel. They all bore marks of a violent death by sword. As Oliver uncovered each man, he saw that some still lay beside the brittle remains of muskets, the chipped stocks of which appeared to have been used as improvised quarterstaves in hand to hand combat against an opponent wielding a large sword.

That explained some of it. A picture began to form in Oliver's mind of the French expedition discovering this canyon and the unspoiled estate located at the far end. They would have begun to explore it, just as their great leader Napoleon had explored the tombs and temples of northern Egypt. Then they came to this chapel and... Oliver pondered what it must have been like for those men to be confronted with the raging corpse of Sephor, armed only with muzzle-loading muskets and bayonets. They must have been courageous to not immediately turn and run. But why had they stayed? Standing against the fiend when it first charged, or even after one or two men fell to it, was one thing, but the soldiers had stayed and fought Sephor long enough that seven men had fallen to him in this place.

What if they hadn't been simply exploring? What if they somehow they knew of the "keys" contained within the chapel's inner sanctum and this scene of supernatural carnage was not the result of a blundering exploration, but a suicidal battle charge?

Oliver searched the bodies of the soldiers and gathered what letters and journals he found, but his cursory scan of each object didn't reveal any clues to the soldiers' mission. These were simple combat soldiers, not officers. They had known nothing of their mission, except that it meant more days of traveling through the torturous heat of the desert.

Disgusted, Oliver tossed the sword aside and strode towards the doorway into the courtyard. He had left Diana with the intent of searching the main house, so he would do just that. Perhaps he would stumble across the body of a French officer bearing a packet of orders, or even a journal in which he described his intended course of action.

Oliver had just stepped out through the chapel entrance when a sudden movement in the corner of his eye caused him to dive forward and reach for his gun. He was too late. A weight slammed into his back and in the same instant an arm, clad in desert camouflage covering living human skin, wrapped around his neck. He landed hard on his chest. The arm around Oliver's neck tightened, cutting off his breath. He flailed ineffectually at his captor, but the unseen assailant was too strong for him. The last thing Oliver saw as his vision darkened was the sandy yellow stone of the garden path.

Chapter Thirteen

"...it mean?" The voice was strangely familiar, but Oliver couldn't place it.

"I don't know. You're looking at the ravings of a dead man. It might not mean anything?" Diana's voice. She sounded afraid.

Oliver's head felt heavy. He was laying face down on a hard surface covered in sand. How had he gotten here?

Another voice. This one also strangely familiar. "Let us give her some incentive." A pause. Oliver heard the sound of feet crunching on sand coming close to him. A sharp pain bloomed in his side and he jerked sideways, letting out an involuntary shout. Oliver's eyes popped open and he found himself looking at Diana.

She was sitting with her back against the wall, her feet bound with white plastic zip ties and her arms behind her. He assumed that they were bound as well. The side of her head was bloodied and the blush of a bruise was already developing just below her hairline, but she didn't appear to have been severely injured.

Turning his head slowly back and forth, Oliver saw a familiar man dressed in bloodied desert camouflage sitting against the opposite wall while a similarly dressed man finished applying a bandage to his right shoulder. A set of booted feet stood beside Oliver and, as he watched, one drew back and swung forward sharply to kick him in the side again.

He coughed and groaned.

"What about it Miss Jordan? Does this bring any thoughts to mind?"

Oliver recognized the voice now. He looked up past the booted foot that had kicked him, along the thick leg, and past the protruding belly to the face of Rais Karim.

"How the hell did you get out here?" Oliver croaked.

Rais looked down at Oliver and grinned. Despite his clean-shaven face and white teeth, the curve of his lips and glint in his eye made it an unpleasant sight. "So our little tomb robber decided to wake up at last. Looks like I'm still a bit more than a deposed bureaucrat after all."

Oliver blinked and tried to clear his head. How had Rais Karim got here? And why was Frank getting his shoulder bandaged? That name brought it together for him. The man on the floor was named Frank. He was a mercenary who had been part of the scheme to sell relics captured from a secret vault in the Cairo museum. Frank and his cohorts had double crossed whoever paid them to retrieve the relics and attempted to sell them on the black market instead. All of this came back to Oliver in a rush, but it still didn't explain how they had known to come here.

Another voice spoke. Oliver turned his head and recognized Frank's partner in crime and business, Kyle. "What about it, Ms. Jordan. Still having trouble translating that text?"

Diana twisted in her restraints and looked pleadingly at Oliver. He did his best to smile and give her a little nod. "There's no point hiding anything, Diana," he said. "If they plan on killing us, there's nothing we can do to stop them. Make yourself useful, and you might get out of this alive."

"A sensible viewpoint." Kyle said, nodding his head slightly.

"Speak for yourself, I'll kill the bitch." Frank grunted.

Kyle laughed and threw a glance towards Frank. "Shut up man. It's your own fault for blundering into the back room without checking it out first."

"The girl was supposed to be some sort of language nerd. I didn't exactly expect her to be sitting back there waiting to plug me." Frank scowled and pushed the medic away, then pulled himself up with his good arm. "Get her working for us, or I'll kill her." He stalked out of the chamber, wincing once as his wounded shoulder brushed the wall.

Kyle waited for Frank to leave and turned back to Diana. "As I was saying, tell us what this inscription says and we'll let you go. It's not as if you can go and report us to the authorities. Even if you can find someone who is willing to listen, I'd love to see how you tell this story without confessing to illegal relic hunting yourselves."

Diana sighed and closed her eyes for a minute. Finally she took a deep breath and said, "What you see on the wall there is little more than the mad ravings of a man driven to insanity by time and rage. I can't promise you that it will be of any use."

"Go on."

"I assume you saw the bodies in the chapel as you dragged Oliver in here?"

Kyle and Rais both nodded and Rais said, "One of them was most certainly a man preserved by supernatural forces. In my early days with the secret police, we encountered one such creature. It killed three members of my squad before we managed to subdue it."

"Oliver knows more about that sort of thing than I do, but yes, I believe that the... thing out there was once an Egyptian general named Sephor. The first line of the inscription appears to be a formal statement of his lineage, like the opening lines of ancient court testimony, but it's hard to make sense of it without any supporting documents."

Diana paused and took a deep breath. She looked to Oliver and he nodded encouragingly, then winced as Rais kicked him in the side again. Diana got a hard look to her eyes, then continued to speak.

"Sephor then refers to the murals on the walls of the inner sanctum, where we are now, as evidence of his greatest victory. After returning the staff to Pharaoh, he was rewarded with this land, where he ordered this estate built and brought his family and retainers to live in luxury. Though he was retired from making war, Sephor was entrusted with the protection of a set of relics that would guide the holder to the temple where the staff was kept, so that he could always find his way to the temple of the staff. But then something went wrong."

Diana shifted uncomfortably in her bonds and took a deep breath, then explained, "Even if the narrative hadn't been written by a madman, you have to understand that it was composed in the mind of a man from a different time. Nothing is written in terms of personal failures, so what I'm about to tell you comes from reading between the lines of an already fuzzy story."

She paused, waiting for some indication that Kyle and Rais still wanted to hear her story. Good, Oliver thought, She's making them hungry for her information.

Kyle crouched down and looked Diana in the eyes. "Go on."

"Well, some time after retiring to this place, the family was attacked by their own guards. At Sephor's command, the priests who served the family in this chapel had created undead guardians to protect the house, but one night, these creatures turned on their masters. Sephor's family and servants were slaughtered or driven away and he was wounded grievously. He fought his way to the chapel, where he forced the last remaining priest to perform a ritual that bound him to the inner sanctum as eternal guardian of the relics."

Kyle snorted and took a step closer to Diana. "Do you really expect me to believe that crap? This is the real world, honey, not some fantasy story."

"You asked me to tell you what the inscription says. I'm explaining a bit of the context, as much as I understand it, but every bit of this is written on that wall."

Rais Karim cleared his throat and interjected, "Don't be too quick to discredit her story, Kyle. You saw that corpse out in the chapel. And you know how well-preserved that scroll was, at least until you destroyed it."

"Shut up old man."

"I will not. You violated a relic of my people that had survived for centuries, all because these two fools outwitted you by pretending that it was not authentic. To my mind, that makes you the greater fool."

Oliver wasn't exactly sure what was going between the two men, but he was beginning to suspect that they were not working together entirely by choice. He had been surprised to see them at first, but as Diana related the translation of Sephor's engraving, he had started to put the pieces together in him mind. After he and Diana had pulled out of the deal in Cairo, Rais must have made contact with the mercenaries again. But that didn't make sense. He didn't have the resources to buy the scroll from them, and he had just accused Kyle of destroying the scroll after Diana told him that it was a forgery. What could have brought these men together?

Kyle's hand slipped down to the holster strapped to his thigh. He stepped closer to Rais, momentarily ignoring Oliver and Diana. "I'm warning you, Rais. You're here to ensure delivery, nothing more."

"Warning me?" Rais's face darkened and he took a step closer to Kyle. "If it wasn't for my intervention, you would have been out on the streets now, begging for work and hoping to find a patron before your old enemies hunted you down. I gave you the name of the hotel where Mr. Lucas and Ms. Jordan were staying. I arranged the trace on their vehicle's navigation system. Without me you'd have no chance of recovering the staff before your employer..."

Kyle pulled out his gun and shot Rais in the chest. Rais stumbled and fell backwards against the wall. His blood splattered across the mural and formed a bright red streak running down the wall as he slid down and came to rest leaning against the wall, just a few feet from Oliver's bound legs. His face was a twitching mask of shock and confusion. He raised one hand to the bloody hole in his chest, probing it with his fingers as if he didn't believe it was actually there.

Kyle shot him again. The old man's head slumped down as he gave one last shuddering gasp, then fell silent.

A loud pounding of booted feet on stone sounded from outside the chamber. Oliver craned his neck around the corner and caught a glimpse of a large man in desert camouflage dodging behind the altar. At the end of the short passage that led out to the main hall of the chapel he saw the tip of a boot poking out around the corner of the wall.

"Commander Sanders, what happened?" a rough voice shouted. "Are you alive?"

"Stand down men." Kyle said, holstering his gun. "Just dealing with a little problem."

"Yes sir," the same voice replied. Oliver caught another glimpse of movement in the chapel as the men out there moved away from the narrow passage.

Oliver looked over and saw that Rais's chin had settled down on his chest. He didn't appear to be breathing, which was no surprise given the two holes in the center of his chest and the pool of blood spreading out around him. Oliver turned to Diana and was relieved to see that she was remaining calm.

He knew that she was strong, but anyone could be excused for getting upset in present circumstances. The wet streaks of tears had etched bright lines of pink in the dust covering her face, but her mouth was firm and her eyes were open.

"Now, about you stopping the bullshit and telling me what I need to know about that inscription," Kyle said, stepping close to Diana. He squatted in front of her and pointed back at the lifeless body of Rais. "I said that I would let you go, and I still might, but only if you don't jerk me around. I've got a lot riding on finding that staff. Got it?"

Diana nodded.

"Good."

Oliver cleared his throat and waited for Kyle to turn and face him. When the mercenary commander looked around, Oliver said, "Look, Kyle, you're obviously angry. I don't want to upset you any more, but Diana's not screwing with you when she talks about undead guardians and ancient priests. I can't read that inscription, but I've had a lot of experience with getting in and out of magically guarded tombs. If you let us help you, we can all get out of this alive."

Kyle appeared to ponder this for a moment. His face remained harsh, but he kept his hand away from his gun, which was good enough for Oliver. He could imagine that it was difficult for a man like Kyle, accustomed to dealing with the gritty realities of modern warfare, to accept the existence of such things as undead warriors and skeleton guards.

"What sort of tomb robber are you if you don't even read the language?"

"The sort who usually stays far away from Egypt, and will be happy to return to that modus operandi if allowed to keep breathing."

That got Kyle to crack his glowering expression just enough to let a crooked smile through. He let out a short chuckle and said, "I almost like you, man. Even if your girl here shot Frank."

"Listen, Kyle, I don't know what your situation is, and really don't want to if it'll make me end up like that old bastard." Oliver nodded in the direction of Rais's body. "But I've got this hunch that you're under a lot of pressure to find a particular ancient staff. Diana and I were in a similar situation when we met you in the book shop. What do you say we put the past behind us, figure all this out without any more killing, and go our separate ways?"

Oliver was playing a close game here and hoped that he hadn't pushed too far by mentioning the pressure Kyle was under. It seemed to work though, because Kyle nodded his head and looked thoughtful, then said, "Help me get to the staff and I'll keep my word on not killing you both. If you screw with me though..."

He let that hang in the air as he looked between Oliver and Diana. They both nodded.

"Good. Now, tell me where to find that temple."

Diana sniffed and cleared her throat, then squared her shoulders and said, "Sephor describes the temple as being located on an island in the middle of a desert lake, three day's journey west of his estate."

"That can't be far from here. That was thousands of years ago, they couldn't have traveled very fast." Kyle said. He paused and looked thoughtful for a moment. "But I don't know of any lakes in this area except those three lakes north of here."

Diana looked to Oliver. Oliver didn't like giving the mercenaries the location of the temple, but at the moment, he was more concerned with staying alive. He shifted his legs to get Kyle's attention, then said, "I don't know for sure, but if we looked at some satellite imagery we might be able to find a dried lakebed that matches the description. You've got to remember that this inscription was written by someone who was trapped in this chapel for nearly five thousand years. That's plenty of time for a spring to dry up, or a stream to shift course."

"Alright. Let's go take a look."

Kyle stepped up to Diana and pulled out a long knife with one serrated edge. He bent over her and set the knife against the plastic bindings around her ankles. Then he paused and looked up at her. "No funny business. You try to kick me, or run away, or anything else, and I'll shoot you."

He waited for Diana to nod her head, then used the serrated edge to quickly saw through the thick plastic bands that held her feet together.

"Frank, you out there?" Kyle shouted.

An unfamiliar voice called back, "Frank went down the the chopper, Commander."

Kyle shook his head and muttered a curse, then called back, "Alright. The girl is coming out. Waverly, take her to the chopper and pull up some satellite maps of the region for her to look over. Make sure she doesn't have a comlink."

"Yes, sir."

Kyle grabbed the front of Diana's shirt and hauled her to her feet. She stumbled and almost fell against him, but managed to catch her balance. Kyle pointed towards the doorway and Diana began walking towards it, stepping gingerly around the pool of blood that now surrounded Rais's body.

Once she was gone, Kyle crouched down beside Oliver and asked, "Are you still working for that damn Senator?"

That caught Oliver off guard, even as it confirmed a theory he'd been working out. Not even Rais had known that he was working directly for Senator Wheeler, so this Kyle character must have some additional source of information.

"No. I left his employment after Mr. Karim over there told me that you wanted half a million for the scroll. Senator

Wheeler told me he couldn't swing that sort of cash, so we went our separate ways."

"And you decided to go after the staff yourself anyway."

"He seemed satisfied with my explanation. I don't like the man, so I saw it as an opportunity to break free."

Kyle chuckled and shook his head slowly. "Well, Oliver, I wish I could get away that easy. Let's get down to the chopper."

With that Kyle swiped his blade through the plastic strips binding Oliver's ankles and pulled him roughly to his feet. Oliver leaned against the wall for a moment, working first one leg, then the other, until he felt steady enough to walk again. Standing there, watching Kyle gather his and Diana's bags in one hand and look around to see if anything else of importance remained, Oliver decided to try and get a bit more information out of him.

"Tell me to shut up if this question makes you want to shoot me too, but how did you and Rais Karim end up working together? That old bastard hated foreigners touching Egyptian relics."

Kyle ignored Oliver's question and gestured for him to turn around. He cut the plastic restraints off of Oliver's wrists, then thrust the backpacks into Oliver's newly freed hands. "Carry your own crap. Walk ahead of me and don't try to run."

Oliver complied. They left Rias's body in the inner sanctum and walked through the short passage into the main chapel chamber. There Oliver saw a lone guard leaning against the altar smoking a cigarette as he waited for them to emerge. Kyle waved for him to follow them and he stubbed out the cigarette on the altar and slung his submachine gun up onto his back. The three of them walked in silence out of the chapel and around the outside wall of the house, backtracking the steps that Oliver and Diana had taken a few hours before.

They reached the front of the house and Oliver looked up the canyon to where he and Diana had parked their Range Rover. The vehicle still sat in the shadow of the high canyon wall, but Oliver's view of it was now obscured by a large helicopter that had set down on the flat canyon floor between the car and the crumbling walls of Sephor's estate. The helicopter was painted in a mottled pattern of dull beige and tan colors that succeeded in camouflaging it well enough that Oliver had difficulty picking out the exact edges of the aircraft. As he watched, Oliver saw Diana and her guard emerging beyond the wall and plodding towards the helicopter.

"Plenty of room for us all." Kyle said. "Don't ever believe someone who says that war doesn't pay well, Oliver. That baby is a top of the line desert transport. Even the engines are designed for hellholes like this. See, you've got to minimize the sand getting in through the crank shaft so it doesn't gum things up, then there's the issue of filtering the air intake."

Oliver nodded in acknowledgement of Kyle's obvious enthusiasm, but didn't say anything. He had ridden in helicopters before, but always civilian models that he chartered for getting quickly in and out of remote sites that would otherwise have taken days, or weeks, of harsh backpacking and climbing to access.

Kyle looked over at him and laughed, then clapped Oliver hard on the shoulder. "What do you say, man? Ever give a thought to making your living as a soldier of fortune?"

"Can't say I have. My interests tend more towards avoiding dead things than making more of them."

"You're serious about that thing in the temple being, what, some sort of zombie?"

"Not a zombie, no. But it was certainly an animated corpse."

"And it attacked you?"

Oliver nodded.

Kyle motioned for them to keep walking. As they reached the bottom of the wide front steps and began crossing the courtyard he said, "You asked about Karim. Well, I'll tell you the basics. Your senator tracked down our employers and applied some pressure. Let me tell you, Oliver, if there's one thing that my bosses don't like it's bad news from Washington. Well, the shit rolled downhill like it always does and now I need to get that staff and ship it back the the States ASAP, or my team and I are out on the streets."

"I guess they're less likely to overlook a little private enterprise when it comes back to bite them."

Kyle chuckled at that. "You got that right."

"How did you manage to get Rais Karim to work with you?"

"That's where you are completely lost, kid. That old bastard has been in on the deal since the beginning."

Oliver stopped in his tracks, nearly dropping the bags he was carrying. Of course, that was the missing piece. Now Oliver understood why Rais had been willing to put him in contact with the dealers, and why he had simply been making noise, rather than mercilessly hunting them down and murdering them.

"Weren't expecting that one, were you?"

"No. Not at all. But I suppose it makes sense."

"Of course it does. You think that man felt any loyalty to Egypt after he was booted out of office? Where did you think we learned about the secret vault?"

They reached the helicopter and found Diana sitting on a camp stool just outside the door of the helicopter, already engrossed with pinching and swiping her way through satellite enhanced maps of the surrounding desert on the screen of a tablet computer encased in a heavy rubberized case. A guard stood five feet behind her, smoking a cigarette with an expression of utter boredom written clearly on his face. Kyle left Oliver with Diana and climbed into the helicopter to check on Frank, leaving instructions with the guard that she and Oliver were not to go anywhere until he returned.

Once Kyle was gone, Diana looked up and gave Oliver a half smile, then returned to her work. Oliver stood behind her and put a hand on her shoulder, then leaned down to look at the screen on her lap. Keeping his voice level, he asked whether she had made any progress on finding the tomb.

"A few possibilities, but nothing that jumps out and bites me."

"Need any help?"

Diana shrugged and waved at the screen in her hand. "If they've got another one, maybe you could look too, but for now..." She sighed deeply and allowed a brief look of frustration to cross her face. "I'm trying to find a hidden temple in thousands of square miles of desert, based on a description that is thousands of years old."

"Don't forget that the author of that description was an undead warrior, driven mad by thousands of years of solitude." Oliver said with a wink, squeezing her shoulder.

Diana didn't laugh, but she did manage a tired smile. "Thanks, Oliver."

"I've got to be useful somehow. Don't want our hosts to think I'm worthless and kill me too." He flashed a cheesy grin at the mercenary standing a few feet away, but if the man had heard the remark he didn't give any sign. He gazed blankly back at Oliver for a full half minute before Oliver broke eye contact and looked back to Diana.

"They know who we are and why I came to Egypt. Seems that Senator Wheeler decided to take matters into his own hands and apply pressure from above. Kyle and Frank must have led the museum raid using unauthorized company resources to score a little extra cash on the side. Now they have to deliver what the Senator wants or they're out in the cold."

"That's bad."

"Exactly. We already knew Frank was jumpy from his little performance at the book shop, but now Kyle's under a lot of stress. I think that's the only reason he even told me what's going on."

"What do we do if we manage to find the staff? Do you really think they'll let us go?"

Oliver had been pondering exactly those questions for the last half hour and he still didn't have an answer. He gave Diana a crooked smile and shrugged. "We'll just have to play this by ear. If we make it to the temple alive, I think we'll be able to work something out." He didn't tell her that it was their only choice for the moment. If they refused to help the mercenaries, or gave obviously false advice, they would certainly be killed. Oliver was secretly harboring a hope that they would find the temple intact and that whatever guards had chased away the French soldiers would distract the mercenaries long enough for him and Diana to escape.

Diana nodded solemnly and looked out across the canyon towards the estate while she took a few slow, deep breaths. Then she blinked, shook her head, and turned her attention back to the tablet perched on her lap.

Oliver patted her on the shoulder again, then straightened and stepped toward their guard. The man stiffened and slipped his right hand from the butt of his assault rifle to the handgrip. Oliver waved genially and announced, "I need to take a leak. I can do it on your shoes or over behind the Range Rover, your choice."

The guard narrowed his eyes and said nothing, so Oliver reached to unzip his pants.

"Alright." The guard growled, nodding towards the car. "Make it quick and keep where I can see your head." He patted the side of his weapon significantly.

Oliver got the point, nodded and strode towards the car. He moved slowly, not wanting anyone to think he was trying to make a run for it, keeping his stride casual, as if he frequently went for a walk in the sights of an assault rifle. Once he reached the far side of the car, he placed both arms in front of him and used one hand to take care of his business while he slipped the other up to the front zipper pocket of his vest. He worked the zipper as fast as he could without moving his arm too much. The entire operation took only seconds, but it felt like an eternity passed before his fingers felt the warm glass corner of his phone nestled in the zipper.

He had felt the bulge of it in his vest as he lay on the floor of the inner sanctum, curled up in a ball from Rais kicking him in the gut. He hadn't dared to believe at the time that they would leave his phone on him, but when the opportunity arose, he couldn't resist checking. The mercenaries had taken Oliver's gun and presumedly searched him for more weapons while he lay unconscious in the chapel, but if they had noticed the narrow bulge of his phone they hadn't considered it worth removing. Of course, they might have been distracted by Diana shooting Frank as he blundered through the doorway into the inner sanctum.

Ducking his head to see what he was doing, Oliver saw that he had a single bar of signal. Not much, but it would be enough for his purposes. He used the thumb of one hand to launch his Twitter app and tap out a quick message:

Blown. Leonidas security did it on senator's orders.

He tapped the send button and slipped the phone back into his pocket. He zipped up his pants and made a show of stretching his arms and back, then quickly zipped up his vest pocket again as he turned. He hoped that the action of concealing his phone and zipping the vest had been lost in all the motion of his stretching, and was relieved to see that the guard by the helicopter was only watching him out of one eye.

Oliver returned to the helicopter and sat beside Diana. He spent the next three hours trying not to think about his message. Amber might see his message right away if she was at her computer or had her phone nearby, but if she was asleep or busy it might be hours before she saw his cryptic little message. Even if she did read it immediately, there wasn't much that she could do. Oliver's Twitter accounts were intended primarily as a means of keeping his closest friends and family appraised of his general location in the event he disappeared for days on end, and as a high speed low bandwidth secure communications network to share updates with clients. The best he could hope for was that Amber would forward the message to his father, who might be able to get the Senator to back off.

The more Oliver thought about it, he considered that sending the tweet might have put them in deeper danger. Even if his father managed to contact Senator Wheeler and convince him to stop applying pressure to Leonidas Security, they might decide to cut their losses by ordering Kyle and Frank to kill him and Diana. Even if the company didn't give the order, it was clear now that Kyle and his team had been working for themselves for a while.

But there was no point in fretting over the situation. Oliver had sent the message and at the least, Amber would know who to go after if she got the urge to avenge his death.

Over the next three hours, Oliver and Diana managed to identify seventeen possible locations for the temple. The tablet was running a mapping application containing high resolution satellite imagery of the entire country, which could be overlaid with a detailed topographical map to verify the contours of the desert. Diana estimated that the "three day journey" could be anywhere between thirty and one hundred fifty miles, depending on whether the directions assumed traveling on foot, by camel, or in a chariot. Given the accuracy of ancient desert navigation techniques, she also suggested searching north and south of the indicated path in a widening search pattern. The upshot of this was that they ended up swiping the tablet map slowly north, then a little west, then south and a little west, and then north again across an ever expanding triangle of desert that encompassed over seven thousand square miles. They took turns swiping at the screen and gazing over each other's shoulders, stopping occasionally to blink and gaze out at the shifting shadows of the canyon walls. Kyle stopped by now and then to berate them for not producing results fast enough, but for the most part he stayed with Frank, who sat sullenly in the padded copilot seat of the helicopter, smoking cigarettes and badgering the medic to administer more morphine.

Chapter Fourteen

"You're telling me that we need to check seventeen different locations?" Kyle exclaimed, as Diana pointed to the various possible temple sites marked on the map. "Do you have any idea how much it costs to fly this chopper? How difficult it is to keep out of the sights of Egyptian radar systems?"

Diana shrugged and gestured at the canyon surrounding them. "Just look around you. Thousands of years ago this was a lush valley with a stream flowing through it. There would have been fields of grain bordering the stream. That sandy plaza surrounding the chapel would have been a garden filled with trees and flowers, probably with a few pools of fresh water stocked with fish. The rooms of the house were filled with dozens of living people."

"Get to the point."

"My point is that a lot can change in over three thousand years. The message describes the temple sitting in the center of a lake far out in the desert, but there are no lakes west of here for over a thousand miles, so Oliver and I had to look for geological formations that could have been that lake long ago. Let me tell you Kyle, it's not easy to find a lake that is not there."

Diana had managed to keep her voice level for most of the explanation, but by the end, she began to enunciate each word with a sharp clarity that Oliver knew she only used when truly angry. He couldn't blame her.

Oliver put a hand on Diana's shoulder to calm her, then said, "You asked us to find the temple. Our best guess is one of these locations. Some might be nothing more than shallow valleys with rock formations at the center, but if one is the temple..." He waited, hoping that Kyle would get the point.

Kyle glowered over the tablet for a few minutes, ignoring Oliver, Diana, and his own men, who had begun to cluster around. There were seven in all, including Kyle, Frank, and the medic. They were of varying heights and skin tones, but all shared the muscular build and cold expression of their leader. Oliver had developed the impression in the last few hours that each and every one of Kyle's men would have gladly shot him in the back on command, but was otherwise content to ignore him. Every man, except Frank, who had repeatedly expressed his desire to kill Diana, and Oliver also, in revenge for her shooting him in the shoulder.

Finally Kyle nodded to himself and tapped an icon on the screen that activated a navigation mode in the mapping program. A line appeared on the screen, tracing a path through the air between their current location and the nearest marked waypoint.

"Alright. Load up. We'll head to the nearest spot now. It should only take about twenty minutes to reach the first waypoint. Depending on how long it takes to inspect each site we should be able to get through half of these waypoints before nightfall."

Frank made a disgusted rumbling noise at the back of his throat and flicked his cigarette at Diana. He reached up with his left arm, grasped a strap hanging from the roof of the helicopter, and hauled himself up out of the seat. He was shirtless but wore a tan camouflage jacket over his shoulders to keep off the sun. His right arm was in a sling and Oliver could just see a large bandage wrapped around his upper chest, with thick layers of gauze packing the right side of his body.

"Excuse me for asking, but why are these two even alive?"

"We need their help." Kyle replied, glancing over his shoulder at Frank.

"No, we don't.

Kyle ignored Frank's comment and waved for his men to board the helicopter. One of them stepped up behind Oliver and pushed him towards the open door of the helicopter. Diana moved past him, climbing up into the helicopter and moving to the end farthest from the cockpit, where Frank still stood glowering. She sat on the bench seat and pulled the webbed belt across her chest and lap. Oliver hopped up and was about to follow Diana to the back when he heard heavy boots clanging on the metal grid of the floor.

Frank stalked down the length of the helicopter, eyes fixed on Oliver. He stopped an arm's length from Oliver.

"Kyle, tell me exactly what this guy is good for."

Kyle twisted back around the side of the pilot's seat, his head already clamped into the shell of a helmet, wires jacking him in to the helicopter's radio system spiraling down from a junction box in the roof. He looked on in silence for a few seconds, then flipped the visor of his helmet down and replied, "We need the girl to translate any old writing we find. Do what you want with him." He went back to flipping switches on the control panel.

Diana made to unstrap herself, but was restrained by the mercenaries sitting to either side. Frank grinned and lunged forward, striking out with his massive left fist in a powerful blow that would have knocked Oliver flat if it hadn't been thrown off target by the constraining bandages wrapped around Frank's chest. Oliver staggered back, easily dodging Frank's awkward attack. A glance told him that Diana was completely helpless, but at least the other mercenaries didn't seem interested in helping Frank kill him.

The helicopter motors coughed to life and settled into a deep thrumming sound that Oliver could feel in his chest. Frank swung at Oliver again. Oliver dodged to the side, letting the blow slip past his face by mere inches, and grabbed Frank's forearm. He jerked hard on the arm, adding his own weight to the momentum of Frank's attack. The wounded mercenary stumbled forward and crashed into the bench seat, nearly falling into the laps of his comrades. Frank roared in frustration and scrambled back to his feet. Instead of going after Oliver with his fists again, Frank grabbed the assault rifle resting between the knees of the man he had just fallen on. The rifle was secured to the mercenary by a webbed strap, so it jerked back and fell as Frank raised it. Oliver took that as an opportunity to jump out of the helicopter.

He hit the ground hard and allowed himself to fall to the sand and roll up into a crouching run. The blades of the helicopter had begun to spin over his head, pulling air downwards and whipping the sandy canyon floor into a hurricane of gritty dust. Oliver ran in a crouch until he was beyond the downdraft of the blades, then stood and ran as fast as he could, heading in the general direction of the Range Rover, but throwing in the occasional zig or zag. Oliver was grateful for the obscuring cloud of sand whipped up by the blades of the helicopter, but he knew he was dead if he didn't get to cover. He reached the Range Rover just in time to see the glass of the passenger window shatter and hear the crack of a shot rip through the low thrum of the helicopter blades.

Oliver dropped to the ground and tumbled behind the front wheel of the Range Rover, putting the heavy steel of the brake assembly and engine between himself and Frank's rifle. He prayed that Kyle was simply letting Frank blow off some steam. If the mercenaries took off right away he might get out of this alive, might even be able to rescue Diana, but if Kyle held the helicopter at ground level while Frank got out and hunted Oliver down, he was a dead man. More shots crackled through the air and Oliver covered his face to protect his eyes from chips of stone and glass that spattered up around him.

He waited.

The sound of the helicopter reached its zenith in a dull thwaping pulse that he could feel in his chest, but hardly hear. A part of Oliver's mind not entirely concerned with surviving the next minute noted that he must have not heard the mercenaries approach because the helicopter employed some sort of stealth design to reduce the noise of the rotors. The shots ceased and Oliver rolled onto his belly and slipped under the car, keeping the dense mass of the engine block above him as he slithered back to the side where the helicopter had rested. It was gone. The dust was beginning to settle and the pulsing noise and impact of the rotors was already fading.

Oliver waited until the noise was entirely gone before slipping out from under the Range Rover. The vehicle was a complete wreck. Multiple bullet holes deformed the side panels and only the rear window remained intact.

Looking around, Oliver saw his and Diana's backpacks laying on the ground not far from where the helicopter rested. He walked over and looked down at them for a moment, pondering the likelihood that they had been booby trapped and left for him, just in case he had survived the gunfire. After a moment's hesitation, Oliver slowly unzipped the bottom access panel of his bag and found his camera, still safely nestled in the padded pouch. He closed the bottom panel and worked his way through each compartment, unzipping each slowly and using the flash light of his phone to peer in through the narrow opening and check that no explosives waited for him. It took nearly ten minutes, but eventually Oliver was satisfied that the bags had simple been left behind in the scramble to board the helicopter, or perhaps they had been intentionally abandoned to ensure that Diana and Oliver were dependent on their captors for everything.

Oliver transferred Diana's emergency rations and water to his own pack. He pulled the memory card out of her camera, but left the camera in the bag. As much as he hated to leave it, there was no point in carrying the extra weight of it.

Oliver was pleasantly surprised to find Diana's spare ammunition clips in a side pouch of her pack, as well as his own backup gun still tucked away in the very bottom of his bag. It was increasingly evident to Oliver that Kyle had grown sloppy in his desperation to save his own skin. He was grateful for that because, along with Frank's desire for revenge on someone after being shot, it had allowed him to escape and provided these supplies. On the other hand, Diana was now trapped alone with Kyle and his men and Oliver could see no way of rescuing her.

Oliver tossed Diana's pack into the back of the Range Rover and sat down in the bullet riddled passenger seat to think. He pulled out his phone and saw that he now had no service, so there was no chance of calling for help until the antenna somehow managed to catch a signal, which might happen when he left the cage of the car. He pulled up a map of the area and did his best to mark the locations he and Diana had identified on it from memory. Even if he couldn't chase the mercenaries, he could hope that they would let Diana live or, at worst, abandon her at the temple. If they did that he might be able to track her down before she died of dehydration.

Oliver heard a stone tumble across the sand, clattering against other rocks as it fell down the canyon wall.

He grabbed for his gun and dove out of the car through the open door. Looking back towards the entrance of the canyon he saw nothing out of place. He spun, scanning the canyon walls, and saw a party of five figures in light colored desert robes and headscarves emerging from a narrow cleft in the rock about two hundred feet away. The shortest of the group, Oliver now saw was a young woman holding the arm and hand of an old woman, supporting her as they hobbled across the sand. The three remaining figures continually swiveled their heads back and forth in apparent watchfulness. Glancing upwards from the group, Oliver noticed a narrow trail cut into the side of the canyon wall, switchbacking up to the desert floor high above.

The party spotted Oliver. The three guards pushed aside their robes to reveal automatic rifles, which they shouldered and pointed at Oliver. They began shouting in Arabic for him to drop his gun and lay down on the ground. The young woman wrapped her arms around the older woman and dropped to the ground, rolling to put her body between Oliver and the woman she had been leading.

Oliver sighed deeply and dropped his gun. This day just kept getting worse and worse. He stepped back from the gun and held his hands up, but did not drop to the ground. He had no idea why these people were in the canyon, let alone threatening him with guns, but he intended to find out.

"I am now unarmed." Oliver shouted in his best Arabic. "I mean you no harm. My partner was recently kidnapped, that's why I had my gun out."

The men with rifles glared at Oliver and continued to keep their weapons leveled at his chest, but they stopped shouting.

"My name is Oliver. I am an archaeologist. Who are you?"

The older woman began shouting at her younger counterpart in a dialect that Oliver did not recognize. The young woman was doing her best to keep her elder down on the ground, out of danger, as they argued. One of the men turned around and joined in the discussion. Oliver had no idea what they were saying, but got the impression that the older woman wanted to get up and look at him, while the others were concerned for her safety. Ultimately the woman won the argument, using her guardian's shoulder as a prop to push herself to her feet.

The old woman moved towards Oliver with a tottering step, her wrinkled brown hands stretched out towards him. Her assistant leapt to follow, skirts spraying sand as she hurried to the old woman's side and took her arm.

One of the men approached Oliver, keeping his gun pointed at him the whole time. He came almost within reach, then stopped and said, in Arabic, "We heard shooting and saw helicopters moving west. What happened here?"

"I told you. My research partner was kidnapped. The men who took her were trying to kill me. They probably think that they succeeded." He nodded towards the bullet-riddled remains of the Range Rover.

The man nodded his head gravely and glanced back at the others. The old woman was still shuffling forward. She was not far away now. He called out to her in the dialect that Oliver could not understand. She replied with a burst that sounded to Oliver like questions.

"Why are you here?"

"I might ask you the same thing."

"You might, but you are... what, British? American? You speak Arabic with an accent... and I'd wager you don't have a permit to excavate here."

Oliver couldn't have explained why, but he didn't get the impression that these people were a threat to him. Something about the way they all seemed to defer to the old woman, who now stood just behind his interrogator and had fixed Oliver with a piercing gaze. He slowly lowered his arms and hooked his thumbs into the pockets of his trousers. He tried to relax, despite the guns pointed at him, and decided that the best course of action was to tell the truth, mostly.

"My name is Oliver. I'm a photographer and treasure hunter. I found some clues that suggested I might find a powerful relic here. Since I don't read hieratic or hieroglyphs very well, I brought along a colleague who does. While searching the house down there, we were attacked by a group of American mercenaries who are also looking for the relic. They killed an Egyptian agent who was helping them and kidnapped my partner, then went to track down the actual resting place of the relic."

It all spilled out of Oliver and when he was finished, he deflated. His shoulders sank and he lowered his head, feeling utterly exhausted from the stress of the day.

The men said nothing, but Oliver noticed that their faces had gone completely blank, where before they had been animated and angry. It was obvious that something in his story had caught their attention, but they were trying to hide it. The young woman was busily whispering in her elder's ear, apparently translating Oliver's story. The old woman nodded slowly, her wrinkled face betraying little as she assimilated the information. When her assistant had finished, the woman turned her intense gaze back to Oliver and uttered a few short statements.

This time, the young woman translated for Oliver. She had a soft, melodic voice, but there was an intensity to her speech that commanded Oliver's attention, especially when she addressed him flawless English.

"The priestess asks whether you saw anything else while you were in the house, and what parts of the estate you explored."

Oliver hesitated. He wasn't so much surprised by the young woman speaking English, since it was the common tongue of mass media throughout the world, as he was uncertain how much to say. There was no going back now though, and he still had that niggling feeling that this woman would understand his story and it would bring him no harm to tell her. He returned the old woman's gaze and did his best to speak in a level tone, switching to English as he said, "We explored the front hall, throne room, and a guest room of the main house. We were following a passage to the back of the house when..." He paused, then shook his head and said, "When we were attacked by a living skeleton."

He waited for a sign of surprise from the young translator, but she simply nodded and began speaking to the old woman. The woman did not appear surprised, so as soon as the young woman stopped speaking, Oliver continued.

"We also entered the chapel in the rear garden. There we were attacked by the living remains of an Egyptian general named Sephor. I destroyed him and we were in the midst of reading an inscription that he made on the wall of the chapel when we were attacked by the mercenaries."

Oliver did catch a look of surprise cross the young woman's face when he claimed to have defeated Sephor. The surprise passed, darkening into something that Oliver feared would spell his doom. Before she could finish translating he quickly said, "I have photographs of the inscription. Sephor apparently carved it into the wall some time after he was transformed into an undead guardian himself."

The young woman shot him a cold look, then turned back to her elder and continued to translate what Oliver had said. The old woman's eyes widened as her assistant translated. She looked at Oliver with an expression that seemed equal parts horror and respect.

As the translator finished speaking one of the men raised his rifle and strode closer to Oliver, pointing the gun at his head and laying his finger alongside the trigger. His impassive mask had fallen and now his face was etched deeply with rage. He shouted back at the women in their dialect, spittle flying from his lips and flecking his dark brown beard. Without waiting for a reply from the old woman he switched to Arabic and shouted at Oliver, "You bastard! You filthy heathen bastard! How dare you defile this place? What right do you have to come here and destroy our holy places?"

Oliver put his hands up and stepped back, thinking fast. Most of the sites he raided were so remote, so obscure, so long forgotten that there was little risk of encountering human devotees of the shrines he violated. Still, he had encountered relic cults on couple occasions and been able to talk his way out of a fight more often than not. Generally he would lie to them, perhaps even try to insinuate himself into their sacred myths as some sort of holy messenger or invulnerable herald of evil, but he had already told too much of the truth to start lying now. Not to mention that they were clearly modern people who were unlikely to fall for such a rouse.

He looked straight at the man holding the rifle and spoke calmly, keeping his voice low as he said, "I had no intention of damaging anything. I came to take photos and look for clues to the location of a temple that has been lost for thousands of years. The guardians of the house and chapel attacked me, so I defended myself."

This had no visible calming effect, but the man did not shoot Oliver between the eyes, so he continued.

"Please, tell me who you are. Perhaps we can help one another."

The old woman pushed her enraged guard aside and took Oliver's right hand in her own. She gripped his finger tightly with one hand and reached up, stroking his face with the palm of her left hand as she looked deeply into his eyes. The skin of her fingers felt like brittle paper against his cheek. Oliver swallowed hard, trying to suppress the thought that she could read his mind or peer into his soul. This was just a crazy old priestess, accompanied by her acolyte and guards, drawn here by the sight of helicopters and the sound of gunfire.

The woman cupped Oliver's chin in her hand and began to speak to him. Her voice quavered at times and the expression in her eyes shifted wildly. At times her eyes bored into Oliver with such intensity that he would have looked away, had she not held his chin, and at others she appeared on the verge of tears. She paused at times, to allow her assistant time to translate, then continued before Oliver or the men with guns could interject.

"Your presence here is a sign of evil, American. You have witnessed violence and caused damaged in a sacred place where my ancestors once lived in peace. Dangerous men have followed your trail here and even at this moment I feel the threat of them growing. Despite this, you are not an evil man yourself. That which you have destroyed was... profanely sacred... so I both abhor and thank you for its destruction. You are hungry for knowledge that is beyond you. Beyond what humanity should know. I cannot compel you to cease your quest, but I can help you stop a great evil."

The woman released Oliver's chin and dropped her hand to his shoulder. She looked over her shoulder to the armed men and spoke. Her assistant translated for Oliver's benefit, "We will return home now. This man will accompany us. Tomorrow he will set out to bring an end to the evil that he carried with him to our lands. Then I will return here to see that which we have guarded unseen for over an hundred generations."

Oliver allowed himself to relax and took a deep breath. He didn't fully understand what had happened, or how he was expected to bring an end to an evil he had brought, but he figured that it had something to do with stopping the mercenaries. The old woman released his hand and began walking back towards the cliff path. One guard, the one who had threatened Oliver, ran ahead of her and began to jog up the path. Her assistant glanced back at Oliver and said, "We will speak more on the way." Then she followed the old woman, taking her arm to help her up the path.

One of the remaining guards slung his rifle under his robe and enveloped Oliver's right hand in a double-handed grip. "I am Zaid Ahmad, chief guardian of the Elder." He said in Arabic.

"Oliver Lucas. Photographer and international trouble-maker."

Zaid did not smile, but something in the set of his shoulders gave Oliver the feeling that he got the joke and approved.

"Take your bag and follow us. You will forgive me for keeping your gun in my possession until you depart from our company."

Oliver nodded and returned to the wrecked Range Rover long enough to grab his backpack and slip it on. He picked up his phone from where it had fallen on the bullet-riddled floor. It showed one bar of signal, but no reply to his tweet to Amber. He slipped the phone into a pocket of his vest and rejoined the guards.

They marched up the narrow path. Zaid walked in the front with Oliver behind him and the still unnamed guard taking up the rear. It didn't take long for them to catch up with the old woman and her young assistant, who introduced herself to Oliver as Hadiya.

"You speak English very well, Hadiya." Oliver commented between panting breaths as they marched up the steep incline.

"Thank you. I participated in a student exchange program in New York for two years while I attended university."

"What did you study?"

"The closest equivalent in English would be something like Women's Rights in International Relations."

"That's very modern."

Hadiya shot Oliver a sharp look. Her dark eyes cut into him and he had the distinct impression that he had offended her.

"I might be from a small village, but we aren't some backwards tribe scrabbling in the dust of your modern empire, you know. We have electricity. We have medicine. I was encouraged by my parents to attend university so I could get a bigger picture of the world. I did well there, then returned to the village out of respect for my family's honor and my grandmother's beliefs."

"I didn't mean to offend you."

"Oh really?"

"Certainly, Hadiya. All I meant was that your choice of major reflects an interest in society that many people lack, no matter where they come from."

She looked away from Oliver and appeared to consider this for a few minutes as she helped the old woman, who Oliver now assumed to be Hadiya's grandmother, keep her balance on the steep path.

Eventually she said, "I apologize for snapping at you. My grandmother appears to trust you, so I will try to do the same."

"And I apologize for bringing trouble to your people. Can you tell me more about yourselves? For starters, how do you know of Sephor and his estate?"

"My family are the leaders of a village several kilometers southeast of this place. For over a hundred generations the women of our line have been priestesses and chief elders, while their husbands and sons served as defenders of the people."

"A matriarchal society here in Egypt. One that has persisted for over a thousand years. That's interesting." Oliver commented.

"Yes. Well, we believe ourselves to be descended from the wife and servants of Sephor, those few who escaped a terrible slaughter. For the most part we live as you might expect any other small village centered around an oasis. We grow crops. We raise animals. We pray that the spring does not fail. We never grew large enough to concern the Pharaohs, or Caliphs, or Generals, because our Elder women always reminded us of Sephor and how he grew too proud until one day his pride destroyed him."

"I find it hard to believe that nobody in your village ever sold the secret of the estate to an archaeologist or grave robber. That nobody ever attempted to plunder Sephor's house for riches."

"Some did. Those we caught were executed for blasphemy. Those we did not were never seen again. The guardians of the estate saw to that."

"The undead skeletons."

Hadiya thought about that, then nodded. "Yes. I suppose so. I have never seen them myself, thank God, but my mother would tell me stories of walking skeletons to keep me from straying outside the village as a child."

Oliver smiled at that. He was still trying to take in the idea that he might be speaking to an actual descendant of the people who had lived in the canyon estate before it was destroyed. As they spoke, the party had reached the top of the slope and trudged across the rocky surface of the desert towards a large white passenger van parked about a quarter mile from the canyon wall.

Zaid noticed Oliver looking at the van and said, "We parked a few hundred meters away from the cliff so that our approach would not be heard by anyone in the canyon."

"How often do your people visit this place?"

Hadiya answered him saying, "Six times a year my grandmother comes to bring offerings to the Old Gods. My mother accompanies her. One day my mother and I will take over the duties... or at least, so I had always expected. Now that you claim to have destroyed Sephor, who knows what will become of the rituals."

They reached the van and Hadiya helped her grandmother into the center bench seat while the men took their places in the rear bench and driver's seat. Once the old woman was settled, Hadiya turned to him and said, "I don't know what to think of you, Oliver. You show up out of nowhere, bringing my grandmother nightmares and visions of death, confess to destroying our sacredly profane ancestor, and tell us that a relic we have worshiped from afar for generations is in peril. Part of me still wishes that grandmother had let the men shoot you down in the canyon. But then... this is a strange day."

She turned away, shaking her head, and climbed into the van beside her grandmother.

Oliver paused briefly, unsure what to say. He still wasn't certain whether these people were grateful or furious that he had destroyed Sephor's undead body, and he wondered whether he would survive the day. These people kept using such a strange term to describe Sephor, sacredly profane. He thought he had an idea what they meant, but it was so vague he couldn't be sure. Zaid called for Oliver to ride along in the front passenger seat. Oliver climbed in and settled into the seat beside Zaid, who was driving.

They set off southward, the rim of the canyon on their left as they drove. Zaid kept the van on rocky terrain and hard packed sand, steering clear of large rocks, ravines, and deep dunes where the wheels could become bogged down in soft sand. The men said nothing the entire journey, but Hadiya and her grandmother spoke constantly in the dialect Oliver could not understand. At times their voices rose and he could sense anger in the unfamiliar words, at others the old woman nearly wept as she spoke.

Oliver said nothing. Even for one accustomed to dangerous situations and supernatural events, this day had been filled with more than its fair share of startling revelations. He tried not to think about what Diana might be going through, or of the mercenaries who held her and might at this moment be standing at the entrance to the forgotten temple. He listened to the rhythm of the women speaking behind him and allowed his eyes to drift. Before Olive realized it was happening, he was asleep.

Chapter Fifteen

Oliver felt a hand on his shoulder shaking him awake. A voice he recognized, but couldn't name, was shouting at him in Arabic, "Awake! We have arrived!"

Oliver opened his eyes and saw that the van had stopped in front of a two story mud brick building with a rusted tin roof. He saw more low brick buildings in the distance, each with a small array of solar panels bolted to the roof, and a small crowd of children and dogs surrounding a well at the center of a paved plaza. Streets radiated off from the plaza in five different directions, running between the buildings in narrow strips of dusty gravel.

The voice came again, a little louder this time and he felt a slap on his right shoulder, and Oliver snapped his head right to see Zaid holding the van door open with one hand as he shook Oliver's shoulder with the other. "Good, you're awake. Hadiya and Elder Layla are already in the house. They will be wanting to speak with you."

Oliver pulled the door handle and slid out of the van. He stretched his back, legs, and arms tiredly, feeling a dull ache settling in. It was only mid-afternoon and he had already been attacked by an undead warrior, knocked out by a professional killer, kicked repeatedly in the ribs and gut by a disgraced Egyptian spook, and used for target practice by an enraged mercenary. His body was in desperate need of some good rest and the short nap he had taken in the van had only served to make his muscles seize up and drain him of adrenaline so his bruised flesh and stressed muscles had started to hurt.

He grabbed his bag from the floor in front of the passenger seat, swung the van door shut and stalked around the front of the van towards the open door of the mud brick house, his body aching the whole way.

A woman who looked remarkably like an older version of Hadiya opened the door in response to Oliver's knock. She was dressed in a simple dress of white cotton that hung from her shoulders to her ankles. Delicately embroidered hieroglyphic designs ran down the front of the dress and across the shoulders and sleeves. The beginnings of wrinkles creased the corners of her eyes, which glinted at Oliver from behind large multifocal lenses.

She spoke to him in a strongly accented English. "Welcome to my home, Mr. Lucas. I am Duha, mother of Hadiya and daughter of the Elder Layla."

Oliver bowed his head and replied, "Thank you for having me. I appreciate your mother sparing my life and bringing me to this place."

Duha stepped back and waved for Oliver to enter, saying, "You are our honored guest. Please, come in."

He stepped into a combined kitchen and dining room. An electric stove and refrigerator stood against one wall, under several rows of shelves built into the brick wall. Water pipes and electrical conduit ran along the baseboard of the room and disappeared through a hole knocked into the ancient bricks and patched with plaster. Small statues of the gods of ancient Egypt stood in nooks set into the walls around the room. The old woman, Elder Layla, reclined in a rattan seat beside a heavy wood table at the center of the room. Hadiya was nowhere in sight, but Oliver though he could hear running water from the back of the house and guessed that she had stepped into the bathroom.

Duha closed the door and moved to a seat across from her mother. She lowered herself into the chair and picked up an embroidery frame from the table. Oliver dropped his backpack beside the door and waited beside it until Duha waved him to a seat at the table. He settled into the seat, nervously hoping that the creaking rattan would support his weight.

Elder Layla began to speak. Her daughter translated, never looking up from her needlework as she spoke, "My honored mother asks you to describe what you seek. She spared your life in the sacred canyon because she believes you to be a good person, but desires to know what artifact you expected to find in our sacred land." She paused in her stitching and tilted her head down to look at Oliver through the top of her glasses, "I know only what my daughter shouted on her way through the door, so I also look forward to hearing your explanation."

Oliver proceeded to explain everything that had happened since the Senator pressured him to take the job searching for the staff that had belonged to Moses. He explained bringing Diana into the effort because of his unfamiliarity with Egyptian script, how the mercenaries had become involved, and how he and Diana had double-crossed the mercenaries to gain the information they needed. Hadiya came in while he spoke and busied herself chopping onions and garlic at the counter beside the stove. She set the knife down and turned around to lean against the counter with her arms crossed as Oliver described exploring Sephor's house and chapel. This event was clearly the highlight of his story, as even Duha laid aside her needlework to gaze intently at Oliver as he described fighting Sephor's living corpse. Both she and Elder Layla had several questions for Oliver on that regard, which he did his best to answer.

The old priestess seemed especially concerned with Oliver's feelings about having destroyed Sephor. He answered honestly, explaining that he took no pleasure in destroying ancient ruins, or their guardians, but that he felt no regret at defending his own life.

"I apologize for defiling the body of your ancestor. Had he given me any warning..." Oliver explained.

Elder Layla shook her head and covered her face with her hands. Hadiya stepped up to her grandmother and rested her hands on the old woman's shoulders. Duha grimaced and tapped her fingertips on the tabletop. She opened her mouth as if to speak, then shook her head and remained silent.

"Listen. If there is anything I can do to make amends... I don't quite understand what's going on here."

Hadiya replied, "It's complicated, Oliver. For my grandmother, most of all. We are all trained as priestesses of the old gods and guardians of Sephor's memory, and she has spent nearly a hundred years bearing witness to his fate."

She stepped away from her grandmother and pulled an apple from a basket over the sink. She tossed it to Oliver and looked at her mother. Duha shook her head and picked up her needlepoint. The Elder Layla continued to hide her face in her hands, weeping softly and muttering to herself. Hadiya took another apple for herself, then settled into a chair across from Oliver.

"You see, our worship of Sephor's memory is different from how people perceive worship in your country. We don't pray to Sephor to save our souls, or bring good fortune, or anything like that..." She took a bite of her apple and chewed it for a while, seeming to contemplate how to explain the mysteries of her faith to an outsider, then continued. "Have you ever been to Arlington, the cemetery?"

Oliver nodded, wondering where Hadiya was going with his.

"I went to Arlington once over spring break. The college arranged for us exchange students to visit many sites around your capital, but it is Arlington that I remember the most. They have men there who are sworn to guard the tomb of a nameless soldier. Over eighty percent of those who apply for the duty are rejected before they even enter training. Even then, most of the men who are accepted fail to complete the training. They memorize names, battles, rituals. They take vows that regulate their behavior on and off duty. They march a precise step every day in the sun, the rain, the snow. They do all this out of sense of duty to preserve the memory of the men who died and could not be identified."

Hadiya paused to catch her breath. She had been speaking with increasing rapidity and forcefulness and Oliver was impressed at her passion. She leaned forward on her elbows and continued, "If you can understand that, Oliver, you will understand some of what we feel. The old gods and our ancestor are something to be remembered and honored, even if the rest of the world has forgotten them or written them off as silly tales told by ignorant people in the past."

"You used a phrase when we first spoke: 'profanely sacred'. What does that mean?"

"I, and my mother, and my grandmother, and all the women of our lineage for thousands of years, are sworn to protect the memory of Sephor. What I have not explained is that this memory is not a good one. We remember it as an admonition against lust, pride, and tampering with the powers of the gods."

"As Sephor did, in creating the guardians."

"Exactly. Our legends tell us that Sephor called upon the power of Osiris to guard his house against the corruption of death, and on Setesh to return the souls of the dead to their bodies as eternal guardians of his home and the treasures contained within."

Duha interjected then, speaking in a hushed voice like that which she must have used to tell the story to her daughter, as it had been told to her. "And all was well with the mighty lord Sephor for a time. His lands prospered. His people gave birth to many skilled craftsmen and mighty warriors for the Pharaoh. Until one day the lord Sephor offended a visiting noble by taking his wife into his bed as a concubine. When confronted with his crime, the lord Sephor laughed and told his guest that all things were permissible to him, because the gods had raised him above all men except the pharaoh himself, even blessing him and giving him the strength to defeat foreign gods.

"The nobleman was outraged at his host's lust and pride, but did not strike at Sephor directly. Instead he waited until the middle of the night, when all were asleep in bed except for Sephor's undying guardians. The nobleman took a chisel in his hand and with five mighty blows he struck out the names of prideful Sephor and his family from the great engraving above the household altar. Then he fled into the night, taking his servants with him, but leaving his wife behind.

"That very night, the undying guardians of Sephor's lands fell upon the family in their beds. Many were slaughtered in their sleep. Others awoke to die with screams on their lips before they could rise from their beds. A few managed to fight. A very few slipped away into the darkness beyond the gates of the estate.

"In the midst of this chaos of bloodshed, Sephor fought the undying warriors that the gods Osiris and Setesh had granted him. Abandoning his wife and concubines to what fate might bring, he retreated to the shrine that he had erected to his own glory, in which rested the Guide Stone and Key, relics that served to remind him of his power and guarantee him access to the temple of the staff. It was there that the most mighty, and yet most foolish, of Pharaoh's generals sealed his fate. Standing before the altar to Osiris and Setesh, grievously wounded by the swords of his own undying guards, the lord

Sephor made an offering of his own blood and entrails in exchange for becoming the undying guardian of the chapel, so that he could see his memory protected for all ages."

Duha's voice faded away at the end, as if saying the words hurt too deeply. She laid her needlepoint on the table and wiped at her wet cheeks with the back of a hand.

Oliver watched the women in silence. He was unsure what to say. Never before had he been confronted with a legacy such as this. These women held within themselves the memory of an event drawn from the deepest chambers of history, passed on from one generation to the next over the course of five thousands years.

"As you can see, it is complicated."

Oliver nodded. He swallowed, his throat dry and tight.

Hadiya continued, "I cannot speak for my mother, or my grandmother, but the feeling I have towards you now is a mingling of gratitude and horror. Gratitude that you have destroyed the legacy of foolish pride that we have been bound to remember. Horror that you would dare to defile the monument that we have guarded for so long."

Duha, who had stopped weeping by this time, nodded and said something in their language. The Elder Layla dropped her hands from her face and looked at Oliver thoughtfully for a moment, then replied.

Her daughter translated, "It will be long before I know how to feel about this day. I will continue to tell the story of Sephor's folly to my people until my dying day, and hope that my daughter and her daughter will continue after I am gone. But that is for the future, and it does not concern an outsider such as you. What does concern you is the evil you have brought upon your friend, and the Temple of the Staff. We will speak more of this at dawn tomorrow, when new light brings with it the hope of a better day than this."

As soon as Duha stopped speaking her translation, the Elder Layla put her hand on the table and levered herself out of the tattered rattan seat. She turned her back on the three people still seated around the table and tottered through a curtained doorway into the back of the house.

They sat in silence for a while, each pondering the story that the women had told in their own way. Oliver did his best to stifle a yawn, then stood and stretched his aching muscles. "If I'm to remain in your house, I should probably wash up. It's been a rough day."

Hadiya looked up from the apple core she had been fiddling with and said, "I'll show you to the bathroom." She tossed the core into an earthenware bowl on the counter and moved to the curtained doorway.

Oliver grabbed his backpack and followed her through the curtain into a narrow hall. Framed family photos hung on the wall, dimly illuminated by an old metal lamp with a scrollwork shade resting on a small wooden table.

Hadiya paused before a door and said, "This is the bathroom. Don't be shy about using water for a bath, this village has deep wells and a stream, so we never lack for water. Do try and be sparing with the hot water though. It has to warm in a tank on the roof and my father will still need some when he comes home. There's a towel for you on the toilet seat."

Oliver thanked Hadiya and pushed the door open into a cramped bathroom. An enameled iron bathtub with a roundabout shower curtain occupied half the space of the room. A toilet and wash basin stood opposite to each other beside the tub. An old mirror, the silvering chipped away at the edges, was affixed to the wall over the basin.

Oliver closed the door and set his bag down. He stepped up to the basin and looked into the mirror, examining his reflection with interest. It had been four days since he had last shaved and the red stubble was coming in thick on his face and neck. He had a bruise over his left eye, which he supposed he had gotten when he was knocked out, or while tumbling to get to cover when Frank had shot at him just a few hours ago. Oliver stripped off his shirt and pants and examined the fresh bruises on his sides and stomach from when Rais had kicked him. He probed the bruises, grimacing at the pain but not crying out, feeling for broken bones or the deep ache of organ damage. His ribs hurt like hell, but he was fairly certain that there was no true damage.

Oliver filled the tub with cold water and slipped into it. The icy water felt good on his skin and slowly numbed his aches as he willed his muscles to relax. After resting for about five minutes he sat up and began scrubbing away the sweat and grime of the day. He repeatedly plunged his head under the water and massaged at his scalp, but was still picking grains of sand out of his hair as he toweled himself dry and dressed in his one set of spare clothes. He squirreled away his dirty clothes in a zipped plastic bag in his backpack.

Clean, freshly dressed, and feeling a little more alive than he had fifteen minutes previous, Oliver pulled on his vest and unzipped the hidden phone pocket. He clearly wasn't a prisoner, wasn't about to be executed or coerced to reveal any information, but he didn't know how these people would take to him telling others about their hidden oasis, so he hadn't checked his phone for several hours. He unlocked the phone and saw several messages from Amber waiting in his Twitter client:

Checking Leonidas from this end. Be safe.

This was followed an hour later by another message.

Leonidas is bad news. Get out if you can. Putting your dad on Senator, but risky.

"Great." Oliver muttered to himself. The last thing he wanted was for his father to get involved in this whole mess. It wasn't that Oliver mistrusted his father, but applying pressure to Senator Wheeler and the Leonidas Security leadership might have unpredictable results. If Kyle was to be believed, the mercenaries and Rais Karim had pursued Oliver and Diana precisely because the Senator had tracked down their employer and started applying pressure for them to retrieve the staff.

He selected Amber's most recent message and tapped the reply icon.

In the clear for now, but Leonidas still has Diana. Going to try and rescue her in next 24 hours. Leonidas team led by a Kyle Sanders. Includes a Frank.

He paused for a moment, then added.

Thanks. You and dad be careful, mercs came after us because of pressure from Wheeler.

He locked the phone and slipped it back into the hidden pocket in his vest.

Oliver emerged from the bathroom dressed much as he had been before, with the exception that his clothes were no longer stained with blood and dirt. He found Hadiya and Duha in the kitchen, busily chopping vegetables with large, extremely sharp looking knives. A pan on the stove splattered cheerily and gave off the aroma of browning lamb meat. At the table sat a large man dressed in canvas pants and a light cotton shirt with long sleeves. The naturally tan skin of his face and hands had been tanned a deeper brown by long days spent working in the sun. He looked up from a laptop computer that sat on the table before him as Oliver entered the room.

"You must be Oliver Lucas." He said to Oliver in Arabic.

He rose from his seat and shook Oliver's hand. "Welcome to my house. I am Mahir, husband of one of these women, father of the other, and all-around problem solver in this little village."

Oliver smiled at Mahir, already getting a sense that he liked the man. "Yes, I am Oliver. Your daughter and the Elder Layla found me in the desert this afternoon and rescued me. Elder Layla said she has a task for me to perform, so I thank you for letting me stay the night."

Mahir nodded gravely. "Yes. My wife told me of Elder Layla's plans for you. I don't envy the journey you are about to undertake, but if half of what Hadiya tells me of your exploits today is true, you might just survive this."

"That's my goal."

"They tell me you have photographs of the estate. May we see them? My wife and her ancestors have never set foot beyond the walls in all the years they worshiped there."

Oliver nodded and pulled the camera out of his bag. "Yes, I have many photos. Can we load them onto your computer?"

Mahir nodded, so Oliver ejected the memory card from his camera and passed it to the man. The transfer took only a few moments, during which Oliver explained how he and Diana had come to explore the estate. Once all of the photographs had transferred, Oliver put the memory card into a plastic case and slipped it into a vest pocket. Mahir turned his laptop so that the women could see the screen while they cooked, and for the next hour Oliver took the family on a tour of the estate that they had guarded, but never entered, for a hundred generations.

Chapter Sixteen

Oliver woke the next morning with the rich smell of coffee filling his nostrils. He opened his eyes in the dim light of the common room and rolled over, being careful to not fall off the sofa as he did so. Every muscle in his left side flared to a fiery wakefulness, reminding him of yesterday's events. His eyes fell upon a large mug resting on the table, filled to the brim with a dark brown liquid. He glanced around, but didn't see anybody else in the sitting area or the kitchen.

He swung his legs down to the floor and leaned on his knees for a moment, waiting until the pain subsided into a dull ache, then dropped to the floor and did several pushups. The pain returned, but he pushed through it and kept moving until his arms pumped his body fluidly up and down. He rolled to his feet, wincing as his bruised muscles and organs screamed at the sudden movement. Oliver knew he didn't have any broken bones, but the damage he had sustained yesterday would take at least a week to fully heal.

Oliver sat down on the sofa and pulled on his shirt. He picked up the thick brew and sipped at it experimentally. The liquid was as thick as heavy cream and far stronger than normal coffee. It left a slightly gritty feeling on his tongue, but it was so sweet that he couldn't help but keep drinking it. He sat on the sofa for a few more minutes, mulling over the events of the previous day as the caffeine worked its way into his system.

He was half way through the mug of coffee when Hadiya pushed through the curtained doorway to the family's rooms. "Good, you're awake. I was worried when the noise of making coffee didn't wake you, but thought the smell of a mug right beside your nose might work."

Oliver raised the cup in salute and thanked her, then set it down and began pulling on his boots while Hadiya busied herself at the stove.

"My mother and father are out refueling the Jeep. When they return we will have breakfast, then I imagine you will be on your way to rescue your partner."

Oliver folded the thin blanket that he had slept under and laid it on the arm of the sofa. Then he picked up the cup of coffee and walked to the kitchen table. He watched Hadiya in silence for a moment, sipping his coffee and trying to think of the right words for the question that had been bothering him since Hadiya, her grandmother, and their guards had rescued him yesterday. Finally he said, "Hadiya, I've been thinking about this all night. Why didn't your men just shoot me yesterday?"

She turned from the counter, still twisting a ball of dough in her hand, and gave him a quizzical look.

"Not that I don't appreciate it, but what do you gain by keeping me around? What can I do for you?"

"I know the reason, but it is my grandmother's place to tell you, not mine. Now go get washed up for breakfast."

Oliver watched as she turned back to the counter and tossed the flattened disk of bread onto an oiled cast iron skillet. He drained his coffee mug and set it on the table, then slipped through the curtain into the bathroom.

When he returned he found the Elder Layla sitting in her chair at the table, her hands resting on a wooden box that was polished to such a sheen that it seemed to glow softly in the growing light of the morning sun. Taking his seat at the table across from the old woman, Oliver could smell the rich scent of olive wood that that been preserved by frequent polishing with a rag soaked in olive oil. The light was too dim for him to make out the precise nature of the inscriptions on the box, but he could see the vague outline of several hieroglyphs running across the side of the box facing him.

"Good morning, Elder Layla."

The old woman nodded and replied in her own tongue.

Hadiya translated, without looking away from the stove, "Good morning, Oliver. Are you prepared for the journey that awaits you?"

"I think I am, but I don't know the nature of the journey. Where do I go? How will I save my friend?"

Elder Layla didn't reply for a moment. Her hands caressed the box on the table, crooked fingers slipping into the groves of the engraved hieroglyphs and tracing their outlines. She seemed to look past Oliver and into some distant place that only she knew.

"I am an old woman. For over seventy years I have served the gods of my ancestors and preserved the sacred memory of Sephor's folly, as did my mother and grandmother before me, and their mothers before them. As long as I have lived I expected that my daughter and her daughters would do the same. But now..." She hesitated long enough that Hadiya was forced to pause in her translation and wait for her to continue. She sighed deeply and said, "Now I am unsure what we will do. Sephor has been destroyed and violent men are moving to desecrate the temple that holds the rod of power.

"The men who attacked you are not the first to have sought to take this relic. Seven generations ago a party of French soldiers came upon our village as they explored the land. My ancestors said little to them and they were soon gone, but not before the rebellious son of the Elder, bored with his simple life in this peaceful place, offered to show them the sacred canyon in exchange for a commission into the army. He went away with them, only to return a month later bearing a tale of woe.

"The boy had led the soldiers to the sacred canyon and told their leader, a lieutenant, of two relics said to be hidden in the chapel. They did not destroy Sephor, but they managed to capture the guide stone and the key. The lieutenant was furious with the boy because several of his men had died in the assault, but the boy pled for his life and showed the lieutenant how to use the guide stone to find the Temple of the Staff. He then guided them to the temple and helped them to gain entry. Soon after they entered the temple, they were driven off by the powers that guard that temple. The soldiers who still lived retreated to the north, never to return, while the rebellious boy retrieved the relics from the corpse of the lieutenant and journeyed back to this village."

Elder Layla stopped speaking and caressed the box in her hands. Oliver nodded slowly, the realization dawning that the box must contain the guide stone and key. That would explain why the French soldiers had attacked the chapel in Sephor's estate, but not made any effort to loot the riches of the main house. He recalled the layout of the inner sanctum, where he and Diana had puzzled over the two empty niches in the side walls of the chamber. Those must have been where the guide stone and key had rested until they were stolen by the French soldiers.

He stood then and retrieved his camera from the backpack resting beside the sofa. He pulled a chair up beside Elder Layla and switched the camera into review mode, loading up the images of the inner sanctum from its memory card.

"Hadiya, could you explain to your grandmother that these are photographs I took in the chapel. She didn't see them last night."

Hadiya set her cooking aside and came to stand behind Elder Layla. She spoke softly to her grandmother, translating as Oliver flipped between photos and pointed to parts of the inner sanctum that seemed relevant to the story she had just related. He showed her the bodies of the French soldiers and the remains of Sephor. At the sight of her destroyed ancestor, the old woman began whispering to herself. Hadiya explained to Oliver that her grandmother was praying for the soul of the ancient warrior, freed from torment after so many years. When she grew silent, he flipped to another photo and pointed out the empty niches in the inner sanctum of the temple. He zoomed the image in close enough that Elder Layla could inspect the inscriptions around each niche. The old woman's eyes lit up as she gestured between the screen of the camera and the box on the table. The inscriptions were remarkably similar. Then Oliver flipped to a photo of the roughly carved inscription.

Layla studied the photo of the inscription intently, asking Oliver to zoom in on several portions in turn. Finally she spoke, almost in a whisper. Hadiya translated, "You must leave as soon as my parents return with the car. I will pack supplies for you."

"I am eager to rescue my friend, but why is your grandmother in such a rush all of a sudden?"

The old priestess did not reply to Oliver's question. Instead she began speaking rapidly to her granddaughter. Hadiya pulled a pad of paper from a drawer and began writing as quickly as she could, occasionally interrupting the old woman, apparently insisting that she repeat herself. Oliver watched in silence, waiting for an explanation. After several minutes Hadiya stopped writing. She tore off the paper and folded it up, then handed it to Oliver.

"This is a rough translation of the instructions that Sephor scratched into the wall. He was furious that his relics had been stolen, but was unable to pursue the thieves because of the magic that bound him to the chapel, so he left instructions for his descendants to find the temple and retrieve the staff if the soldiers hadn't already taken it."

Oliver made to unfold the paper and read the instructions, but Elder Layla laid a hand on his and shook her head. She motioned for him to put the paper in one of the pockets of his vest. Confused, he did as she told him.

Elder Layla turned to the olive wood box on the table and rested her worn hands on it. She breathed a few words in what Oliver assumed to be a prayer, then lifted the top of the box. The top half slid smoothly apart from the bottom, revealing a piece of crumbling parchment inscribed with hieratic script atop the thick folds of a finely woven white linen cloth. She set the lid of the box on the table and paused for a moment to whisper a few more words. Then she tenderly moved the parchment aside and laid it atop the lid. With one more murmured prayer she lifted the linen cloth.

Underneath, two objects rested in gentle indentations they had made in another linen cloth. One was a oval disc of alabaster stone about the size of Oliver's palm with a large hole bored through the center. Within this hole was set a large fleck of mica. Carved inscriptions in hieratic and, to Oliver's surprise, a script that reminded him of ancient Hebrew surrounded the hole on one side. The other was a pyramid of polished brass, about an inch to a side, with fine lines of hieratic script scribed into each surface.

"These are the guide stone and key that were stolen from the chapel of Sephor by the French soldiers. With these you will be able to find the temple of the staff and open its outer gates. After that, you must follow your heart and heed the instructions that my granddaughter has written for you. I pray that you will reach the temple in time to save your friend."

Elder Layla lifted the brass pyramid from the box and handed it to Oliver. It was still cold with the night's chill and felt heavy for its size. At Layla's prompting, Oliver slipped the pyramid into a zippered pocket on the front of his vest, pulling out the spare camera battery he normally kept there and dropping that to the tabletop. She then handed him the guide stone and pantomimed holding it up and looking around.

Oliver held the guide stone up to his right eye and looked through it. At first he saw nothing unusual. The fleck of mica set into the hole was clear enough for him to see through, but it distorted the image enough that he had trouble making out the features of the women in the room with him. He turned his head from side to side as Layla had shown him and was about to set the stone down when he noticed something strange. When he turned his head to the right, Oliver could just see a faint reddish orange glow at the edge of the mica fleck. He initially wrote it off as the sun rising outside the front window of the house, but then he realized he was sitting with the window to his left.

Oliver scooted his seat around a little and looked to the right. As he turned his head a narrow line of flickering flame appeared in the fleck of mica. He lowered the guide stone and found himself looking at the side wall of the room. He put the guide stone back to his eye and the flame appeared again, flickering against the wall of the house as if he was looking through the wall at a distant pillar of fire.

Elder Layla spoke solemnly beside him and Hadiya translated, "Follow the fire and you will find the temple. Rescue your friend and prevent the staff of the foreign god from falling into the hands of the violent men. I only ask that when you have rescued your friend you return the stone and key, if you are able."

Oliver looked away from Layla and raised the guide stone to his eye again. Despite his aching muscles and the knowledge that Diana was in danger, Oliver couldn't help laughing out loud.

Chapter Seventeen

Oliver swerved the wheel to the right and gunned the accelerator to dodge around a boulder jutting out of the sands in front of the jeep. The sun was high enough now that it no longer burned bright in his rearview mirror, but it would still be several hours before the desert air whipping through his hair grew unbearably hot. He rested one hand on the wheel and used the other to pull the guide stone out of his pocket and hold it up to one eye as he drove. The flickering pillar of fire continued to burn at the center of the mica fleck.

Duha and her husband had returned to the house, along with the guard Zaid, soon after Elder Layla gave the guide stone and key to Oliver. He had quickly packed his bag, tossing in several parcels of food that Hadiya had wrapped up for him, and filled the bladder of his water pack, then tossed all of his supplies into the jeep. Zaid had returned Oliver's gun and wished him luck. The whole family gathered in front of the house to wave him goodbye as Oliver turned the jeep around and sped up the dusty road leading out of the village and the fertile valley in which it rested.

The jeep was an old ragtop model with zip windows that had long since been lost. The top was a patchwork of the original canvas and dozens of repair patches of differing ages, which served well enough since its primary purpose in this climate was to provide shade from the sun.

He drove west, skirting the edges of canyons, picking his way though fields of boulders, and keeping clear of deep sand dunes. Every ten minutes or so he pulled out the guide stone and checked that he was still pointed in the right direction.

Diana had estimated that the temple was within one hundred fifty miles of Sephor's estate, possibly closer, but couldn't be any more specific acting solely on the information provided in the inscription. They had marked out over a dozen possible locations for Kyle and the mercenaries to search and Oliver had no idea which, if any, of these might be the actual location of the temple. For all he knew they might have arrived at the temple within half an hour of leaving him to die in the canyon yesterday, or they might have just broken camp in preparation for a second day of searching for the temple. Unlike the mercenaries and Diana, Oliver now knew the exact direction to travel and had a key that would help him find the entrance, but he had no way of knowing how far he had to go and had to contend with the obstacles of traveling over the surface of the desert.

As he drove, Oliver tried to formulate a plan for what he would do when he arrived. Any plans he made, however, were contingent upon what he found when he reached the temple. If the mercenaries had already reached the temple he would have to go with his gut and try to rescue Diana before they realized that he had arrived. On the other hand, if they hadn't reached the temple yet, his goals would probably be best served by hiding the jeep under the camouflage netting that Zaid had provided him and attempting to enter the temple himself. Then he might be able to set up an ambush and rescue Diana as the mercenaries worked their way through whatever defenses the temple might possess.

He patted his breast pocket, feeling the crinkling of the paper Hadiya had given him, translated from what Elder Layla had told her. He had not yet had time to read it, but he truly hoped that the old woman was right in saying it would give him a fighting chance in the temple.

Two hours into the drive, Oliver saw a bloom of sand to the north. He brought the jeep to a stop and reached back to pull a set of binoculars out of his bag. Adjusting the focus showed him the swirling clouds of sand pouring out across the desert like the front of a sand storm. Oliver shifted his view upward to the top of the storm and saw the vague outline of a helicopter painted in shades of sandy tan and brown.

The mercenaries.

The helicopter moved across the desert in near silence. The beat of the rotors reached Oliver's ears as a whisper of wind, accompanied by an inaudible pulsing beat that made his chest resonate strangely. As Oliver watched, the helicopter slowed and hovered for a while about two miles farther along his track. Then the beat in his chest slowed and the helicopter dropped out of sight behind the ridge of a sand dune.

So much for getting there ahead of them, Oliver thought.

He shifted the jeep back into gear and continued following the guide stone towards the place where the helicopter had set down. He drove at a slower pace now, wary of alerting the mercenaries to his approach with a plume of sand from his jeep. If this was the temple, then he was already to late to set up an ambush, so he would have to wait and see how the mercenaries fared gaining entrance to the temple, and whether they still had Diana with them.

Oliver parked the jeep at the base of the high dune that separated him from the mercenaries. He pulled out his pack and slung it comfortably over his shoulders, checked his gun, and slipped the guide stone into a side pocket of his vest.

He turned to face the dune, over which lay Diana, the mercenaries, and a temple filled with secrets. He took a long drag from his water tube, stretched his arms and legs, and set off jogging up the face of the dune. He kept running until he thought that his head might show over the ridge. Then he bent into a crouch and ran bent half over until he was high enough that prudence dictated dropping to the sand and crawling the remaining distance on his belly.

Oliver wriggled across the sand until he could just see over the ridge of the dune. The opposite side swept downwards to a deep bowl of sand and rocks, with an immense reddish brown stone jutting up in the center. Atop the stone stood a temple built of carved granite blocks stacked one atop another in a long low structure that covered much of the surface of the rock. A series of stone pillars spaced about twenty feet apart led from the temple rock across the sand-filled bowl of the dry lakebed, and into a high mound of sand several hundred yards to Oliver's left. Each of these were also built of reddish stone up to the upper three feet of their length, at which point the builders appeared to have switched to a more conventional white sandstone.

Examining the scene through his binoculars, Oliver surmised that the site had remained untouched across the ages in part because of its inaccessibility. In its prime this site had been a beautiful temple complex built on a rocky island in the center of a lake. It had most likely been accessed via a bridge built across the pillars, which had since collapsed under the weight of the sand that had drifted onto it over the centuries. After the lake dried up and the bridge collapsed, there would have been no way to reach the temple save making a treacherous climb up several steep, and in places, sheer rock faces. That, and the site's location so far to the west of the Nile, had likely protected it from looters until modern times. As to why nobody had excavated the site in the last two hundred years...

The helicopter rested on the sands of the dry lakebed. Turning his binoculars towards it, Oliver saw the forms of seven men in desert camouflage moving around the exterior of the helicopter. One of them, Oliver assumed was Frank, had a white sling supporting his left arm. As he watched, six of the men, including Frank, broke off into two groups and began stalking around the base of the rocky island in opposite directions. Oliver assumed that these would be searching for an easy route to the top of the rock. The seventh man returned to the helicopter and began gesticulating to an unseen figure inside the crew compartment.

It was clear that the mercenaries were not sure how to proceed, and that Oliver had a snowball's chance in hell of slipping past them and entering the temple first, so he slipped back down the slope a couple feet and pulled the folded paper that Hadiya had given him from his breast pocket and opened it to read the words that Elder Layla had spoken.

The temple of the staff is built upon an island in the center of an oasis lake three days' journey to the west of my estate. If the guards still live they will challenge you when you attempt to cross the bridge to the temple. Speak to them the sacred words of my household and you will be allowed to pass. If the foul warriors in blue have slaughtered the guards, as I fear, your first challenge will be the gates of the temple. These will open to whoever possesses the key, or to one who knows the sacred name of the god whose staff I captured. I pray to Osiris and Setesh that the staff of the Hebrews has been left untouched, for if those who stole my sacred treasures have succeeded in disturbing it you may be faced with the plagues that befell our forefathers. In that event I can only pray that your heart does not tip the balance as you pass between our gods and the sun to enter the inner sanctum. The staff must be kept at the center of the altar, else its power will be unleashed.

Oliver read the letter three times, trying to find some solid clue that might help him survive whatever traps might have been laid by the ancient guardians of the temple, but he could find nothing that explained what he ought to do once he entered the temple. This didn't especially worry him. He had delved into temples and tombs from South America to Iceland with as much information, but Elder Layla's words had given him hope that he would enter this particular temple with more information than usual. And then there was the matter of the mercenaries and Diana. Oliver didn't usually mind working from vague clues because he often had plenty of time to examine the site and puzzle his way through a temple's defenses. That was unlikely to be the case today.

He risked another look over the ridge. The scouting party on his side of the rock was nearly half way along the length. They didn't appear to have selected a place to ascend yet. Back at the helicopter stood a man. Oliver zoomed in as far as he could and saw that it was Kyle leaning against the fuselage of the helicopter talking to someone within. As Oliver watched, the other person climbed out of the helicopter and held a set of binoculars to their eyes to examine the walls of the temple high above.

Oliver felt a great wave of relief pass over him when he focused the binoculars on the person and realized that it was Diana. So much had happened in the last twenty-four hours that it was hard to believe that just yesterday they had been exploring the chapel in Sephor's estate together.

He slipped back down the hill and pulled out his phone to check for a signal and was not surprised to see that there was none. He did have a message though. As he drove away from the home of Elder Layla he had sent a quick tweet to Amber, informing her that he knew the location of the temple and was going after Diana and the mercenaries. He had immediately put away the phone to concentrate on navigating the jeep safely across the desert and had not checked it since.

Don't do anything stupid.

Short and to the point. Oliver smiled as he held the phone up over the ridge and took several photos of the helicopter, the rocky once-island, and the men moving along the base of the rocks. He pushed all of the images into an e-mail addressed to

Amber and his father and hit the send icon. If the phone picked up even a hint of signal it would send his messages right away. Sending the images in this manner would ensure that the geolocation data encoded in them by his phone's GPS chip was preserved.

He put the phone back in its zippered pocket and sipped again from the water tube on his pack as the considered his options.

Arriving within minutes of the mercenaries presented a challenge. If they had been at the site for a few hours, or since the previous night, then there would have been the chance that they were all deep within the temple. If he had arrived first, Oliver might have been able to find a way up the rock and into the temple complex before them. But now he would have to think of a way to scale the rock without being shot while the mercenaries were on highest alert.

Oliver went back to the jeep and pulled the camouflage net from the rear compartment. He then climbed slowly back to the top of the dune and settled down under the net with his camera to watch the men below through the longest zoom lens he had brought with him. He took care to get close up photos of Kyle and the helicopter, as well as the Leonidas Security patches on his uniform. If he made it out of this alive, he intended to make life difficult for these men.

The two scouting groups returned to the helicopter within twenty minutes. The news they brought obviously agitated Kyle because Oliver could hear him shouting all the way from his perch atop the dune. His words were twisted by the winds that carried them, but the tone was clearly thick with frustration. Oliver guessed that he had been hoping they would find a path to the top of the rock, but they apparently hadn't. The men all piled into the helicopter and the blades began to spin, slowly at first but then faster until they were a nearly invisible blur at the center of the dust cloud that had formed around the helicopter.

The helicopter rose into the air and Oliver waited under his net, hoping they wouldn't spot him.

The pilot directed the helicopter to hover over the narrow plaza outside the temple gates, between the closed gate and gap where the bridge had once stood. Oliver wondered why they didn't simply fly to the center of the temple complex and set down, but assumed that they had some good reason for remaining outside the walls. Both the French expedition and the Elder Layla had believed that the temple was guarded by supernatural forces, so perhaps the mercenaries had already seen signs of such guards from the air.

Now that the helicopter was hovering over the stone plaza instead of a deep pool of sand, the cloud of dust surrounding it began to dissipate. A roll of black rope tumbled out of the side door of the helicopter and dangled down to the surface of the plaza. As Oliver watched, six mercenaries slid down the rope one after another in rapid succession, followed more slowly by Diana. Each of them ran to crouch in the lee of the wall, beside one of the large statues that lined the plaza, as the helicopter tilted back and moved away from the plateau to settle down on the sandy lakebed once again.

This was the opportunity Oliver had been waiting for. There had been only seven mercenaries, including Kyle and Frank, at Sephor's estate. That left just the pilot in the helicopter. Judging from the rapid movements of all the men who had repelled from the helicopter to the plaza, that pilot was the injured mercenary Frank. If Oliver could somehow get aboard the helicopter, he could either force the pilot to take him up the the plateau, or disable him and find his own way to the island surface.

He ran down the slope of the dune to the jeep and tossed his backpack and camouflage into the back. Oliver started the jeep and drove southward along the base of the sand dune until it leveled out to meet the desert floor. He turned north west and saw the bowl of the dry lakebed stretching out below. The helicopter was now hidden from view on the far side of the island and Oliver could see the towering white walls of the temple wrapping around the upper edge of the red rocks.

He used the large water bottle in the back of the jeep to top up the reservoir in his backpack, checked that he had a box of spare ammunition in the side pockets of his backpack and two full magazines in his vest, then rearranged the central compartment of his backpack so that the few climbing supplies he had brought with him were on top. That done, he threw the camouflage net over the jeep and marked its location on his phone. If he survived this little adventure, and he had every intention of doing so, it would be faster to follow a GPS track than backtrace from landmarks, though he did take visual note of the jeep's location relative to the temple island and the pillars of the fallen bridge.

Thus prepared, Oliver snugged the straps on his backpack and set off at an easy jog down the slope to the bottom of the dry lake.

It took him nearly ten minutes to reach the rocky base of the island, glancing up now and then as he ran to check that he was not being watched by any of the mercenaries from above. Oliver estimated that the island was about a quarter mile long at the base and half as wide. It narrowed as it went up, but only marginally so the slope of sheer rock, broken in places with outcroppings of wind-scoured boulders, would be almost impossible to climb without more ropes and pitons than he was carrying.

Oliver took a sip of water from his drinking tube and wrinkled his nose. It tasted stale. He hadn't noticed it before, but decided that the flavor was probably a result of mixing his own filtered water with that which he had been given back in the village. He tucked the drinking tube away and set off at a lope around the western side of the island. The helicopter had come to rest on the northeast side, cockpit facing south, so he hoped to come at it from the rear and catch the pilot unawares.

Soon enough he saw the tail of the helicopter around an outcropping of rock. Oliver sidled up the rock and risked a glance around the corner. He didn't see Frank, or any of the other mercenaries. The side doors of the helicopter rested open.

Oliver slipped his gun out of its holster and checked that there was a round in the chamber and no sand blocking the barrel or jammed in the mechanism. He took a few deep breaths, then crept forward, ready to roll aside and fire if Frank appeared holding a machine gun. Oliver didn't relish the thought of killing the man, but Frank had already made it clear that he had no compulsions about riddling Oliver's body with holes.

He heard a voice and froze, listening.

The voice continued, vaguely melodic as it drifted through the dry desert air.

Oliver crept forward and leaned against the fuselage of the helicopter. He could now make out what the voice was saying.

Oliver poked his head around the edge of the helicopter door and grinned. Frank sat in the pilot's chair, an empty morphine autoinjector laying on the textured metal of the deck beside him, white wires trailed from his lap up to his ears where they disappeared under the headphones of his headset. He had clearly raided the medic kit and, assuming he would have a few hours lonely watch, had dulled the pain of his wounded shoulder. His head bobbed slowly in time to unheard music and he sang along out of tune

Oliver pulled himself into the helicopter as quietly as he could, keeping his gun pointed toward Frank. He paused for a moment until he was sure that Frank hadn't noticed him, then tiptoed forward and waited as Frank continued to sing along with Iron Maiden's *Fear of the Dark*. He waited until Frank was just finishing the last line of the chorus in his raspy voice, and swung his arm forward and around, pushing the barrel of his gun up under Frank's chin.

Frank started back in his seat, hand swinging down towards his sidearm, then froze as he recognized the feeling of hot steel and plastic pressing against his throat.

Oliver stepped between the seats, keeping his gun against Frank's throat, and yanked down on Frank's earbud wires. "Recognize me?"

Frank nodded.

"Should have paid attention to the song and looked behind you."

Frank cleared his throat and swallowed. An expression somewhere between fear and rage was welling up in his eyes.

Oliver reached forward with his free hand and relieved Frank of what weapons he could see, slipping the handgun and combat knife into the outer pockets of his own pack. He extracted his gun from Frank's neck and sat down on the edge of the copilot seat, keeping the weapon pointed at Frank's face.

"Strap yourself in. Tight."

Frank complied, working clumsily with his one good arm.

"Obviously, I'm not dead. Right?"

A slight nod.

"So here's how this is going to work. You take this helicopter up to the top and let me down inside the wall, or I kill you now and climb up myself."

"I can't do that."

"I think you can."

Frank shook his head slightly and coughed, then replied, "I can't see inside the walls. It's all dark."

"Don't lie to me Frank. The morphine might block the pain, but I can still put holes in you."

"I'm not lying." He replied through gritted teeth. It was clear that Frank wanted nothing more than to rip Oliver's throat out. "It's like... I don't know... like the walls are filled with oil or something. We couldn't see a thing inside the walls when we first got here."

Oliver considered that. From his vantage point on the dune, he had only been able to see the exterior walls of the temple complex and a few vague shapes that might have been the roofs of interior buildings.

His thoughts were interrupted by a resounding boom that echoed back and forth across the dry lakebed.

Oliver looked out the cockpit window and saw a cloud of dust pouring down from the surface of the island fifty feet above.

"Looks like Kyle got impatient and blasted the gates open." Frank said.

"Idiot!" Oliver shouted.

"Get your panties out of a twist kid. We know how to use shaped charges. I'm sure your girlfriend is just..."

"Shut up and get this thing in the air!"

Frank rolled his eyes and laughed contemptuously. "Why the hell would I do that?"

"Because if I don't kill you first, that stuff might." Oliver grabbed Frank's blond-stubbled chin and twisted his head around, pointing out the window with his gun.

The dust cloud above had already begun to dissipate and through it Oliver could see a roiling blackness welling up on the edge of the plaza above. As they watched, it began to cascade down the side of the island, moving with a slow certainty like warm molasses pouring out of an overturned bottle. The darkness oozed down the slope, cascading across the sheer rock faces and pooling atop boulders before slipping downward again. Though the body of the darkness moved like a liquid, the edges of it whipped away in the desert wind, spreading tendrils of darkness across the sky. Wherever the viscus cloud moved, it covered everything in a profound blackness that not even burning light of the desert sun could pierce.

Frank's neck muscles went slack for a moment as he gaped at the spreading dark. Then he snapped his head out of Oliver's grip and set about flicking switches on the console in front of him.

Oliver felt a shudder run through the frame of the helicopter as the motors spun into sudden motion. A deep thrumming sound started in the engine compartment and quickly ramped up in pitch and frequency as the helicopter shuddered to life. The rotor blades lurched into movement and rapidly built up speed as Oliver scrabbled to find the buckle of his harness and get himself strapped in.

The darkness continued to pour down the side of the island until it pounded soundlessly into the sand of the lakebed and began to pile up on itself in the boiling, swirling mass of blackness. The dark began to spread out across the sand as it grew in height, creeping towards the helicopter in a deepening mass. The downwash of hot air from the helicopter blades pushed back against it momentarily, causing the dark to divert around the helicopter like a stream of liquid turning aside to surround a pebble in its path.

"Get us up!" Oliver shouted.

"This is already an emergency takeoff!" Frank screamed back at him, his words barely audible above the roar of the engine. "If I push it any faster, the engine will burn out." He grasped the control yoke and rocked it gently back and forth but the helicopter didn't move.

Oliver turned his eyes back to the pool darkness that had now completely surrounded the helicopter and begun to pile up around the invisible wall of air thundering down from the blades. As he looked, the black cloud slipped closer along the sands at the edge of the downwash. A single tendril of the darkness slipped forward, skittered back and forth across the sands, battered about by the torrent of air pounding down on it even as it continued to grow thicker and creep closer to the helicopter.

Then the rotors reached their lift speed and the helicopter shot up several feet into the air. As it lifted the surrounding darkness rushed in like walls of dark water. The darkness filled in the space beneath the helicopter and quickly grew deeper as the helicopter climbed into the air.

Oliver pulled the copilot's headset from a hook above his head and slipped it on. Then he grabbed the pilot's headset where it dangled behind Frank's seat and pushed it over Frank's head. The mercenary growled indistinctly and shook himself, tossing the helicopter about in the air, then he settled down and shot Oliver a fiery look. He brought the helicopter to a hover about thirty feet above the surface of the lakebed as the darkness continued to spread below.

Frank looked up from the spreading pool of darkness below and said, "What the hell is that?" He spoke in a soft tone that made Oliver wonder if Frank had ever been this afraid in his life.

"Darkness. A darkness that no light can pierce."

"But what... Where'd it come from?"

Oliver looked at Frank incredulously. "Do you have any idea what Kyle has gotten you into?"

"Artifacts. Duh."

"Not just artifacts. Relics. Objects filled with supernatural power of the sort that the average person never encounters."

"Bullshit."

Oliver gestured to the still expanding pool of darkness below them.

Frank said nothing.

Oliver looked toward the island and saw that the cascade of darkness had ceased to tumble down the rocks. Small puddles of black still pooled in crags of rock, but no other sign of the black flood remained on the rock face.

"Take us higher. We need to check on your team."

Frank complied, adjusting the yoke of the helicopter to pull them level with the plaza just in time to see the last of the mercenaries forcing Diana to walk through the shattered fragments of bronze and wood that were the only remnants of the temple gates. The darkness had slipped past them, seemingly without any harm, and Oliver could see only a few narrow streams of it slipping through the cracks of the plaza.

"Damn it," muttered Oliver. "You know Frank, your boss is rewriting the manual on how to be an idiot."

Frank grumbled something indistinct and started to bank the helicopter away from the temple.

Oliver pointed his gun at Frank again and said, "Nope. You're going to let me down on that plaza or I will shoot you the moment we land."

"And if I don't land?"

"Then you'll have to keep flying until we run out of gas and crash. Either way, you're dead. Or you can just let me down in the plaza and do whatever you want. I'd recommend flying back to Cairo and disappearing before your employers find out what happened out here."

Frank glowered at Oliver, then moved his controls until the helicopter hovered thirty feet above the temple plaza.

The plaza was too narrow for the helicopter to set down without hitting the outer wall of the temple, but stretched along the front wall of the temple for fifty feet or more on either side of the shattered gate. Keeping his gun trained on

Frank, Oliver unbuckled his harness and moved slowly into the crew compartment. He stayed far away from the open doors until he had finished donning a climbing harness from a rack behind the crew seats and snapped the rappel device on the harness onto the rope that was already attached to an anchor point at the center of the cabin. He kicked the coil of rope out the door. He secured his gun in the holster on his leg and grabbed a spare coil of rope from the rack beside the door.

"Thanks for the ride, Frank!" He shouted. Then Oliver jumped out the door of the helicopter.

He slid down the rope as fast as he dared without chancing a broken leg when he hit the ground. As he had expected, the helicopter began to pull away from the plaza as soon as he was out the door. He hit the mud brick pavement hard and was immediately dragged forward on his belly by the rapidly departing helicopter. Fortunately, his hands were already squeezing the carabiner that connected his harness to the rappelling unit. He gave the carabiner a twist and the unit was ripped from his hands and clattered over the edge of the cliff as Oliver skidded to a stop mere inches from the precipice. He got to his feet and dusted the sand from his clothes, watching in silence as helicopter flew away from the plateau of the former island and settled down behind a dune at the edge of the dry lake. Down below the darkness continued to seethe as it spread out to fill the bottom of the lakebed.

He turned to face the ruined gates of the temple.

Chapter Eighteen

The exterior wall of the temple must have once stood at the very edge of the surrounding water long ago before the lake dried and left the island temple resting atop a high plateau. The exterior wall of the temple extended from the very edge of the rocky cliff, where it was stained the same dark red as the stone upon which it was built, upwards in tightly fitted blocks of white stone that reached thirty feet above Oliver's head. The plaza on which he stood jutted out from the face of the island out to the shattered edge which he had nearly fallen over. The gates, so recently shattered by the blast of shaped explosive charges, were flanked by monumental statues of Osiris. At the feet of each statue, its heads only reaching the knees of the god behind it, stood a life sized statue of man holding a brass trumpet to his lips. Remarkably, neither the deities nor their heralds appeared to have been weathered by the ages. Over the gap where the gates had stood, a series of hieroglyphs were etched deep into the stones of the wall. Oliver could not read them, but he assumed they said something about mighty powers of the gods that guarded the temple.

The remnants of the gate, which appeared to have been made from bronze-clad wood which had somehow remained intact through the centuries, lay shattered and charred across the paved floor just inside the temple. Looking between the charred fragments still hanging from the bronze hinges, Oliver saw a courtyard with statues of Egyptian gods arrayed in twin rows. Their various heads, snouts, beaks, and muzzles gazed at one another across the court, which was open to the sky. At the end of the courtyard, a low wall of brick surrounded a sunken area, with smaller statues, which did not appear to depict gods, standing on pedestals flanking the steps down.

Oliver pulled out his gun and ran to the corner of the gateway, intending to peer around the edge and spot where the mercenaries had gone after entering the temple, but his plans were thrown out the window when a mighty blast sounded from the trumpets of the heralds on either side of the gate. Oliver dove to the ground and crouched behind one of the statues of Osiris, cursing his fortune. No such welcoming burst had sounded when the mercenaries and Diana had entered the temple, so it must have had something to do with the brass sphere, which Elder Layla had called the "key," that he carried in his pocket. As he waited, knowing that Kyle or one of his men would come to investigate, Oliver heard the harsh squeal of bent metal twisting and rasping against itself. He risked a glance and saw the shattered remnants of the gates twisting outwards as the ancient hinges rotated to open what remained of the gates.

The echoes of tortured metal died away and Oliver heard the crunch of footsteps approaching over the brick pavement. He ducked low behind the statue of Osiris to the right of the gate, keeping one eye around the base to watch the gateway, and waited for the mercenary to appear.

When he did, Oliver recognized the man as the medic who had been patching Frank's shoulder in the chapel when Oliver awoke on the floor yesterday afternoon. He now held an assault rifle in his hands and had slung his medical kit over his back. The man came around the corner of the gate from the right side of the temple interior, gun up to his shoulder as he advanced rapidly through gate and sighted down the length of his rifle, checking first the left, then right sides of the plaza.

Seeing nothing, the mercenary lowered his gun and turned back towards the temple.

"I don't see anything, Commander."

Kyle's voice shouted back from the temple interior. "There must be something out there. Trumpets don't sound for no reason."

"And what about darkness?" Another voice now. One Oliver didn't recognized but assumed to be one of the mercenaries, though it carried a note of panic he had not heard from any of them last night. "Night doesn't move around like a cloud, Kyle. I say we cut our losses and get the hell out of this place. Take our chances on the free market if Leonidas cuts us off. Hell man, even the water..."

A gunshot sounded. Then the thump of a body hitting the stones.

"Anyone else want to argue?" Silence, as Oliver held his breath and waited. Then, "Right. Adams, get back in here. We're going further in."

The medic shouldered his weapon and walked back through the gateway.

Oliver waited until he could no longer hear the man's footsteps then sidled up to the gateway, hoping with every fiber of his being that the trumpets would not sound again. They didn't. Oliver poked his head around the gate and saw that the central walkway was still empty. He slipped a little further out and saw six figures standing in the shadows of the covered side court, near the low wall that divided the upper court from the sunken area. Kyle was gesturing towards the steps leading down while Diana stood nose to nose with him and waved her hands wildly. Two of the mercenaries bent and lifted a body between them and carried through the doorway of a low chamber built against the right wall of the temple as the other two watched them in silence.

Oliver saw his opportunity and took it. He darted through the gateway and ducked behind the cat-headed statue of Bastet that stood on the left side of the open walkway. He paused, holding his breath and listening for any sign that his entrance had been noticed, but no shout came from any of the mercenaries and Kyle continued to argue with Diana. Their words were still indistinct, but Oliver could tell that Diana was angry about something and, judging from her tone and the rapidity with which she spoke, it probably had more to do with further destruction of the temple than Kyle's methods of imposing discipline among his men.

Oliver surveyed the left side of the courtyard. The light shining in from the uncovered central walkway was bright enough to both illuminate much of the covered area and cast deep shadows behind the supporting pillars and statues of the gods. If he moved quickly and didn't trip over anything, Oliver thought he might be able to reach the   deeper shadow of the lower courtyard without being spotted. Then he might have the opportunity to get ahead of the mercenaries and lay some sort of trap.

He darted from behind the statue and came to a halt behind one of the supporting pillars twenty or so feet down the hall. He waited there, half-expecting to hear a shout or burst of gunfire, but the mercenaries gave no sign of catching on to his presence in the temple.

Kyle's voice echoed across the courtyard. "We're going in, now."

"But the guardians!" Diana cried out.

"If you're so damn afraid of a few skeletons, which, by the way, we haven't even seen, then stay at the back. Hell, stay in the courtyard for all I care. It's not like you can go that far." Oliver glanced around the pillar and saw Kyle stepped closer to Diana and push a finger against her forehead as he spoke, "Just remember, the only reason you're still alive is I might need you to translate something by the end of this. So make sure you stay useful, or I'll put a bullet in your skull."

Kyle strode out of the shadows of the covered courtyard into the light of the central path between the statues of the Egyptian gods. The mercenaries followed a few seconds later, filing out between the legs of the statues, most holding their guns at the ready and glancing about nervously as if they expected the stone deities to spring to life and attack them. Diana did not appear.

Oliver didn't know what motivated her to remain in the shadows of the outer courtyard, be it a vague hope that she could escape from the mercenaries while they ventured deeper into the temple or a true fear of what might guard the inner chambers, but he thought her wise to keep her distance from Kyle and his men. They were skilled and remorseless killers, but had no experience delving into the sanctuaries of relics. If there was one place in the world Oliver would not want to stand, it was at the side of an overconfident neophyte tomb raider as they blundered deeper into the labyrinth of magic and traps that so many of these sites of power were.

Kyle paused at the head of the steps down to the lower courtyard. His men lined up on either side, all gazing down into the area below. When they didn't move to walk down the steps Oliver took a chance and ran lightly to the next supporting pillar, the closest to where the men stood.

"...the hell is going on here?" one of the men, identifiable to Oliver only by the edge of a tattoo peeking up over his collar, was saying. "I've never seen to many bones in one place."

"They're not human." Kyle growled, placing his foot on the first step.

"But... where did they come from? The ones on top can't be more than a few days old."

Kyle didn't reply. As Oliver watched, he strode down the steps and bent to inspect something on the floor. After a moment he stood and flicked something small and white at the nearest mercenary. "They're frogs, or lizards, or something like that. There's nothing to worry about here."

With that he strode forward, his boots making a disconcerting crunch and shuffle sound with every step, and disappeared behind the low wall that surrounded the lower court.

The mercenaries exchanged glances. One of them nodded over his shoulder towards the shadows where they body of their comrade still lay, then stepped forward and followed Kyle. The others followed, their footsteps building the crackle and swoosh of shattering bones under foot to a brutal crescendo.

Oliver crept up to the brick wall surrounding the lower courtyard and waited for the sound of combat boots crunching bone to fade. As he approached, a stench reached his nose, creeping in on his consciousness so slowly that he didn't even notice it until he was almost to the wall. It was a smell of death and decay that reminded him of being a child and coming upon his dog playing with a rotten fish on the banks of the river. He swallowed bile and breathed through his mouth until, a minute or two later, he became inured to the odor. Soon enough the crunching sound faded as the mercenaries left the lower courtyard and disappeared into a dark hall beyond. When they didn't return for a full minute, Oliver risked a look over the wall.

The lower court was sunk about three feet below the level of the upper courtyard. In the places where the mercenaries had trod, he could make out the brick pavement, but everywhere else the floor of the court was covered in a layer of tiny white bones nearly six inches deep. The topmost layer of bones was thinly strung with bits of skin and viscera from thousands of frogs.

"That's not a good sign." Oliver whispered to himself and the words of Sephor's mad message returned to his mind: You will be faced with the plagues that befell our forefathers.

A glitter of golden light caught Oliver's eye and an empty brass bullet casing clattered to the ground a few feet from him. He ducked and raised his gun automatically, pointing it in the direction he had seen the light, even as his rational mind told him that he would already be dead if one of the mercenaries had fired at him from the other side of the upper courtyard. Sighting down the barrel of his gun, Oliver saw Diana crouching against the wall on the opposite side of the open walkway. He allowed himself a smile of relief and lowered the gun, waving for her to come to him. She moved forward to the edge of the open walkway between the statues of the gods, hesitated for a moment, set her shoulders back, and ran across the walkway into Oliver's arms.

As soon he had her, Oliver dropped, pulling them both down below the edge of the wall. Diana clung to him wordlessly for nearly a minute, her body shaking with repressed emotion, though she did not cry. Oliver felt himself breathing deeply as he was filled with joy that Diana had survived her time with the mercenaries. He had kept the thought locked away deep within himself, but now all of his guilt at leaving her behind in the helicopter, even though it had been forced upon him, broke over him like a wave and threatened to draw him down into a sea of shame. He took several deep breaths, allowing himself to enjoy the warmth of Diana's body against his own, then pushed the emotion down and locked it away again. If they were to get out of this temple alive he would have to stay clear-headed.

He bent his head until his mouth was beside Diana's ear and whispered, "I'm glad you're alive."

Her body shivered hard against his several times at that, then she spoke into his ear and Oliver realized that she was trying to keep from laughing. "Thanks, Oliver. Me too."

She leaned back away from him and whispered, "Can you get us out of here?"

Oliver nodded, then hesitated, thinking of the words that Elder Layla had translated for him. "Diana, you lied to them about the inscription on the chapel wall. You only told them about the directions, not the warning."

She looked shocked for a minute, then nodded.

Oliver smiled reassuringly. "That was quick thinking, and brave. They probably would have killed us right there if they thought there was no chance of getting to the staff."

He looked down at Diana. She was still wearing the climbing harness that she had used to descend from the helicopter about an hour before, though it was now covered with dust and grime from the temple and the destruction of the gates. "I've got a rope. We can go back to the plaza and you can rappel down to the desert and use my phone to find the jeep. There's water there, and food, and another set of binoculars. If I'm not back in two hours..."

Diana shook her head. "No way. If you're still going in, I'm coming with you."

He looked at her uncertainly. He had never intended to pull her into such a dangerous situation and, while he was sure she was brave enough to follow through, he didn't want to put her in harm's way again.

"This is all so new to me, Oliver. I've read your posts and listened to your stories for years, but this is the first time I've had the opportunity to actually live them. Do you have another gun?"

Oliver nodded.

"Alright. Give me your spare and a sip of that water. Those bastards wouldn't let me drink since we got up here. Then I'll go in with you."

"You're sure?"

"Yes."

Oliver allowed a smile to creep onto his face as he unslung his backpack and pulled Frank's gun from a side pocket. "You have a holster?"

Diana nodded and patted her belt, which Oliver saw did indeed have a nylon sidearm holster attached to it. "I took it off the dead mercenary. I figured I might be able to snag a gun if one of the others had a run in with whatever traps or guardians are back there."

He passed her the gun and watched as she checked it and secured it in the holster, then handed her the drinking tube from his bag. "Remind me why we broke up all those years back?"

"Because you ran off to the jungle with your cousin and I didn't hear from you for two months."

"Right. After this, I might have to keep you with me."

Diana put the rubber nipple of the tube in her mouth and sucked deeply, a look of anticipatory relief on her face at the thought of finally getting a drink. Then the expression on her face turned to horror and disgust. She threw the tube town and spat dark liquid out on the ground, then gagged, spit, and retched at Oliver's feet.

Oliver picked up the tube and squeezed the nipple, letting a drop of the liquid spill out onto his fingertip. He pinched it between finger and thumb, feeling the smooth viscosity of it like oil against his skin. He sniffed the bitter saltiness of it, then wiped it off on his pants.

"Why the hell do you have blood in your water bag..." Diana froze as the answer to her own question dawned across her face. "The plagues."

Oliver nodded, his face grim. "Napoleon's men must have reached the staff and done something to unleash the power within it."

"Is that possible?"

"I'm afraid so."

Oliver pulled the note Hadiya had written for him from his shirt pocket and examined it again. Elder Layla had said that it would help him survive the temple and reach the staff, but he was beginning to wonder if she had simply been conveying the sentiment in Sephor's half-mad scratches on the wall. He read the note over again, holding it low enough that Diana could read it as well, and looked slowly around the courtyard. The somber faces of the Egyptian gods gazed back at Oliver from their places on either side of the sunlit path, their stony eyes seeming to laugh at his inability to crack Sephor's riddle.

"That's a good translation of the inscription." Diana remarked. "Where'd you get it?"

"An old priestess." Oliver muttered absently, his eyes drifting down towards the lower courtyard and its morbid carpet.

At the far end, nearly hidden in the shadows of the low roof, the wall was carved with a scene of judgment. Ancient Egyptian gods and goddesses were stacked in ranks above a relief carving of a balance scale. On the right side of the scale was a depiction of a man dressed in the garb of a pharaoh. On the left was a set of glyphs that Oliver thought he recognized. He let Diana take the paper from his hand and moved forward to stand at the edge of the foul expanse of rotting flesh and bones. He reached behind him and pulled his camera out of its padded pocket at the base of his backpack then held it up to his eye, using the zoom lens to inspect the mural while snapping a few quick photos.

"I'd love to speak with this priestess of yours. She translated a few words that I couldn't. Here, where she wrote 'tip the balance' I didn't know how translate the phrase. Thought it had something to do with a scale."

Oliver nodded absently. He didn't want to step into the bones until it was absolutely necessary because they would make such a loud crunching noise that the mercenaries were almost certain to hear them coming, not to mention the risk of snakes, scorpions, and traps. They had to find some way of getting to the staff before it could be brought out of the temple by Kyle and his men. He had never before encountered a relic with the power to sow destruction on this scale and hated to think what would happen if it were brought out into the world. Tracking the camera up across the mural, Oliver frowned at an odd dark patch under the radiating arms of a sun.

"Odd, this, but it makes more sense." Diana continued. "She translated the word 'crawl' as 'pass' in the last line."

That gave Oliver an idea.

"Come on. I think I know how to get in there without them hearing us coming."

Without waiting for Diana to acknowledge him, Oliver slipped his camera into its compartment and descended into the lower courtyard. He kicked aside the rotting piles of bones and frog skins as he made his way directly to the mural. Diana pushed the paper into a pocket and jumped to follow.

"How?"

"The priestess who gave that to me said it might help me reach the staff before the mercenaries. I think I see..."

He reached the wall and, feeling a twinge of guilt at risking damage to the ancient wall carving, used the forehead of an Egyptian god and the narrow ridge of the right balance to boost himself up high enough to reach the blank expanse of stone between the sun and the balance. His fist pounded against a thin layer of stone, giving a hollow thud. The stone between heads of the carved figures of the gods and the splayed rays of the sun seemed to be nothing more than a thin cap of slate. He pounded on it again cracking the stone, then shattering it and sending shards tumbling down over his shoulders to the bones below, revealing a dark crawlspace leading back into the temple.

Oliver reached into the side pouch of his pack and pulled out small, but intensely bright, LED flashlight. He clicked it on and examined the entrance to the crawlspace. There would be plenty of room for Diana and him to move through, but he probably wouldn't fit with his backpack on. He could push it ahead of him but that would make a loud scraping sound and slow their progress, negating the point of taking this path. He jumped down and turned to see Diana standing amid the bones a few feet away.

"I'm going through that tunnel. If you still want to come with me you can follow behind. If not, you can take the rope from my pack, climb down, and head for the jeep."

"I'm coming."

Oliver stepped past Diana and set his backpack on the steps to the upper courtyard, then returned to the mural and laid a hand on Diana's shoulder.

"You think you can get up there on your own?"

She shook her head. "No. Not tall enough."

"Right."

Oliver passed her the flashlight, then bent and cupped his hands. Diana got the hint and used Oliver's hands as a step up to grab the edge of the tunnel. She pulled herself up into the hole and crawled forward. Oliver repeated his balancing act on the stone ridges and pulled himself into the tunnel behind Diana.

They crawled down the tunnel in silence, the sound of their own breathing and the shuffle of their knees and hands loud in the dark stillness. There was remarkably little dust on the floor and walls, though Oliver did occasionally brush up against a sharp fleck of stone that had chipped away from the blocks as they were set into place and gone unnoticed in this cramped space. His initial concerns that they might encounter some dangerous pest were soon brushed away as they crawled deeper into the space between the walls without encountering any sign that this passage had played host to living things in the last five thousand years. The air was cool and had the intense, skin-pricking dry quality that is only felt in places surrounded by literally tons of moisture-deprived stone.

Every few feet, the tunnel would slope abruptly downward, then continue on straight for a while before going down again. Reflecting on the layout of the temple courtyard, Oliver came to the conclusion that the chamber which housed the staff must have originally been located below the waterline of the lake that had once surrounded the island. He wondered if this had been done for ceremonial purposes, keeping the staff lower than the water to restrict its power, or as an act of religious politicking, placing it lower than the chambers dedicated to the gods of Egypt. There was no way to be sure now, unless they found an engraving or scroll that explained the purpose of the temple's layout, but judging from the damage seemingly wrought by the staff, its power had been in no way diminished by its location within the temple.

They proceeded several dozen yards down the passage and Oliver was just allowing himself to relax when a blood-chilling scream filled the passage. It seemed to seep through the very stone surrounding them, then echo down the passage from the opening behind them. The scream was followed by distant shouts and the noise of automatic weapons firing.

"They've encountered the guardians!" Diana shouted.

"Whatever they might be. Keep moving!"

They continued down the passage, moving more slowly now, flinching whenever another scream of burst of gunfire sounded around them. Oliver knew that sound moved in deceptive ways in ancient temples, or any other place that consisted of a maze of corridors separated by stone of varying thickness. A noise that seemed to come from far away might be just on the other side of a thin wall of stone, while a seemingly close noise could have echoed from one twisted corridor to another, up through a hole in the floor, and into your ears from an incredibly distant source.

"There was a warning inscribed above the gates." Diana whispered when no more shots had come for over a minute. "It spoke of the eternal guardians of the temple, sworn to protect the people of Egypt from the wrath of a foreign god."

"Did it describe them?"

"No. Do you think any of them are still alive?"

"The mercenaries? Probably. The French soldiers got in deep enough to break whatever wards kept the staff under control and they didn't have machine guns. Of course... " He paused, thinking of the bloody water, darkness, and countless dead frogs. "Who knows what happened when the two powers clashed."

"We might be about to find out. This is the end."

They had come to a solid wall of slate with a narrow bead of gray mortar running along the edge where the gray slate met the yellow sandstone. Diana knocked on it and it echoed hollowly. She put her ear to the cool stone and listened while Oliver waited anxiously, wishing that he had been at the front. He hadn't traveled with a partner for several years, so he had grown unaccustomed to trusting the judgement of others when exploring.

Diana twisted around and said, "I don't hear anything from the other side. Maybe they're all dead, or we've gotten ahead of them by running straight down the length of the temple."

"Get your gun ready and try to knock out the stone. See if you can just chip away a section of it with the butt of the flashlight and peek though."

Diana nodded and was about to jab the light at the stone when it dawned on Oliver that they might be about to break into a chamber guarded by the supernatural guardians of at least two pantheons. He called out and Diana froze, arm poised awkwardly in the air beside her.

"Take this. It may keep the guardians at bay." Oliver whispered. He passed her the engraved brass pyramid that Elder Layla had called the key. It had already caused the guardians of the gate to welcome him into the temple with the sound of trumpets and swing wide the gates, or what remained of them after Kyle and his men had blasted their way in, so he thought that perhaps it would give Diana a measure of protection against whatever lay beyond the cap of slate. In fact, now that he thought about it, that could explain how the French soldiers had managed to disturb the staff. If the key granted access to the temple, perhaps they had passed through unharmed until the moment that they touched the relic itself.

"What about you?"

"I've got something as well, though I don't know if it will protect me. Even if mine doesn't work I have more experience dealing with, well, this sort of thing."

She nodded and tucked the brass pyramid into the pocket of her khakis. It bulged awkwardly against her hip, but appeared secure against falling out.

Oliver nodded and Diana flipped the flashlight over and stabbed the rugged metal end of it into the slate. The thin stone shattered where the flashlight struck it, sending a spray of shards into the space beyond and spidering cracks across the surface of the slate. Diana lowered the flashlight to the floor in front of her and Oliver saw, through the random speckling of yellow dots still clouding his vision, a pale blue light pouring into the tunnel through the crack. She put her eye to the hole and Oliver heard her breath catch in her throat.

"What is it?" he whispered.

Diana's voice, when she finally replied, was barely audible. Her eye remained fixed to the crack as she said, "I can see the staff."

Chapter Nineteen

Oliver felt a familiar grin creasing its way across his face. He recognized the tone in Diana's voice from the dozens of times he had felt the same joy at the discovery of a true relic in some ancient tomb or long abandoned temple. No matter how hard he had to work to find the place, how far he had to crawl through mud, how many armed rivals he faced, or how many supernatural wards stood between him and escape, that moment of first beholding a genuine fragment of refined cosmic power always brought a grin to Oliver's face and a chill to his spine.

"It looks like the tunnel opens just above some sort of viewing platform, behind a statue of some sort. I can see the chamber through the statue's legs. Below the platform there's an altar. The staff is laying on the ground beside the altar, amid a pile of bones."

"Break through. We'll see if we can get to the staff before Kyle and his men get here."

Diana did as he said, smashing away the remainder of the slate with the butt of her flashlight and slipping out to crouch behind the left leg of the statue. Oliver followed her and knelt behind the statue's right leg to survey the room.

It was as she had described. They knelt upon a raised stone plinth, which supported a larger than life statue of a man. Oliver could not see the face from where he crouched, but looking up past the man's back he saw that the man was depicted wearing the headdress of a pharaoh. Over each shoulder he could just see the tops of the crossed scepter and flail that were the symbols of his rank.

This must be the Pharaoh Ramesses II. Oliver thought. Standing here in the room where the symbol of his ancestors' shame was kept subject to the power of all the gods of Egypt.

Another statue, smaller, but still larger than life, stood a dozen or so feet to the right of the one they crouched behind. Oliver immediately recognized the proud profile of that effigy as Sephor, an assumption supported by the oversized bronze sword clasped in the hand of the stone general.

Looking out beyond the Pharaoh's leg, Oliver saw that the room was built in a perfect square, with a high observation platform surrounding a depression in the center. Eight stone pillars stood around the central area, two on each side of a set of wide steps leading down to an altar of cast bronze. Spaced out around the edges of the platform, only faintly visible in the dim light that gleamed out from narrow slits in the ceiling, were a number of shadowy niches cut into the stone of the walls. At least a dozen scorched and shattered skeletons, some bare and others swathed in layers of tattered cloth, lay in various poses of disarray around the platform and down the steps. Many of the clothed skeletons lay beside the rusted and splintered remains of French army swords and muskets.

At the center of all this stood the altar, bathed in the soft glow of daylight that had traveled far through numerous passages too narrow for any man to crawl through, at the lowest point of the room. The altar was built of a pure white stone and inscribed with densely packed hieroglyphs running in rows across its surface and sides. Atop the altar rested two simple curved stones, each notched at the top as if to hold a rod in place so it would rest without rolling away. But that rod, the very shepherd's staff that Moses had carried with him into Egypt and used to call down the wrath of the Hebrew god upon the Egyptians, had then carried with him through their sojourn in the desert, had used to draw forth water from desert rocks and channel divine power to strengthen his troops in battle, did not rest peacefully upon the altar.

The Staff of Moses lay atop a pile of bones and tattered cloth at the foot of the lowest step, surrounded by long streaks of soot scorched across the stone, as if the man holding the staff had been struck down by blast fire as he turned away from the altar.

Oliver couldn't make out the details of the staff from this distance, but it appeared to be nothing more than a simple length of yellowish wood, one end blunted from pounding against thousands of miles of sand and rocks of the desert, the other polished to a dark sheen from years of being grasped the the hands of its owner. For all its simplicity, the staff emanated a sense of potency and command that Oliver couldn't help but believe to be real power.

They waited in silence until Diana took a deep breath and whispered, "I can hardly believe this is real."

He nodded, but remained silent as he surveyed the room.

"Should I..."

"Stay here." Oliver interrupted. "I'll go get the staff, then we can take the tunnel back up to the surface and get out of here."

Before she could protest, Oliver jumped down from his position behind the Pharaoh's leg and dropped into a roll on the stone floor seven feet below. He glanced up at Diana and was not surprised to see that she was fuming.

"Relax. I'll need you to pull me back up when..."

His consolation speech was interrupted by the look of horror crossing Diana's face. She opened her mouth to shout and Oliver dove to his left, pulling his gun and spinning around to face the room as he came up out of the roll.

From the shadows of the alcoves around the perimeter of the platform, they emerged. Men and women, their naked skin shriveled to thin leather over their creaking bones. Their eyes glowed a pale blue, and streaks of dark blue light, like faintly glowing smoke, streamed out from holes and slashes in their leathery skin. They were accompanied by ferocious dogs with mottles of white and red fur and eyes like glowing embers. The dogs began to growl and Oliver could have sworn he saw white smoke drifting out between their teeth and smelled the faint reek of sulfur.

The desiccated human form nearest to Oliver opened its dry lips and growled out something in a language he didn't recognize, its voice screeching past dry vocal cords and lips like wind rushing through dry branches. The fiend finished speaking and waited silently, as if it expected a response, its hollow eye sockets glowing with a dim blue light that seeped out and dripped down its sunken cheeks like smoke. Oliver raised his gun and centered his sights on the fiend's skull. He slipped his left hand slowly into the outer pocket of his vest and pulled out the guide stone.

"I come in the name of Sephor," he shouted, holding the stone out in front of him. Though he didn't look through it, Oliver could see that the fleck of mica at the center of the stone was awash with flickering flames.

At the sight of the guide stone, the nearest fiend nodded silently and raised its left hand in salute and rattled out a string of words in the dead language of ancient Egypt. The other creatures likewise saluted, the dogs sitting back on their haunches, and stopped advancing towards Oliver.

Keeping his gun trained on the nearest fiend, Oliver took a hesitant step forward. None of the creatures reacted, so he took another step with the same result.

Oliver had reached the steps down to the altar when one of the dogs growled fiercely and gave a deep bark that echoed throughout the chamber and spewed flames across the stones before it. The other fiends turned as one and Oliver froze, thinking they were about to charge him. There were fourteen human-shaped fiends, as well as seven dogs, and he had only fifteen bullets in his magazine and one spare clip loaded in a vest pocket. He was just deciding whether he should shoot at the undead humans or dogs first when he heard the same words that had been spoken to him uttered again.

He turned and saw Kyle standing in the shadowy doorway between the statues of Ramesses and Sephor, an assault rifle clutched in his hands, his clothes and face streaked with blood. His face was pocked with bright red welts, as if he had been bitten by dozens of horseflies. Oliver imagined that Kyle must have faced several other rooms of fiends and plagues before reaching this chamber. He had left the courtyard with four other men, only two of which appeared behind him, each staggering out of the dark doorway with wild eyes, guns pressed to their shoulders prepared to shoot anything that moved.

Kyle's eyes found Oliver's and they locked. Neither spoke for a long moment.

Then Kyle laughed. There was no mirth in the laughter, only a deep hysterical irony that convinced Oliver that Kyle had snapped.

Oliver dove down the steps and rolled behind the altar as Kyle roared and began firing bursts of lead from his gun.

The fiend nearest to Kyle jerked backwards and flopped over onto the floor, its body folded at an unnatural angle as a burst of bullets shattered its spine and ripped through its frayed muscles. The unholy blue fire that animated it blazed bright in the fiend's eyes and it dragged itself across the floor towards Kyle on rigid fingers, roaring hatefully before Kyle silenced it with another burst of gunfire that shattered its skull. The glowing blue smoke burst out of its body and drifted away into nothingness.

Reacting to the scream of their fellow, the other fiends roared, filling the chamber with a skin-prickling blast of noise like a hurricane ripping through a forest of dead trees. The dogs howled, spewing gouts of red fire that blasted into the stones of the floor and spread out in burning arcs, leaving dark cones of charred stone in their wake. The monsters threw themselves at Kyle and his last remaining man, screaming and barking as they charged across the platform. Strangely, not a one of them descended the steps to cut across the low area in which the altar stood, instead they all ran the long way around the upper platform.

The mercenaries remained in their place by the door, firing around the base of the statues at the approaching fiends until their magazines ran dry. Five human fiends and one hound fell under the force of their fire, but that did not stop the remaining creatures from charging towards them. Kyle met their assault, leaping forward into the room and slashing the bayonet of his rifle across the neck of nearest fiend, then slamming his booted foot into the chest of the creature as it clutched at the gout of blue smoke pouring from its throat. One mercenary, his face already bloodied from wounds sustained somewhere along his journey through the temple, followed Kyle out into the platform, only to be smashed in the face by a fiend that emerged from behind the statue of Sephor. He lashed out with the butt of his rifle, shattering the fiend's skull. The undead guard roared, blue smoke oozing out through cracks in its skull, and threw the man across the platform to strike with a crunch against a supporting pillar, then fall down into the shadowy corner between two sets of steps. The final mercenary slammed a new magazine into his rifle, took aim, and shot at one of the fiery hounds as it charged towards him. The beast dropped and rolled forward over itself, spewing flame in all directions before collapsing into a pile of dry skin and bones.

As the barrage of automatic gunfire slowed, Oliver risked a glance around the side of the altar and saw the two mercenaries fighting off the undead. They fought fiercely, though Oliver couldn't tell whether they were driven by desperation to live or absolute madness, but it was not enough. The fiends plowed forward towards them, the human ones slashing cruelly with unfeeling fingers and snapping with preternaturally strong jaws without a care for scraped skin or shattered teeth, while the dogs darted around, barking out flames as they attempted to roast or bite the mercenaries without being shot or clubbed. As Oliver watched, one of the dogs blasted the remaining mercenary with a spurt of flame. The man screamed and dropped to the floor, rolling and slapping at the flames on his clothes to put them out. The man slammed into the wall of the chamber and slapped away the last flicker of fire on his leg just in time for one of the dogs to pounce onto his chest. Oliver looked away, but not before he saw the beast growl and dart its massive jaws down at the man's face.

He saw that Kyle was now a quarter of the way around the perimeter of the room, still fighting hand to hand with the fiends. He had managed to slip a new magazine into his gun and was using short bursts of bullets to keep the fire-breathing dogs at bay as he dispatched human fiends with merciless slashes of his bayonet and rapid kicks to the chest.

Oliver decided that this was probably his best chance. He darted out from behind the altar and grabbed the staff with his left hand as he ran towards the statue of Ramesses.

As his fingers closed on the wood of the staff, worn smooth by years of hard use in the wilderness, Oliver felt a surge of energy shoot up his arm and into his brain like an electric shock. Everything around him and inside of him seemed to slow down until, in a moment of utter silence between heartbeats, he could hear the scrape of a fire hound's claws on the stone and trace the slow arc of a cartridge as it was ejected from Kyle's rifle. His entire body convulsed and he suddenly felt as if he was standing face to face with the most charismatic person he had ever met, blubbering his way through an explanation of his quest to track down relics and re-assemble the bronze mechanism and prove, if only to himself, that a powerful agency lurked in the shadows of the world. His perception was drawn to the staff, still gripped in his frozen hand, and his mind went blank except for thoughts of the staff and what he could do with it if he were to wield its power. He fought back, reaching for memories of Diana, Amber, his quest, and even his father, focusing on them instead of the staff, which had begun to grow hot in his hand.

Oliver was struck with guilt as he considered that his hunt for relics was selfish and had caused him to hurt himself and others, but the guilt faded as he focused on his motivation for the quest. The thing that drove Oliver was an insatiable hunger for knowledge, not greed or the desire for power. The image of the staff grew large in his mind again, this time held in the hand of another man, who appeared to flux constantly between the forms of Senator Wheeler and Kyle. Even as the world around him continued to slow, with the flames spurting out of a hound's open mouth seeming to stand still in the air, Oliver saw the men rising to power as they summoned the magic of the staff to defeat their enemies.

In that moment, Oliver knew what he had to do.

Then the world snapped back into action and Oliver charged up the stairs, staff in hand, screaming Diana's name. He reached the platform and skidded to a halt beside the statue of Ramesses II. Diana appeared beside the leg of the stone Pharaoh and he hurled the staff up to her.

"Go! Meet me at the gate."

Before she could reply, Oliver had spun away and dashed through the doorway and up the stairs.

"Get back here!" screamed Kyle, sending another burst of gunfire into a fiend and turning to follow Oliver. The remaining fiends and their canine companions gave chase, screaming and howling in rage as their quarry disappeared up the slanted ramp on the other side of the dim doorway.

Oliver had no idea where he was going, but he knew that he needed to keep Kyle away from Diana as she carried the staff up the tunnel to the courtyard. Still running up the steep stone steps, he reached into a side pocket of his vest and pulled out an emergency chemical light. He bent and slammed the plastic tube against his knee, bursting it to eerie green life in the dark of the tunnel.

Gunfire sounded from behind and Oliver dropped to the ramp. He threw the light stick down behind him and lurched to his feet, firing his gun blindly down the ramp twice as he pounded upwards in the dim green light. Kyle scream a curse at him from below, then let out a string of profanity as the green glow of the chemical light was washed away by the hellish blaze of fire spewing out of the mouth of a hound that had reached the doorway. Oliver risked a glance back and saw Kyle, simultaneously silhouetted against the red fire and illuminated by the glow of the chemical light, leaning against the wall of the ramp and firing his rifle down at a press of fiery hounds and reaching, screaming human fiends pushing their way through the narrow doorway. His maniacal laughter joined in a cruel chorus with the din of gunshots and the screams of the fiends.

Oliver turned away and kept running. In the dim light he could see the end of the ramp leveling off into dark room.

The instant he reached the end of the ramp, Oliver leapt sideways to put the heavy stone blocks between himself and Kyle. He pulled his last chemical light out of his vest and hurriedly cracked it, to reveal a small room with statues of Egyptian gods arrayed around the edges, all facing inwards towards a stand on which rested a large bronze bowl. Oliver searched the perimeter of the room for an exit, his gaze faltering over bloodstained floor and the mutilated corpses of the last mercenary and five large dogs with pointed ears and black, heavily muscled arms where their front legs should have been. The mercenary's throat had been torn out by the jackal-headed monster that rested atop him, nearly shredded by dozens of bullet holes ripped into its back and side.

Oliver spotted the exit and ran, the noise of Kyle laughing and shooting echoing up the ramp behind him. He had to trust that Diana would carry the staff up to the courtyard, and that whatever force had infiltrated his mind when he first touched it would leave her unharmed and allow her to carry the staff to the surface. That was a risk, but one he had to take. There had been no time for him to climb up to the tunnel and if he didn't escape Kyle and the guardians she might still manage to escape with the staff, or at least destroy it before Kyle could find her.

He passed through the doorway at a run and found himself in a narrow corridor of stone. He darted along it for about twenty feet, then came up to a wall with a small nook set into it. Painted images of an Egyptian god in with a crocodile head surrounded the nook, in which was set a bloodstained altar of white stone. Rows of hieroglyphs were etched into the curved wall of the nook above the alter.

The corridor split here, one passage running right and the other left on either side of the altar nook. Oliver looked frantically for a sign of which way the mercenaries had taken when the entered the temple. It only took him a moment to find the line of white chalk, glowing an eerie green in the chemical light, marking the passage to the right. Looking down he saw bloody footprints on the floor, approaching the altar nook from that same passage. Oliver turned right and moved down the narrow passage as quickly as he could.

He soon came to another sacrificial nook, at yet another split in the passage. He continued to follow the chalk marks and bloody footprints past two more turns and altars. It was now clear that this room was a maze. That would explain why it took the mercenaries so long to reach the room where the staff had been kept. At one point he came to a split where the chalk marks indicated that he should turn left, but the bloody footprints continued on ahead. He paused for only a moment, then heard Kyle's voice screaming a threat to him from somewhere behind and turned to follow the chalk marks. The mercenaries must have explored that passage as they worked their way through the maze, and one of them must have fallen to a gruesome trap.

He moved more quickly now, following the chalk marks past a dozen more altars to the gods of the Egyptian pantheon as Kyle continued to shout his name and threaten brutal recriminations, until Oliver turned one last corner and saw the faint glow of light at the end of the passage. He ran forward and saw that the light was seeping under and around the tattered remnants of a heavy curtain. When he reached the curtain, which had once been dyed a rich crimson but was now faded and tattered with age, he pushed it aside and stepped into a chamber that had clearly been designed as a ritual bath.

Bright sunlight poured in from the open door to the courtyard, illuminating the wide shelves built into the walls, some still bearing frail piles of ceremonial robes that looked as if they would crumble at a touch, and a deep bath with cut steps leading in from one side and out the other. The faint stench of rotting frogs returned to Oliver's nose as he paused to catch his breath and listen for any sign of Kyle catching up behind him. The shattered skeletons and torn skins of amphibians poured into the room through the door, reaching nearly to the bath at the center of the chamber. Many had been ground to small pieces and scattered across the floor as the mercenaries tracked through this room less than an hour before.

Oliver knew that Kyle couldn't be very far behind. He could continue into the courtyard and hope that Diana was there waiting, but then they would have to make it all the way down the length of the courtyard, across the plaza, and down from the plateau of the island. Somehow Oliver doubted that that they could accomplish half of that before Kyle stepped into the courtyard and shot them in the back. He must have been running low on ammunition by then, but if he still had any, his assault rifle would be accurate at a much greater range than Oliver's handgun so he would only need a few rounds to take them down.

Oliver made up his mind. It was time to bring this chase to an end.

He jumped down into the ceremonial bath and crouched in the corner nearest the curtained door. He leaned against the side of the bath to steady his aim and take some of the pressure off his aching calves, then rested the barrel of his gun on the edge of the bath and sighted about three feet above the floor of the doorway. Only the very top of Oliver's head was visible over the edge of the bath and Kyle would probably not even see that as he came through the curtain.

He waited, breathing as softly as he could. He didn't have to wait long.

Kyle burst through the curtained door moving fast in a low crouch. Oliver pulled his trigger twice, allowing his aim to buck upwards with each shot. The first round slammed into Kyle's right thigh just above the knee, sending him twisting down and to the right with a scream of agonized rage. The second shot slammed into his chest. Kyle hit the ground hard and his rifle clattered across the stones.

Oliver jumped up the stairs three at a time and delivered a vicious kick to Kyle's shoulder, flipping him over and eliciting a groan of pain, then pointed his gun directly at the mercenary's face. Kyle's eyes were dull and unfocused, but still alive. Oliver looked at Kyle's chest and saw no blood. The man must have worn a light body armor under his camouflage. The shot to the chest had wounded him, but done no serious damage.

Oliver pressed the muzzle of his gun under Kyle's chin and bent to release the cover on the mercenary's sidearm case. He pulled out the gun and tucked it into his own belt.

He glanced at the spreading pool of blood around Kyle's wounded thigh.

"You have two choices: Keep your mouth shut and I'll get you out of here. Say a single word, and I mean so much as a 'but' or 'please' and I'll shoot you in the other leg and leave you to try and crawl out of here and hope that your last minion is still around to help you."

He stood, keeping his gun pointed at Kyle's face. "Blink your eyes. Option one, or option two."

Kyle looked at Oliver with undisguised hatred. He didn't blink.

"So you think there's a third option do you? There isn't."

Oliver stepped back, lowering his gun. Kyle continued to stare at him defiantly. The edge of his mouth twisted up in a vicious smile, even as his eyes started to water from the effort of keeping them open. Oliver shrugged, aimed, and calmly shot Kyle in the left knee.

He turned away from the screaming mercenary and collected the man's assault rifle before walking through the doorway to the courtyard.

Chapter Twenty

Summer was in full swing in Washington D.C. The air was hot, humid, and heavy with the scent of automobile exhaust from the thousands of vehicles that sat in gridlocked traffic around and throughout the city. Oliver strode down K Street with his hands in the pockets of his jeans, a camera slung around his neck and a backpack hanging loosely over his shoulders. He smiled to think that the security guards lining the streets would assume he was nothing but a tourist, even down to the bright red tan, bordering on sunburn, on his face and arms.

It had taken Oliver and Diana only four days to get back to the United States after the events in the temple.

He had emerged from the bath chamber, followed by Kyle's screams of pain and rage, to find Diana hiding behind a statue of Horus half way down the way of the gods. She held the staff in one hand as she hugged Oliver tight, but said nothing. They had used the rope from his pack to climb down the rock face to the bed of the dry lake then hiked to the jeep as quickly as they could, the darkness that covered the entire basin of the lake to a depth of a foot or more dissipating to nothing as they ran through it. When the reached the jeep Oliver was immensely relieved to find that the water in the five gallon jugs was still fresh. The two of them had each drunk nearly a gallon before Oliver got the jeep started and drove back the way he had come.

Diana hadn't said a word to him until the jeep was underway, bouncing and skidding across the desert sands as Oliver followed a route on his GPS that would, eventually, return them to the wide loop of highway surrounding Al Fayyum Lake. When she did, it was only to ask Oliver what he planned to do with the staff.

He had remained silent for a minute, then glanced at Diana as he replied, "I'm going to break it."

Diana had nodded. They were both silent for several kilometers, then Diana had said, "That's the right thing to do. It... it felt angry, and powerful. We can't let anyone get their hands on it to use as a weapon."

Oliver had stopped the jeep then, there in the middle of the Egyptian desert, and looked toward Diana. She had returned his gaze for a moment, then leaned forward and put her hand on his cheek and kissed him gently on the lips. They now shared an understanding of something that went beyond their personal history, or their shared belief in ancient powers and conspiracies. Both had now touched a relic of awesome power and been judged worthy of determining its fate.

Oliver slowed his pace as he approached Founding Flounders, an upscale seafood restaurant only three blocks from the White House that was increasingly popular with executive office staff. Oliver pushed through the rotating door and introduced himself to the hostess, explaining that he was expected by one of her more private diners. She checked the reservation book, nodded, and passed Oliver off to a waiter who led him back past the crowded bar and whitewashed walls featuring caricatures of political figures as fish, to one of the private dining rooms at the back of the restaurant. The waiter knocked on the door. The door opened to reveal a burly man in a dark suit.

The guard examined each of them in turn, then nodded towards Oliver's bag. "I'll need to look in that."

"Have at it."

The suited bodyguard unzipped Oliver's bag and got a puzzled look on his face. Oliver smiled at that. It wasn't every day that a sunburnt tourist met with a former presidential candidate carrying piece of wood.

"What's this?"

"A gift. It's harmless."

The guard cleared his throat and pushed the wood back into the bag before tossing it back to Oliver. He nodded at the waiter, who turned and hurried away.

"Go ahead." The guard stepped aside to reveal Senator Wheeler sitting at the far end of a large table set for sixteen, sipping a glass of whiskey on the rocks.

"Good to see you alive, kid." Senator Wheeler exclaimed, setting the glass down and waving for Oliver to approach.

Oliver stepped past the guard and strode to a chair two seats away from the Senator. He dropped into the seat and tossed his backpack into the chair between them.

"Your father called and said you need to meet with me about our little project. I was under the impression that it had come to an end."

"Yes. I suppose you were." Oliver leaned back and crossed his legs under the table, enjoying the confused look on the Senator's face. "Thanks for meeting with me, though I suppose you had to after the whole screwup with Leonidas Security."

"I'm not sure what..."

"Please, Senator. You can be honest with me. After all, I'm the man you hired to clean up your mess."

The Senator was silent for a moment. He worked his jaw back and forth contemplatively, then reached for his glass and took a swallow of the amber liquid. He coughed and said, "I'm not sure what you mean."

Oliver nodded towards the guard. The Senator got his meaning and told the man to wait outside the door.

They both waited until the door was closed, then the Senator said, "I had nothing to do with the raid on the vault. That was all Rais Karim."

Oliver pulled a large brown envelope out of his backpack and slid it down the table towards the senator. "Take a look in there."

The Senator unclasped the envelope flap and peered inside without dumping out the contents. His face darkened and he gave Oliver a cold look, then he closed the envelope, folded it sharply in half, and slipped it into his suit coat.

"Blackmail is a crime, kid. I hope you know that."

Oliver laughed out loud. He had been afraid of what Wheeler could do to him when this whole adventure started, but recent events had given him a sense of confidence that was hard to shake. He laughed long and hard, pushing himself to continue even after the genuine hilarity of the moment had passed simply to relish the growing expression of fury on Senator Wheeler's face.

Finally he sat upright in his chair and steepled his fingers in front of his face, then said, "I think you'd have a hard time convincing anyone that this is blackmail, Senator, assuming that you let any of this come to light. Blackmail assumes that one party is offering to cover up potentially damaging information in exchange for some sort of payment. All that packet contains is screenshots from a video of some Leonidas Security contractors attempting to sell an illegally obtained Egyptian artifact about two weeks ago. You can see the timestamp there at the bottom left of the image. But that's not an issue, right? Obviously you know nothing about the internal operations of your biggest campaign contributor. It might look bad, but there can't be anything that could be traced to you."

Oliver leaned forward, a cynical smile creeping across his face as he spoke, "Certainly not phone records and visitors logs showing that you had extensive conversations with the

Leonidas executives the day this video was taken, and again a week later when one of their men was arrested in an Egyptian hospital for selling relics on the black market."

The Senator took another sip of his whiskey and said nothing.

He set his glass down on the table and clutched it for a moment, long fingers turning white as they flexed tightly around the heavy glass. Oliver didn't think he had pushed the man too far, but he tensed his muscles to dodge out of the way just in case the Senator hurled his glass across the gap between them.

"You don't have to answer. Frankly, I'm amused by the situation. Hiring me was at least discreet. Putting pressure on a major contractor, then checking in on them after the job fell apart, that was sloppy. But with Leonidas Security out of the picture now, I would appreciate being paid for delivering the goods."

Senator Wheeler's expression of quietly controlled rage shifted to one of confusion. He pushed the glass away with a flick of his finger and asked, "The goods?"

Oliver pointed to where his backpack rested on the chair between them. "Take a look for yourself."

Senator Wheeler lunged forward and grabbed at the backpack eagerly, nearly knocking over his chair in his eagerness. He laid the tattered and sun-faded bag on the table before him and scrabbled with the zippers as Oliver amused himself by wondering if the burnished oak table at which they sat had ever supported such a shabby bag. He didn't imagine it had. The Senator threw the bag open and gasped in shock at what lay before him.

Resting between the splayed sides of the bag, wrapped loosely in a long strip of cotton cloth, was a piece of wood about seven inches in length and two in diameter. At one end it curved, hooking around into the curve of a shepherd's crook.

The Senator lifted the wood reverentially and laid it on the table before him. He shoved the bag across the table towards Oliver and sat gazing at the broken staff for a moment, eyes wide open as his mouth worked unintelligibly. He reached a trembling hand forward and untucked a fold of the cloth, revealing the jagged splinters of wood at one end where the staff had been broken.

"Is this it?"

Oliver nodded. "I couldn't bring you the whole thing, but this is the genuine article."

Senator Wheeler glanced at Oliver, as if to judge the truth of his words. Apparently satisfied, he took a deep breath and returned to gazing at the fragment of Moses's staff that Oliver had delivered to him.

Oliver waited in silence, allowing the Senator his moment of reverie.

Finally the old man spoke, "How can I..."

"Simple." Oliver interjected. "The money you offered."

"Of course. You will have it by the end of the day."

"And a promise that you'll behave yourself if you are elected."

The Senator looked away from the shard of the staff and gave Oliver a puzzled look. Oliver doubted that the man had been this unguarded in decades, but he couldn't fault the Senator for being overwhelmed in that moment.

"I have another fragment of the staff. Behave yourself in office and I'll deliver it to you as a retirement gift in a few years. Keep working with bastards like Leonidas and the other shard will appear in a museum somewhere, with papers clearly linking it to the antiquities collection of a respectable Saudi family."

For an instant, rage flashed across the Senator's face again, but it was washed away as he glanced at the shard of the staff laying before him on the table. His eyes locked on the ancient fragment of wood, tracing the curve of the crook down to the splintered end. He took a deep breath. Then he looked back to Oliver and nodded.

"Then I'd say our business here is at an end." Oliver rose to his feet and grabbed his backpack, zipping it up before tossing it over one shoulder. He lifted his camera from where he had set it on the table and stepped towards the door.

Senator Wheeler cleared his throat and touched the length of wood again before draping the cloth across it. He stood, one hand still resting on the shard of the staff in his pocket, and stepped around the table to shake Oliver's hand.

"Thank you, kid."

"Always a pleasure doing business with honorable people, Senator."

Oliver held the Senator's grip for a moment. The Senator nodded. Oliver released his hand and turned away to walk out the door.

He strode past the diners at their tables and government staffers at the bar, dropped a small tip on the hostess's podium, and pushed his way out through the revolving door into the blistering heat of a Washington D.C. afternoon. A blue convertible idled at the curb, parked in the taxi lane, with Amber at the wheel and Diana in the passenger seat. Oliver swung off his backpack and hopped over the closed rear door, dropping the bag into the seat beside him and pulling on his seat belt as Amber pulled the car into traffic.

"Did he bite?" Diana asked.

"He's hooked." Oliver replied, leaning forward so he didn't have to shout to be heard over the growling noise of the traffic around them.

"And you're sure there is no power in the shard you gave him?"

Oliver reached into the left pocket of his jeans and pulled out a soft leather pouch. He unfastened the neck and pulled out a piece of wood about the size of his thumb. The fragment was a darkly colored irregular knot, streaked with lines and swirls of brown and black, and perfectly smooth on all sides. It appeared to glow darkly in the sunlight, as if it had been carved, sanded, and oiled with care.

The knot of wood, and its more lightly colored twin, had fallen free of the staff when Oliver had climbed out of the battered old jeep in the middle of the Egyptian desert and, with Diana's help, split the staff against the fender of the vehicle. The staff had splintered in two places and given up the two tightly wound burls of heartwood. From that moment neither of them had felt anything when they touched the staff, so Oliver had judged it safe to give the powerless relic to Senator Wheeler.

Oliver and Diana had each taken one of the smooth knots of wood as a memento of their expedition. Diana now wore hers on a silver chain around her neck, while Oliver kept his in the leather pouch.

He smiled to himself, feeling the gentle prickle of restrained power against his palm. If he closed his eyes and listened, he knew he would feel the twinge of a power beyond his understanding pressing softly against his mind.

"Oh, I'm sure."

Made in the USA
San Bernardino, CA
03 October 2014